Dear Mr. Carson

Dear Mr. Carson

ELIZABETH RIDLEY

THE PERMANENT PRESS
Sag Harbor, New York 11963

Copyright © 2006

Library of Congress Cataloging-in-Publication Data

Ridley, Elizabeth.
    Dear Mr. Carson / Elizabeth Ridley.
        p. cm.
    ISBN 1-57962-125-2
        1. Overweight children—Fiction. 2. Teenage girls—Fiction. 3. Camps
    for overweight children—Fiction. 4. Milwaukee (Wis.)—Fiction. I. Title.

    PS3568.I3597D43 2006
    813'.54—dc22   2005056383

Printed in the United States of America.

In Memory of Jan and Trevor Johnson

No writer could ask for better friends

The awful daring of a moment's surrender
Which an age of prudence can never retract
By this, and this only, we have existed

T. S. Eliot, *The Waste Land*

For Johnny

CHAPTER ONE

Doc and the band sound great tonight. The jazzy music licks my earlobes, tickles my collar, settles in my chest. A fist, not my own, beats inside me. I quiver behind the multi-color curtain; in the cold darkness, totally alone. I peek up at the monitor. Ed, on the end of the couch, laughs madly like a happy grandpa. Johnny, my darling Johnny, perches at his desk, tapping and bopping and having a grand old time. He's in a good mood tonight and all of America knows it.

Johnny cues Doc to cut the music. The commercial ends. Johnny hunches his shoulders and looks straight into Camera One. The audience settles as Johnny bends toward the microphone.

"Welcome back. Now folks, we'd like to bring out a very special guest. This young lady comes to us from Wa-wa-tot-zee—Did I get that right?" Johnny glances anxiously off-stage.

Producer Freddie de Cordova signals "no" and passes the proper pronunciation to Ed, who relays it to Johnny.

"Wauwatosa. This young lady comes to us from Wauwatosa, Wisconsin. She's thirteen years old and she's the Academy Award-winning director of the feature film, *Girl on the Lam*, starring Kristy McNichol. Would you all please give a warm welcome to Wilma 'Sunnie' Sundstrom!"

The curtain splits in a kaleidoscope of colors. Thunderous applause. An unseen hand pushes me forward, into the light. Breathless, I count the steps. By eleven, I reach the platform. By fourteen, I'm at the desk. Johnny stands. He smiles. Dazzling. He shines. His eyes are very blue. He is beautiful. He reaches out and takes my hand. He bends as if he might—yes, he just might—kiss me. On the lips. This is going to be way better than kissing Bobby Hickey after gym class. I close my eyes and sigh, trembling in expectation. Suddenly the floor slides out beneath me. I fall forward and hit the ground hard.

"Sunnie! Sunnie? Are you OK?"

"She looks dead." Was that Todd Wombat's voice? "Somebody harpoon the beached whale."

"She just fainted. Alice, get the nurse." *Mrs. Tooley. Social Studies. Must be fourth period. Eleven-thirty A.M. God, do I have to open my eyes?*

"Sunnie?" Mrs. Tooley sounded worried. I had to get up.

I sat forward and swooned. The eighth-grade classroom shattered into stars. When I blinked, the stars scattered. My head throbbed.

"Sunnie?"

"I'm OK. Just give me a sec." Mrs. Tooley knelt beside me, eyes pinched with concern. The whole class huddled behind her, a wavy sea of worried faces, except for Todd Wombat, who picked his nose and pretended to fling it at me.

"Do you know where you are?" Mrs. Tooley's seashell bracelet rattled as she stroked my hand.

I rubbed my eyes. "Truman Junior High?"

"Do you know what day it is?"

I thought for a moment. "Monday. April Twenty-fourth. 1978." The Twenty-fourth! Oh my gosh—'Our Dairy Heritage' reports are due. Suddenly I remembered. I had been standing at the blackboard, reading my report aloud. I had just reached the fascinating fact that some cheese curds need to cure for a full eighteen months when I felt hot. My pants—elastic waistband, size thirteen "Huskies for Her"—got tight. My head was sweating. Everyone could see the fatness bulging out of me. My palms turned cold. I tried to hold on, just keep reading, but the room got spotty. Tiny black fish shivered behind my eyes. Next thing I knew I was backstage at *The Tonight Show* waiting, as I had so often, for Johnny to invite me out.

"Come on Sunnie, let's get you up." Mrs. Tooley grasped my arm and pulled, grunting softly.

"You'll need a forklift," Todd cracked. "Ten Ton Sundstrom." The boys all laughed. Mrs. Tooley ignored them but a splash of color stroked her cheek.

"Sunnie, sit here while we wait for the nurse." Mrs. Tooley sat me in the desk beside her and scanned the class. "Todd, you're next. Sunnie can finish when she's feeling better."

"Unfair! It's not my fault Flintstone fainted." Todd hiked up his pants and rubbed his runny nose. "I'm s'posed to go tomorrow."

"Five points extra credit," Mrs. Tooley promised. Todd, a straight-D student, couldn't resist. He grabbed his report and trudged to the blackboard.

"'Our Dairy Heritage,' by Todd L. Wombat." Squinting, he drew his report closer. "Our state, Wisconsin, is very very famous for its many numerous dairy products. Such as milk, cheese, yogurt, cream and sour cream and ice cream. Lots of people like dairy products for breakfast, lunch, and even for their supper."

My head settled as I watched Todd, chief of my tormentors, with his scrawny neck and stick-up hair. Parts of his body didn't belong together: he had huge feet but tiny hands; thin shoulders canopied beneath a wide, jutting jaw. Why did he hate me so much? Mom said he secretly liked me, and that was how immature boys show their emotions. I doubted that. I think he didn't like me because I took up too much space.

My eye was caught by a flurry of paper a few desks away. I looked over where my best friend, Emily Rankin, sat fanning her *Close Encounters of the Third Kind* notebook. Pushing up her John Lennon granny glasses, she opened the notebook to a page where she had scribbled, "Romulan #1," and below that, "Is so gay." "Romulan #1" was our nickname for Todd Wombat. I smiled and gave her the thumbs-up.

Emily held up another page for me to see. "Any news yet from Mr. C?" it asked with a big smiley-face.

I gave the thumbs-down. It had been three weeks since I sent a letter to Johnny Carson and I hadn't heard a word. What if one of the Mighty Carson Art Players had opened my letter by mistake?

"I hope you're all paying attention to Todd," Mrs. Tooley interrupted. "You will be quizzed later." I sneaked a peek at Mrs. Tooley's desk. She was making a list in her grade book with a bright red pen. *Wonder Bread, Rice Krispies, Karo Syrup . . .*

A page into Todd's report, Alice Andrejewski returned with the school nurse, Nancy "No-Nonsense" Nellis. A volley of whispers rose up behind me.

"Ten Ton's going to the nurse's office."

"Yeah, No-Nonsense does experiments back there."

"Maybe she's got a potion to make Flintstone skinny."

"Fainted again, I see." Nurse Nellis squared her hips and loomed over me with folded arms. Her gruff voice edged on menacing, but Nancy was the nicest grown-up I knew.

Mrs. Tooley quickly covered her grocery list. "Sunnie was reading her report when she collapsed."

"The whole room shook," whispered "Romulan #2" Ricky Rinaldi.

"Right. Sunnie, to my office. On the double." Nurse Nellis offered her hand.

I looked at Mrs. Tooley, who nodded. As I stood, sand poured into my limbs and my stomach clenched. The room got spotty and my head started to sweat. Nurse Nellis clamped her hand on my shoulder and guided me between the rows of desks while Todd resumed reading. "Milk comes out of cows' udders when the farmer milks them . . . "

We reached Nurse Nellis' infirmary behind Principal Henderson's office and she motioned me up on the shiny exam table. Once I was safely in place, she felt my forehead and peered into my eyes. I could hear Principal Henderson in the next room, warning Eddie MacArthur not to release any more grass snakes during class. I met Nurse Nellis' steady stare, trying not to blink. Nurse Nellis was a broad, solid woman dressed in black with a thick neck and fleshy hands. Her narrow eyes were dark and deeply set, nearly disappearing beneath her heavy brow.

"How are you now?"

"Not too bad, Nancy. A little dizzy." My fainting spells had left us on a first-name basis.

"What have you eaten today?"

"Umm, skim milk." I accidentally kicked the exam table and it wobbled with a metallic echo. "Half a glass," I added.

"Half a glass?" Her tiny eyes expanded.

"Four ounces," I recounted proudly. "Only forty-five calories."

"Any solid food?"

"Nope."

She frowned, delving a troubled "V" between her eyebrows. "You've fainted four times this month. A growing girl has got to eat." Her voice was chiding but I imagined, hopefully, that it held some love. "You need a full breakfast every day. Lunch too. And supper."

She stepped across the room and yanked a thin fabric curtain, revealing the "Five Major Food Groups" chart, complete with a speckled fish, a loaf of French bread, a watermelon, and a rare T-bone steak. 'Just drawings,' I thought, but I was hungry enough to eat everything, even the cartoon fish with the tail and fins still on.

"Promise you'll start eating." Nancy's concern was both embarrassing and deeply cool.

"I can't. I'm on a diet."

"Diet?" She folded her fleshy arms. "Diets are not for thirteen-year-olds. Do your parents know about this?"

"It was my Mom's idea. I have to lose eighteen pounds or else."

"She'll put you up for adoption?"

"Worse. She'll send me to fat camp." My voice broke and I drew in a breath, holding it hard near my heart.

"Fat camp?"

I nodded, realizing that Nancy, in her early fifties, came from a different era. In her day, people were probably judged by their character, not by their Kate Jackson figure or Farah Fawcett hair.

"It's a 'Summer Slim-Down Retreat' in Minnesota. Mom saw an ad in *Family Circle*." Shame clogged my throat and my bottom got bigger, spreading hotly on the metal table.

"Oh honey, there's got to be another way." She squeezed my shoulder, pinching off the blood. "You're giving yourself a nervous breakdown." She consulted her watch, then trained her beady eyes on me. "It's noon. Ready to return to class?"

"It's my lunch hour."

"Did you bring anything to eat, or money for hot lunch?"

I sighed. "Do you know how many calories are in Salisbury steak, tater tots, and tapioca pudding?" I had memorized the hot lunch schedule for the next three weeks. A week from Thursday would no doubt test my willpower: carrot sticks, lemon Jell-O, and a choice of Chicken Fried Steak or Sloppy Joe.

She motioned me down from the table. "You better stay here and rest."

"Thanks, Nance. You're a pal." I jumped off the table and adjusted my pants. "Should I?" I reached for the battered black-and-white TV on her desk.

"Go ahead."

I tuned the TV to the opening of *Days of Our Lives*. "Like sands through the hourglass, so are the days of our lives . . . "

I plopped down on the green Naugahyde couch and put up my feet. Nancy opened the freezer/fridge, which usually held only Bactine Spray, Pepto-Bismol, and Jerry Junkett's diabetic lunch, and pulled out tray of frozen grape-juice-and-toothpick treats. She banged the tray on the sink, loosening the cubes.

"You can eat this." She handed me one. "Only thirty calories." I held the cube to my tongue and felt all its deliciousness; darkly sweet and exquisitely cold. The ice melted quickly and the juice dribbled down my chin. The sugar hit my stomach and filled me, spreading out from a warm little circle that stopped being hungry. I smiled, even as I knew I'd never be thin, and that meant never being happy.

The fourth period bell rang and a moment later the halls echoed with the tinny symphony of kids dashing to class. As quickly as it began, the music ended when the second bell rang.

Nancy and I were quiet, focused on *Days of Our Lives*. Marlena's evil twin and Don's mysterious daughter were threatening Don and Marlena's marriage.

14

"Will Marlena stay with Don or is he too much trouble?" I asked Nancy.

She squinted at the TV, pursing her lips. "She'll stand by him."

"What about his affair with Lorraine?" I sat forward, anxious for her answer.

"She'll forgive him."

"For sure?"

Nancy sighed. "A man like Don—tall, romantic, passionate—doesn't come around but once in a lifetime." Nancy got up and went to the fridge, pulling it open with a pneumatic 'pop.' "A woman's got to suffer for that kind of love."

"Was the late Mr. Nellis tall and romantic?" I pictured a young Nancy batting her eyelashes and accepting a single red rose.

As she chuckled, her neck wobbled and her cheeks turned red. "Bernard was only five-foot-seven. With a limp. His idea of romance was buying a new ironing board."

"Oh." The disappointing Mr. Nellis made me sad. "Would you marry again if you met a guy like Don?"

"In Wauwatosa? If he exists, pass along my number." Nancy took another grape juice cube and offered me the tray. I shook my head. I couldn't afford thirty more calories—I had to weigh in the day after tomorrow. I sat back on the couch, adjusting the green plastic pillow. *Tall, romantic, and passionate,* I noted. This information might come in handy someday. *A woman has to suffer for that kind of love.*

The journey home from Truman Junior High was only about a quarter mile, but it was a quarter mile fraught with dangerous distractions. First came the Baskin-Robbins 31 Flavors, where at least 29 flavors were ones that I liked. High school kids with pimply skin, winged hair, and tight Calvin Kleins loitered in the parking lot after school, drinking Mad Dog 20/20 from brown paper bags. I walked quickly, my baritone horn in its big plastic case bumping my hip with every step.

"Hey Baluba, play us your tuba." I stopped and looked across the lot. It was Ronald Wombat, Todd's older brother, sitting on the hood of his rusty purple Gremlin with two other boys, chucking pebbles at the broken pavement. "Ba-loooo-ba! Play the tuba!" I walked faster with their laughter ringing in my ears. I was too scared to stop and explain the difference between a baritone and a tuba; not that they would care anyway.

After Baskin-Robbins came Dunkin' Donuts with its greasy glass windows and clouds of deep-fried sugary smoke. The aroma brought tears to my eyes. My throat burned, my lungs ached, but I kept steady, counting my steps and chanting, "Nothing tastes as good as being thin, not even a glazed doughnut with sprinkles . . . "

The final challenge was the White Hen Pantry on 116th and North. The boarded-up window, piles of trash, and rough gravel parking lot gave no hint of the wonders within: a circular display case of Slim Jims; racks of Little Debbies and Hostess Fruit Pies; a cash register manned by friendly Mr. Chan offering free samples of his wife's egg roll. "Stay strong," I told myself. "You're almost home. Remember, Johnny will like you better when you're skinny."

I reached our little black-and-white Colonial on West Hadley Avenue thankful to have made it home in one piece, with my baritone still intact. Ever since eighth grade began, I had learned to appreciate minor miracles. I dropped my baritone in the front hall, where it landed with a brassy rattle.

"Sunnie, is that you?" Mom called from the kitchen.

"Yep." I grabbed Nancy's note—*Fainted 4x month*—from my book bag.

"Something special came in the mail."

Mail? Johnny! I dropped my books and ran into the kitchen. Mom stood over the stove, battling a big pot of boiling potatoes. Steam covered the windows, trickling into the curtain's yellowed hem. Mom lowered the burner, wiped her sweaty forehead, and took a swig of Dr. Pepper.

"There on the table." I turned around and knew right away that this wasn't it. The envelope was orange. Johnny Carson would never send an orange envelope. The return address said "Summer

16

Slim-Down Retreat" above a photo of two smiling girls in matching bikinis.

"It's from the fat camp." I sank into the chair and ignored the delicious scent of creamy chicken bake with sour cream and mushroom soup.

Mom wiped her face with a napkin, grabbed her pack of Virginia Slims, and pulled up a chair beside me. "I hope you don't mind I opened it." Mom lit a cigarette and stole three quick puffs, squinting as if under surveillance. "I was so excited, I couldn't wait until you got home."

I peeled back the envelope's broken flap, pulled out the information folder and flipped through it. The pages were full of thin, tan, long-legged girls roasting marshmallows and paddling kayaks. Beneath the pictures were bold captions like, "FIT FOR LIFE!" and "A HEALTHY GIRL IS HAPPY!"

"They sure look busy." My throat ached at the thought of struggling into a swimsuit, even last summer's long-line one-piece with the puckered skirt in front.

"That's why the program works—all that exercise." Mom's green eyes glowed. She looked plump and happy; her damp, dark hair curled over her delicate ears and her freckled cheeks were pink and shiny. I couldn't show her Nancy's note now.

"I have six weeks to lose eighteen pounds." I rubbed the folder's shiny cover with my thumb. "I might not have to go."

"Sunnie, it's not a punishment, it's an opportunity. I wish I had the chance . . . " Mom's voice trailed away as she looked longingly at the *TV Guide* photo of Suzanne Pleshette on the fridge. Mom had pasted her own face on Suzanne's body and beneath it had written, "Goal: Size 6 by Christmas." Of course, that had been Christmas, 1976.

"How was school?" Mom jumped up to drain the potatoes.

"It was OK."

"Any trouble from the boys?"

"No more than usual."

Everyone else's dinner that evening consisted of creamy chicken bake, mashed potatoes, buttered green beans with shredded cheddar cheese, and strawberry-rhubarb cobbler for dessert. I had a grilled chicken breast and one boiled potato with a teaspoon of pepper; no butter or salt. My stomach tightened as I took my place between my nine-year-old brother, Max, and Mom's mother, Grannie Lassen, across from Mom, Pop, and Ingrid's empty chair.

"Where's the sullen Swede?" Pop asked as he slid into his seat. My sister Ingrid was sixteen and ever since she'd been accepted to study in Sweden in the fall, she spent most evenings in the basement, smoking unfiltered cigarettes and listening to ABBA records on the hi-fi.

"Ingrid's downstairs," Mom said, piling Pop's plate with chicken and mashed potatoes. He waved his hand, motioning for more.

"Pining for the fjords, no doubt." Pop chuckled.

"Fjords are in Norway, not Sweden," Max said.

"It's a joke, Einstein." Pop's pale face darkened as he dug into his food.

"Geography is no laughing matter." Max had an IQ of 160 and was slightly hyperactive. He resembled an alien with his big square head, pale skin, and round, gray-blue eyes behind black-rimmed glasses. He loved dissecting things and had his own microscope and chemistry set. Weird-smelling smoke often escaped from his bedroom. I was convinced he would either be a famous scientist someday, or a serial killer.

Pop flattened *The Milwaukee Journal* beside his plate. "Patty Hearst!" he exclaimed through a mouthful of mashed potato. "The little terrorist is afraid of jail. Should have thought about that before robbing the bank."

"Peter, no angry talk." Mom spooned gravy over Grannie's plate.

"Ingrid in the basement again. Something wrong with that child." Grannie cut her chicken into tiny strips.

"Ingrid's just moody," Mom replied, moving on to Max.

"Moody?" Grannie held her knife aloft. "Needs medication if you ask me. In that dark basement all night, brooding. She'll wind up like cousin Margrete, in the sanitarium, strapped to a chair and talking to horseflies."

"Mama! For shame! Not at the table." Mom frowned, nodding at Max and me.

"Sunnie and I are familiar with the etiology of mental illness," Max said, grabbing his glass of gritty Ovaltine with both hands.

"Popularity of President dips to thirty-nine percent, a new low!" Pop scoffed and turned the page. "What do people expect when they elect a peanut farmer President?"

I watched Pop scan the newspaper. People considered him handsome, although he boasted about never spending more than a dollar-fifty for a haircut. He had a full head of wavy blonde hair with a precise side part, hazel eyes, and a thin, high-bridged nose. As he read his cheeks paled and his lips pursed tighter.

"Son of Sam suspect fit for trial," he read aloud. "Damn right he is!"

Mom pushed her plate aside, then grabbed her cigarettes and tapped one out of the pack.

"Stina, eat your dinner," Grannie commanded, pointing at Mom's plate.

Mom clenched the cigarette between her teeth. "I've been slaving all day," she said sadly. "It just doesn't taste the same to me."

"Shame. It's really quite good." Grannie turned to me. "Wilma, did you get an 'A' today?" I was about to answer when Mom jumped in.

"Sunnie got something in the mail." Mom leaned forward, pushing away the potatoes. "Sunnie, do you want to share it with the family?"

"Not really." I fought down the last of my dry chicken breast.

"Go on, it's exciting," Mom encouraged.

I sighed. "I got an application from the Summer Slim-Down Retreat." Saying the words made me feel like a failure.

"The success rate for dieters is less than ten percent." Max pushed up his glasses. "Long-term weight loss is unlikely."

"It's not." Mom stabbed her cigarette into the ashtray and ground it down. "The focus is on physical fitness."

19

"Physical foolishness." Grannie dabbed her lip. "At her age."

"It better be worth it." Pop turned the page. "For that kind of money."

"Peter!" Mom shot him an angry glance.

"I know I'll be losing weight. In my wallet." Pop's eyes darted down the next column.

"How can you put a price on your daughter's health and happiness?" Mom fumbled for another cigarette, then crumpled the pack along with the cellophane wrapper.

"It should be cheap, Christina. Less food."

"This isn't summer camp. They have nurses and dietitians." Mom coughed. "Wish I'd gone at Sunnie's age."

Everyone looked at Grannie, who continued cutting her chicken. "You weren't overweight, Stina."

"Yes, Mama. I was."

"*Fie deg!* You're giving Wilma a complex."

"She'll thank me someday." Mom squared her chin.

"She's not fat!" Grannie's pale cheeks caught fire. "She's just growing unevenly."

"Mama, no one grows unevenly."

"Of course they do. Wilma, stand up." Grannie waved at me. "Show your mother."

I swallowed hard. "Do I have to?"

"Just for a minute," she said. "Show us your legs."

I pushed out my chair and stood beside it.

"Walk around the table." Grannie circled the air with her fork. "Just once. So we can see."

I plodded around the table, feeling the dishes shake with my every step. Max poked my ribs as I passed.

Grannie held out her hand and stopped me. "See? Built like my sister Lena. Wilma will be tall and shapely someday." She nodded confidently. "Unless she gets a complex first."

I crawled back into my chair and contemplated my cold shiny potato.

"They want to raise the postal rates!" Pop pounded the table, rattling the silverware. "Fifteen cents to send a letter! Socialists! Might as well move to the U-S-S-R."

"Sending children away to lose weight," Grannie marveled. "Whoever heard of such a thing?"

I closed my eyes and imagined I was on *The Tonight Show*, sitting beside my beloved Johnny in the plaid fabric chair.

"Sunnie, you're in such great shape," Johnny was saying. "You've got the hectic life of a director; one day you're here in L.A., the next you're in Rio or Paris or Dakar or jetting off to Cannes. How do you stay looking so good?"

"Well John, I play a lot of tennis, just like you . . . "

Before bed I tiptoed to Grannie's room and knocked softly on her door. When she didn't answer, I knocked again, a little louder.

"Come in," she said. I entered quietly. Grannie, in her rocking chair, was wrapped in a quilt stroking Magda, her old tabby cat. The lights were dim as Grannie stared at the darkened window. I imagined Grannie had special access to the past, in flickering images like a movie playing out behind her eyes. Granddad Lassen, who died when Mom was seventeen, would be there, along with Grannie's five dead sisters. In photos Granddad Lassen looked stern and tall and unforgiving, with a pale thin mustache and broad boxy shoulders, but Mom said he was comedic, and liked drinking beer and singing fight songs. When he sang, and when he drank, his fair skin turned crimson and even his ears grew red. He had eight brothers and always, at least one of them was drunk.

"Grannie, can I sit with you?" I whispered. I dared not speak louder for fear of breaking the room's gentle tension.

Grannie nodded. "Of course, Wilma. Come and sit a spell." To Grannie I was always Wilma. To everyone else I was Sunnie; had been since infancy, when I cried a lot and Mom thought a happy nickname would cheer me up. Even teachers called me Sunnie, but to Grannie I was Wilma, named after her sister who died at thirteen.

I sat on Grannie's bed as she continued to rock. Magda's green eyes glowed as she stretched, yawned, then collapsed in Grannie's lap.

21

"You seem subdued tonight, Wilma. Are you mindful?"

I shook my head. I wondered how Grannie knew me so completely, as if all my secrets were visible on my skin.

I cleared my throat. "Grannie, will Johnny Carson answer my letter?"

She kept rocking, staring at the past. "Yes. I believe he will. He looks, on the television, to be an honorable man." She stroked Magda. "His eyes are a bit close but his brow is smooth."

I kicked off my shoes. "It's been three weeks."

"Good fortune's worth waiting for." She sighed, sinking into herself. "I'm tired, Wilma. Would you let out my hair?"

"Of course." I went to Grannie's nightstand and found her coarse wooden hairbrush among a collection of old-fashioned ointments, salves, and lotions. Grannie leaned forward and I grasped her long gray braid. Magda, irritated, arched up and jumped from Grannie's lap.

I pried off the rubber band and freed the braided sections with my fingers, careful not to pull the tiny knots. "Tell me the next part of your motion picture story," Grannie asked as her hair unwound, circling the wooden chair back.

"Where did I leave off last time?"

"Our heroine had just left the orphanage."

"OK, after Stormy leaves the orphanage . . . "

"That's Kristy McNichol?" Grannie held up her hand, pale and steady.

"Right. She runs away to find her real parents. They're French royalty, but Stormy doesn't know that because she was kidnapped as a baby."

"Oh, so violent?" Grannie shuddered.

I brushed her hair vigorously, from the roots to the ends. "Don't worry," I said. "The movie's rated 'G.'"

I continued the story, past the point when Stormy goes to New York and meets Eric, played by Robby Benson, a gifted painter with a brain tumor. I worked the front, back, and sides of Grannie's fine gray hair and pushed it forward in two sections over her shoulders so she could admire the shine in the subtle half-light.

Grannie nodded. "That's a fine story, Wilma. Must Stormy meet the young man, though? That's a bit grown up for you."

"She has to," I explained. "Eric's father was Stormy's parents' lawyer. He knows the secret to her past."

Grannie sighed. "If you insist. You're the author."

I felt myself blush, even in the cool darkness. "Not really. It's just pretend."

"It is real," Grannie insisted. "Don't let anything derail your dreams."

"You're thinking about your tap dancing."

She didn't respond at first, and I feared I'd made her angry. "Wilma, that was a long time ago," she said evenly. "I never think about that foolishness now."

I helped Grannie into bed, lifting her feet as she leaned back on the mattress. I folded the blanket under her chin as Magda purred on the pillow beside her. I leaned in to kiss Grannie goodnight and she held my arms firmly, peering into my eyes.

"What?" I asked.

"Nothing." A sly smile tugged at her lips. Was she guessing the ending of *Girl on the Lam*? Picturing me winning an Oscar for Best Director and thanking her from the stage at the Dorothy Chandler Pavilion? Maybe she was looking for some sign of her sister Wilma in me.

I listened to Grannie's deep breathing as I cleaned her hairbrush with the fine-tooth comb and tidied her nightstand.

"Wilma?" she called quietly.

"Yes?"

"You're fine just as you are."

I squeezed the hairbrush until my fingers hurt.

"Did you hear me?"

"Yes," I replied.

"Don't listen to your mother. I think you're fine."

The ten o'clock news was starting as Pop came up to bed, cursing beneath his breath. No doubt the news had upset him, souring his stomach and darkening his mood. I sat at my dresser beneath the movie star lights, plying my eyelashes with Vaseline and rubbing lemon on my chin, as recommended by Suzanne Somers in *Beauty Secrets of the Stars*.

I tallied my daily calories in the notebook beside my bed. Half a cup of skim milk, one grape juice cube, a chicken breast, a plain potato. Two-hundred-ninety-five calories. My stomach ached as I realized I could eat something else—an apple slice, half a banana, or two Ritz crackers.

Downstairs the kitchen floor felt cool and accusing against my feet. The fridge opened with an enormous creak that I imagined would wake the whole house. I held my breath and heard only Ingrid in the basement, practicing her Swedish beneath the melody of *Dancing Queen: "God dag. Jag heter Ingrid. Vad heter du?"*

The strawberry-rhubarb cobbler called from the fridge's bottom shelf, teasing me with its loose skirt of plastic wrap. I contemplated the crunchy top. One bite couldn't hurt. I grabbed a fork. The first taste was exquisite: sweet strawberry and sour rhubarb beneath brown sugar and oats. My willpower withered as I dug in, stopping only for a gulp of milk, straight from the bottle. My vision narrowed. There was no Johnny, no diet, no fat camp; no Baluba and her tuba, no Marlena on *Days of Our Lives*; only this cobbler entering me like medicine, swirling inside me, filling my veins. A warmth swelled my stomach. I felt whole.

The warmth lasted only until I reached the staircase, where my legs grew heavier with every step. By the top, I weighed a ton. I didn't even glance in the mirror for fear of confronting all that fatness.

It was ten twenty-nine as I turned on my TV. The local news ended and Johnny's theme song began. "And now, heeeeeere's Johnny!" Ed McMahon's voice boomed through my bedroom. The striped curtain separated and out stepped Johnny, slim and shiny in a tan checkered suit and solid brown tie.

"Do Aunt Blabby, do Aunt Blabby," I whispered, crossing my fingers. "At least do 'Stump the Band.'" Johnny, rocking on his heels, joked about Patty Hearst, President Carter, and runaway inflation. Above the TV I could see my reflection in the movie star mirror. My face looked dark and flickering, with dramatic shadows beneath my eyes. With the blanket pulled up to my chin, no one could tell I was chubby. Johnny would love me someday. He would at least answer my letter. The screen went white after the commercials and I saw that I'd been crying.

CHAPTER TWO

April gave way to May, a month I despised for its short-shorts, cork sandals, and tube-top weather. I wished I could move to Alaska and wear Grannie's hand-knit knee-length Nordic sweaters all year long. Worse than the warmer weather was watching weeks go by with no word from Johnny. While Johnny vacationed in Europe, George Carlin sat in as guest host and I worried that George might accidentally answer my letter. I wasn't sure what I'd do with a letter from George Carlin, especially if it included those seven dirty words.

I lost four more pounds and could almost wear last summer's size twelve "Huskies for Her," until I gave in to Mr. Chan's free egg roll offer and, deciding the whole diet day was ruined anyway, bought an Almond Joy, a Baby Ruth, and a $100,000 Bar. Four times I fainted in class; three times for real and once so I could watch Rex and Maggie get married on *Days of Our Lives*.

On May 26th, Principal Henderson announced that Wauwatosa's own Rambert Specialty Jams was sponsoring a banner design contest for Truman School. The winning banner would hang in the school gymnasium while the winning artist would speak at commencement and receive a lifetime supply of jam. We started our banners in Miss Hill's fifth-period art class.

"Right brain off and left brain on," Miss Hill advised, turning her fist like a knob. "Let those creative juices flow." Miss Hill was a former flower child who hadn't left the sixties. She drove a Volkswagen Beetle, covered her desk with peace signs, and crocheted her own clothes out of hemp.

"Let your imaginations run wild!" Miss Hill was a big believer in creativity and, even though it was art class, she let me hand in sections of *Girl on the Lam* for extra credit.

Emily, smelling strongly of Vicks Vapo-Rub, leaned over my shoulder. "Wish I could win that jam." She pulled in a clogged breath, trying to clear her sinuses. "My stepmom would have more money for groceries."

Miss Hill didn't believe in conventional seating plans so our desks were arranged in four-person pods, making it easy to talk to Emily.

"You've got a good chance to win," I said. "As good as anybody." In truth, Emily wasn't much of an artist. Instead she was a human calculator and Star Trek fanatic. Her independent study project involved the Vulcan mind-meld.

As Miss Hill passed out sheets of plain newsprint I imagined my design. I would highlight the T-R-U in "Truman" and connect that to the word "truth," then tie the M-A-N to "humanity" in a gold circle around a silhouette of the school. I was so excited that I started sketching on my wooden desktop.

Emily thrust her fists under her chin and kicked her desk. "I'll help you with your design, if you want," I offered.

"It's not that."

I stopped sketching. "Problems with Jerry?" Jerry Junkett was in love with Emily but she just wanted to be friends. Undaunted, he scribbled love sonnets on crumpled lunch bags, avoiding the greasy Cheetos stains, and pinned them to her locker.

"It's not Jerry." She looked at Kim Melman and Debbie Schneider, the other members of our pod, who were painting their nails. Gauging their lack of interest, Emily wheezed in my ear, "I kinda like the Bay City Rollers."

"Emily, you can't!"

Kim and Debbie looked up. Miss Hill's love beads rattled unhappily as she handed me a sheet of paper.

Emily blushed, scratching an eczema patch on her hand. "My sister got the new *Tiger Beat*. Eric looked sexy in his kilt."

"Derek is tastier," Kim offered, blowing on her hands.

"Derek has like a gazillion zits." Debbie painted her little fingernail. "Ian is the ultimate fox."

"Emily, not the Bay City Rollers," I pleaded. "You promised." Emily and I, the "Geek Girls," had a pact not to like Shaun Cassidy, Scott Baio, Parker Stevenson, or any teen idol. Along with my love for Johnny Carson, I encouraged Emily's burgeoning interest in Leonard Nimoy.

"I'm sorry, Sun." Emily twirled her marker pen. "But my sister says Johnny Carson is gro-tesque."

"You like Johnny Carson?" Kim flipped a wing of her perfectly-parted blonde hair. "He's as old as your dad."

"Or even your grandpa," Debbie added, testing her nails with the tip of her tongue. "You could never kiss him—he's wrinkly."

My cheeks felt hot. Either I was embarrassed, or the incense burning on Miss Hill's desk hurt my eyes. "Johnny is a major part of my life," I said. "My mom watched him when she was expecting me, and then when I was a baby, crying all night. Johnny lets me dream."

"About what?" Debbie asked.

"Being on his show someday." I squared my shoulders and sat up straight.

"*You're* gonna be a movie star?" Kim raised one penciled eyebrow.

"A director, not a movie star," I explained. "Anyway, Johnny doesn't just have actors and actresses on his show; he has singers and child stars, dolphins and hog callers and potato chip collectors. Anyone can be on Johnny Carson, or at least dream about being on Johnny. He connects Hollywood to the rest of America."

I drew a circle on my banner. I didn't care what Kim Melman and Debbie Schneider thought, but I worried about Emily. If she liked the Bay City Rollers, there was a chance she'd become popular. Her eczema could clear up anytime; Melman and Schneider might invite her into their clique. I'd have only Jerry left as a friend, and his dad was threatening to move the whole family back to Ohio. Maybe Nurse Nellis would eat lunch with me every day, but I doubted it.

The fifth period bell rang and as we filed out of the classroom, Miss Hill took me aside. Smiling, she pulled out a folder from beneath her macramé poncho and handed it to me. It was the section of *Girl on the Lam* I'd given her two weeks earlier. Scrawled across the top was "A++ Excellent Imagination!"

"I'm looking forward to the next twenty pages." She straightened her poncho's beaded fringe. "It's a pleasure having such a talented girl in class."

"Thank you, Miss Hill." I tried to sound grateful, but what good was being talented if you had no friends? Maybe Miss Hill would eat lunch with me. I looked up and decided no. On the field trip to the Capitol in Madison I had watched Miss Hill unwrap her lunch of sunflower seeds, brown rice, and bean curd. It would never work between us. "In the next section of *Girl on the Lam*, Stormy finds out that her real parents died in a plane crash," I said suddenly.

Miss Hill's smile dissolved.

"Don't worry, though." I tried to cheer her up. "It's not as violent as it sounds."

That afternoon's walk home was uneventful, even though Mrs. Chan's egg roll smelled especially heavenly and I knew that, at the back of the White Hen Pantry, new issues of *Gossip* and *Rona Barrett's Hollywood* waited stiffly in the wire racks, potentially filled with pictures of Johnny. Johnny on a beach, Johnny on a yacht, a tan Johnny playing tennis under the sun. Still I hurried home, anxious to work on my banner.

"Sunnie, you got a letter," Mom announced as I pushed through the front door. "Upstairs on your bed."

"From the fat camp?" My arms sagged from the weight of my baritone.

"No. California. It looks important."

California? I took the stairs two at a time, afraid to get my hopes up but knowing it could be from Johnny.

I threw open my door and there it was, a big white envelope propped up between my "Visit the Sears Tower" pillow and

Curious George. My hands shook as I read the name and address neatly typed on the front:

Miss Wilma Sundstrom
11529 West Hadley Avenue
Wauwatosa, Wisc. 53226

The return address said:

NBC Studios
3000 West Alameda Avenue
Burbank, Calif. 91523

Burbank? Beautiful downtown Burbank! Johnny talked about it all the time. This was it! Black stars circled my eyes and I had to sit down. "Please," I whispered, tearing the envelope, "oh please let it be . . ." It was! An autographed 8" x 10" black-and-white photo of Johnny Carson! I pressed it to my chest, not daring to cry for fear of smearing the ink.

"He knows I exist." Pride swelled inside me, yet I felt humbled, touched. For the few seconds that Johnny spent signing this photo, our lives overlapped; our souls were as one. This was something Kim Melman and the Romulans and even Emily didn't understand. I was real to Johnny, for an instant. I had reached out and touched something bigger than myself. My life would always count for something, from now on.

I crossed my legs and took a deep breath. "Don't be so emotional," I told myself. I held the photo to the light, judging with a rational eye. In the photo, Johnny was standing in front of the striped curtain, most likely during the monologue. His hands were jammed in his jacket pockets, his chest puffed up, and his head thrown back in laughter. His silver hair glowed and small crinkly lines softened his eyes. Rational went out the window: clearly, this was the most handsome man in the world.

I savored the signed photo, noticing every detail: the shine of Johnny's jacket buttons; the height of his hairline; the crescent dimple in his chin. I felt life flowing around me: Mom in the kitchen fixing dinner, Max in his room mixing flammable liquids, Ingrid in the basement brooding. Grannie was soaking her feet after spending all day delivering *The Good News Gospel* to the Home For Aged Lutherans. Life went on around me and I was aware of it, but separate; able to witness it without taking part.

"Sunnie, it's suppertime," Mom called up the stairs.

"Be right there." I felt a twinge of sadness as I laid the photo aside. Of course I wanted everyone to know that Johnny and I were like satellites aligned in orbit, but I also knew that the minute I showed my family the photo, the spell would be broken. Johnny wouldn't belong just to me anymore; everyone else would have a share of him, just by being able to say, "Sunnie has a photo signed by the real Johnny Carson."

Supper consisted of pork chops with gravy, fried onions, buttered noodles, and applesauce, with pineapple upside-down cake for dessert. I had a plain pork chop trimmed of fat and one cup of boiled white rice but for once I didn't mind. All my suffering hunger had been rewarded. Johnny Carson knew I existed.

"Russians optimistic on new SALT pact," Pop read aloud. "I'm glad they're optimistic. I'm sure as hell not."

"Peter! No swearing at the table." Mom heaped noodles on Pop's plate.

Max stirred his smear of applesauce. "Did you know that scabs are made up of white blood cells?" he asked. "They collect at the surface of the skin and dry out."

"Fascinating," Pop replied, turning the page.

"D'you know what happens if you put a scab in peroxide?" Max's blue-gray eyes glowed. "It fizzes, then dissolves."

"Don't you dare experiment on your scabs!" Mom grabbed her Virginia Slims. "If I find a mess upstairs I'll . . ." She paused to find her lighter. ". . . I'll take away your rock tumbler."

"Why my rock tumbler?" Max blanched.

"So you know when you're being punished."

"Life is a punishment." Ingrid yawned.

"That reminds me. Ilsa Larsson passed away," Grannie said.

"The lady with the begonias?" Mom lit her cigarette.

"No, you're thinking of Elsa Larsen. Ilsa was the redhead. Married to the admiral."

"Oh, I remember. Nice lady." Mom blew a smoke ring.

"Had a stroke." Grannie pushed an onion to the edge of her plate. "Just fell over dead."

Max leaned forward. "A stroke is actually the result of fatty substances slowly building up in the blood vessels of the brain." He stirred his Ovaltine, looking satisfied.

"Fatty substances, my eye. The Lord has a plan for us all." Grannie swallowed loudly.

"Life is pointless." Ingrid shook her head. "You're born, you suffer, you die."

"Three thousand dollars to study abroad and that's your attitude?" Pop slid the paper aside and looked straight at Ingrid. "Well? Is it?"

"Peter . . ." Mom got up to slice the cake.

"Maybe you'd be happier staying home," Pop challenged.

"Happiness is an illusion," Ingrid mumbled, stabbing another pork chop with her fork.

I looked at the two slices of pineapple on my dessert plate; no syrup, no Cool Whip, no cake, and realized I'd never been happier than I was at that moment. My family's squabbles meant nothing to me—not since Johnny Carson knew I existed.

"I'm going to make a documentary film about Johnny's early years in Iowa, before his family moved to Nebraska," I announced. "This will be after I win an Oscar for *Girl on the Lam*, of course. For now, I'm gonna put Johnny's picture in a bag so I can take it everywhere. Mom? Can I borrow a plastic baggie?"

"Sure." Mom patted my arm. "I'm proud of you, Sunnie. You aren't afraid to have big dreams."

Pop scraped his plate. "It isn't proper. Sending photos to thirteen-year-old girls."

"Don't be mean, Peter." Mom eyed him evenly. "Sunnie will treasure this forever."

That night I placed the photo on Grannie's nightstand while I undid her hair. In the soft light Johnny's face looked even gentler, as if he were laughing with us, at a joke we three shared.

"Isn't he handsome?" I asked Grannie.

"Yes. Very handsome."

Grannie had always approved of Johnny Carson, and Doc Severinsen too, because they had good Scandinavian names. I didn't tell her I once looked up "Carson" in a Heraldry book at the library and learned that the name was Scots-Irish in origin.

"He's handsome and he's nice, don't you think?"

Grannie nodded. "No doubt. He answered your letter."

I separated the braided sections of hair with my fingers, letting them fall loose. "Grannie, will you come with me to California?"

She pulled the quilt around her shoulders and shivered. "When are you leaving?"

"September."

"This September?"

"No. 1982. When I start at UCLA." I had already chosen UCLA because of its famous film school. Now that I knew Johnny, maybe I could stay at his Malibu mansion on weekends, entertaining Michael Landon and drinking dry martinis.

"You won't want me with you." Grannie shook her head. "You'll be having fun with the other young people."

I parted her hair with the brush's pointy tip. "We could live together in the dorm."

"The dorm?" Grannie lifted the quilt, letting Magda jump on her lap. "Wilma, I'll be dead by then."

My stomach dropped and I stopped brushing. "It's only four-and-a-half years."

"At my age, a year is an eternity." Grannie scratched Magda's ears as the cat purred happily.

I looked at Johnny's photo on the nightstand. He would be fifty-three in October; forty years older than me. Grannie had turned sixty-eight in March. I wanted the world to stand still so I could catch my breath.

"I don't worry about you, Wilma." Grannie spoke softly, holding Magda close. "But Ingrid troubles me. Why is such a pretty girl so sad? And Max is too smart for his own good. His type ends up plotting against the government." Grannie sighed. "But you'll turn out just fine. Make us all proud."

I lifted the brush and pulled out a handful of hair. The tangled hair looked like a swirl of silver in my hand; glowing and electric, throwing metallic sparks. Tossing it in the garbage felt like giving something precious up forever. "Tell me the tap dancing story," I asked carefully.

"Again?" She sounded weary. "You've heard it so many times."

I nodded towards Johnny. "But he's never heard it. It's the first time for him."

The rocking chair creaked as Grannie sat back. "All right then. The year was 1930," she began slowly. "I was nineteen and the best tap dancer in Wilton, Iowa."

She stopped for a moment to collect her thoughts. "I was better even than Arlys Whiteacre, and she was very good. A motion picture director named Busby Berkeley was looking for tap dancers to put in his next film. He didn't want slick city girls with the taint of the town; he wanted big-boned girls from good Scandinavian families. There was an audition in Chicago. I was all set to go, had my train ticket and everything, but then Horace Hellesen knocked Wilma down with his motor car. Racing down Main Street, he hit her and didn't stop. Never even slowed down."

I stepped to the nightstand and stood with my back to Grannie. I had heard the story countless times but whenever she reached this part, I turned away. My hands quivered as I straightened the delicate glass bottles, the tubes of ointment, the golden-orange salves.

"Wilma was in a coma a long time." Grannie began rocking slowly, back and forth in time with her story. "We moved her to the bedroom upstairs, above the parlor. I stayed home to help Mama. She was just about crazed with grief, and there were four little ones still at home." Grannie paused and swallowed. "After Wilma passed, my father offered to buy me a ticket to California so I could audition for Mr. Berkeley in person, but it was too late. You see, while Wilma lingered, I fell milking the cows and broke my ankle. Not a bad break—it healed sure enough—but there was just a little weakness there. It still aches sometimes, at the end of the day."

Grannie's voice sounded sad but steady. The facts were the facts and she was long past grieving now, but I still had it in me to feel every word she said. I sat down on Grannie's bed, letting the events play back in my mind, so alive and so vividly real: the racing motor car with its ooga-ooga horn; the fragile thirteen-year-old Wilma lying lifeless in the road; her pale, limp body being carried to the room above the parlor; the clutch of lumbering cows huddled by the barn door, heavy with milking. We weren't allowed to cry in the house—good Scandinavians don't do that—so I held my breath, pressing it deep into my chest.

"What's wrong, Wilma?" Grannie squinted towards the bed. "You look a little peaked. Do you have a belly ache?"

"Nope." I dug my fingers into the bedspread and squeezed hard.

She pointed to the nightstand. "There's Milk of Magnesia in the drawer. With a measuring spoon and everything."

"That's OK. I don't need it." I drew up my knees and held them tightly. I looked at the photo of Johnny. He was smiling, so I smiled too. After a moment the sadness passed and my tears stayed hidden beneath the surface, aching like an apple lodged sideways in my throat.

Friday, June 2nd was my last weigh-in before the fat camp application deadline. I weighed in before breakfast because even half a cup of skim milk could fool the scale into thinking I was fatter than I actually was. Standing naked in the bathroom I felt scared but hopeful. I needed to hit 159 to stay home, and I'd been at 160 a full week earlier. The luck of Johnny was with me, offering encouragement, promising it would be OK.

As I waited for Mom I went over my weigh-in preparations: I had clipped my nails, both finger- and toenails, right down to the quick; I trimmed my bangs with the black-handled scissors; I peed twice, really hard both times. I wrapped a Coppertone beach towel around my shoulders and shivered. There was nothing else to do but wait and pray. "Please send me one-fifty-nine," I pleaded, fingers and toes crossed tight. "I'll be in a whole new decade of numbers. My 'Huskies for Hers' will hang loose. Todd won't call me Ten-Ton anymore. Let me open my eyes to find my beautiful 159."

Mom rapped on the door. "Sunnie? Can I come in, hon?"

I cracked open the door and she slipped in, smelling of peanut butter sandwiches and cigarette smoke. "Ready?" Her green eyes were round and excited as she rubbed her freckled hands.

"I guess so." I pulled out the scale, dropped the beach towel, and was about to step on when I remembered my gum. It had to weigh several ounces, at least. I took out the big pink wad and balanced it beside the sink.

"Here goes." I took a deep breath and stepped on the scale, closing my eyes until the needle stopped.

I opened my eyes and looked down. One-sixty-one. Oh no. How could it be? I stepped off, blew all the air out of my lungs and got back on. The needle again stopped at 161 as every bad thing I'd eaten in the previous week came back to me: a handful of Fritos, a bowl of Count Chocula with chocolate milk, seventeen pieces of Pez from Jerry's "Princess Leia" Pez dispenser. Seventeen pieces of Pez! All of them were grape and I didn't even like grape; I only ate them so Jerry wouldn't feel bad. Now, because of that, I had to go to fat camp.

Mom stroked my back. "It's OK, Sunnie."

"No, it isn't." I grabbed the beach towel and covered my eyes. "Look at me."

When I didn't move, she peeled back the towel. "Honey, you've lost sixteen pounds." She reached to hug me but I pushed her away. Sometimes her love felt like pity, even when she didn't mean it to.

"I still have to go to fat camp." I tucked the towel under my armpits. "Right?"

"I don't know." Mom searched her apron pockets but, not finding a cigarette, instead folded her arms. "I suppose you could stay home and diet here."

36

"Really?" The hope I felt surprised me, rising up my throat.

Mom leaned against the doorframe. "Sunnie, the retreat wasn't meant to be a punishment. I just don't want you ending up like me."

I felt myself blush. "You're not that bad, Mom."

She stole a glance in the bathroom mirror and frowned. "I was a chubby kid, but I got down to one-hundred-eight pounds by junior year."

She flicked a dark curl off her forehead. "I had a closet full of Pendleton skirts, blouses with Peter Pan collars, patent leather shoes. I dated the star quarterback." She bit her lip. "OK, he was only JV. Still, he played football. Then the summer before senior year my father died and I got mono, I gained a lot of weight, and it was all downhill from there." She played with the faucets, squirting the water off and on.

I hated seeing Mom this way. "At least you had us," I offered.

"Yes. I have my children." She turned away from the sink, squared my shoulders, and looked me straight in the eye. "I want the best for you, Sunnie. In everything. The truth is, fat girls have fewer choices in life." I tried to wriggle away but she held me tightly.

"No, listen. This is painful, but true. You'll never be the center of attention; never the belle of the ball. No one gives fat girls the benefit of the doubt. Skinny, pretty girls get the best of everything. We get whatever's left." She dropped her hands and sighed. "But I won't *make* you go to the camp. You are a wise child. I know you'll do what's best." She forced a smile, even as her round green eyes seemed to retreat.

"Thanks, Mom."

She squeezed my shoulder. "I'll let you get dressed."

She slipped out of the bathroom and hurried down the hall towards Max's room. "That better not be smoke I smell," she warned. "I said 'no' to that Bunsen burner." Max closed his door quickly.

I grabbed my clothes and struggled into my bra. Soon I'd need a Playtex Cross-Your-Heart Full Figure bra like Mom's, full of complicated buckles, hooks, and wires. Then I'd need a girdle too, like Mom's and Grannie's, that I'd have to unzip after the all-you-can-eat Torsk Bake at the Sons of Norway lodge.

"At least you've got a signed photo of Johnny," I told my face in the mirror. I hated the girl who looked back at me. I hated her dirty-dishwater blonde hair, her pasty complexion, her turned-up nose. I hated her from her double chin down to her size nine, C-width feet. *You'll never be thin,* I told her. *And you'll never be pretty. You'll never direct feature films or meet Johnny Carson. You'll spend the rest of your life in Wauwatosa, squinting at the bathroom scale.*

I wasn't even thinking about fat camp as I walked home from school later that afternoon. Instead I was dreaming, as always, about Johnny.

"Well, John," I said. I'd noticed that Johnny's closest friends never called him "Johnny."

"Well, John, I started writing *Girl on the Lam* in 1977. I had admired Kristy McNichol's work . . ." On talk shows it was always good to "admire someone's work."

"I had admired her work since the ABC television series *Family* and it occurred to me . . . "

Suddenly something brushed my back. I stopped quickly, taking the full thrust of the baritone against my hip. Nothing. I took a few steps forward and felt something else. This was harder, like a rock or stick, thrown from a distance. I took off running but the baritone in one hand and book bag in the other held me back. In a matter of moments Todd Wombat overtook me on the edge of an overgrown lot, two hundred yards from the White Hen Pantry. Even if I called for help, Mr. Chan wouldn't hear.

"Where you goin', Ten-Ton?" Todd blocked my path with feet squared and fists on hips. I turned around but it was too late: pulling up behind me was Ricky Rinaldi with his wavy black hair, porcelain skin, and bright green eyes. He would have been cute if he wasn't such a demon.

"Baluba and her tuba," Ricky chanted, skipping in a circle.

"Leave me alone." I was breathing fast and my chest ached. Traffic roared down 116th Street but no one stopped to help.

Todd stepped closer. "Fat chance, fatso. Ricky, hold her down. She's gotta have candy."

I closed my eyes and swung the baritone as hard as I could, hitting Ricky in the ribs and sending him sprawling to the sidewalk. I fell on top of him and the baritone landed at my side.

"Gross! Flintstone germs! Quits!" Ricky pushed me away, spitting wads of phlegm and scrambling to his feet. Todd pulled the book bag off my shoulder, turned it upside down and shook it over the grass.

"Stop it," I yelled. I reached for the bag but Ricky grabbed my hair and jerked my head back. My scalp burned as I saw tiny black stars. I turned quickly, aiming a kick at Ricky's wiener region. Jerry once confided that that was the worst place to hurt a boy, but Ricky was too agile for me. He laughed, showing his clutch of tiny white teeth, and danced out of reach. I did a semi-pirouette and fell to my side. Ricky pounced on top of me, drawing my arms up behind me and pressing my chin to the pavement.

Todd tossed aside my history book, my algebra notes, and my social studies folder as his gangly arms reached deep into the book bag. "What's this?" He pulled out the picture of Johnny and removed it from the plastic bag.

"Answer him, Ten-Ton," Ricky said, grinding my jaw to the ground. A bitter fluid filled my mouth and I couldn't speak.

"That old fogy from TV?" Todd squinted at the picture. "My Mom let me watch him when I was up vomiting."

"You're queer, aren't you, Flintstone?" Ricky's breath smelled like breakfast sausage, making my stomach churn.

"You wanna kiss this old guy?" Todd swung the picture between his forefinger and thumb as a stiff breeze ruffled his dirt-brown crewcut.

"Forget the picture, Todd." Ricky nodded toward my scattered homework. "See if Baluba has any candy before she infects us with her ugly germs."

"Yeah, you're right." With a glint in his eye, Todd tore the photo slowly down the middle, then doubled the halves and tore them again before tearing the remaining quarters into tiny shreds. The pieces looked like shiny black-and-white confetti as they drifted to the sidewalk, where a small breeze scuddered them into the grass.

Todd kicked his huge feet through my homework. "There's no candy here. Ten-Ton musta eaten it all. Let's go."

Ricky released my arms and I sagged to the ground. For a moment I was too weak to move, as if all the blood had drained from my body. My head was still on the pavement as I watched the Romulans running down 116th Street exchanging high-fives.

I got to my knees and brushed off, swallowing hard and fighting the tears. I wouldn't cry. I just wouldn't.

I was still stuffing my homework into my book bag when Mr. Chan ran towards me from the White Hen Pantry.

"Sunnie, Sunnie, you fall down?" His thin legs kicked through the long grass as his apron strings bounced in the breeze.

I shook my head, afraid his kindness would break my heart. "It's OK, I'm fine," I sniffled.

He stopped and bent down, struggling to catch his breath. "You have hurted your lip." He touched my chin, then showed me the smear of bright red blood. "You come to my shop, I fix you right up." I glanced down at the confettied photo, then followed Mr. Chan back to the White Hen Pantry.

Ignoring Mrs. Higgins, who waited at the register to buy a case of toilet paper, Mr. Chan took me to the back room and sat me on a folding chair amid a throng of mop heads and cardboard boxes.

"You should walk in street, not grass. Grass too slippery."

My hands were still shaking as I watched Mr. Chan fashion a cold compress out of ice cubes and an old gray tube sock. I pressed the sock to my burning lip and Mr. Chan handed me a sachet of mysterious herbs. "Drink this with tea, you feel much better." I sniffed the little fabric sack that smelled like lemon, oregano, and old gym shoes.

"I can get toilet paper just as cheap at the A&P," Mrs. Higgins yelled from the checkout counter.

Mr. Chan raised his eyebrows to ask if I was OK. I nodded, pressing the compress more firmly to my lip.

Several customers came in after Mrs. Higgins, and Mr. Chan was busy ringing them up. After about ten minutes I placed the melting sock in the rusted sink, grabbed my book bag, and went out front.

"I better get home before my Mom worries," I told Mr. Chan. He turned to the cash register, grabbed a rolled magazine, and handed it to me, bowing at the waist. I unrolled it, revealing a copy of *Rona Barrett's Hollywood.*

"For you. New issue. Just arrive. Not even on stands yet." Mr. Chan smiled so broadly his dark, deep-set eyes nearly disappeared.

"I don't have any money on me." I touched my pockets and shrugged.

"No, no." His eyes turned serious as he waved his hands. "No money. Free gift for you. Customer of the month."

I looked down at the cover photo of Natalie Wood and Robert Wagner dressed in matching suede jackets and bell-bottom pants. The banner headline screamed, "Can this marriage last?" I didn't know what to say.

"Thanks, Mr. Chan," I whispered before my throat snapped closed, and the reinforced glass-and-wire door rattled shut behind me.

I waited until Mom had finished washing the dishes after supper before telling her my decision. I peeked through the den's beaded curtain, gathering my thoughts. Mom on the sofa leaned close to Pop, her nose circling his ear.

"Who's my little cubby-wubby?" She put her hand on his knee and he pushed it away. He craned forward for a closer look at the TV screen. David Banner was busy transforming into "The Incredible Hulk," popping his shirt buttons and stretching his pants to dangerous dimensions.

"Please, Christina." Pop shrank against the sofa's side. "I'm trying to watch the program."

"Come on, honey bun, just a little nibble." Mom moved closer.

Pressed open on the coffee table was Mom's dog-eared copy of *If Life's A Bowl of Cherries, What Am I Doing in the Pits?* by Erma Bombeck. Only I knew that she hid a copy of *My Mother, Myself* under the sofa cushions to read while Grannie volunteered at the Home for Aged Lutherans.

"Mom?" My voice shook as I parted the beads.

Mom turned quickly to face me, her cheeks flushed red. "What is it, Sunnie?"

"Can I talk to you?"

"Sure." She patted the spot beside her on the plaid fabric sofa. There was plenty of room with Pop pushed into the corner.

"In the kitchen?" I asked.

Pop chuckled, sounding relieved. "Girl talk. Must be that time of the month."

Mom batted his arm playfully. "Shush. You're supposed to be supportive, Peter. Remember? That was the deal." She grabbed her cigarettes from the coffee table and stood, straightening her embroidered denim blouse. "Let's go."

She followed me into the kitchen and I sat at the table, motioning to the chair across.

"Sunnie, is something wrong?" She looked worried.

"Not exactly." The kitchen clock ticked loudly while the plaintive flute and distant drums of ABBA's "Fernando" drifted up from the basement. I looked to the sink, where stacks of dishes sat drying in the rack.

"You don't need to see the talking doctor again, do you?" Mom asked carefully.

"I never needed to see him in the first place."

"The scissors . . ."

"That was an accident." I took a deep breath, wrapping my toes around the kitchen chair. "What I want to say is that I've decided to go to the Summer Slim-Down Retreat."

42

Mom's eyes lit up. "Really?" Suddenly she frowned, tipping her unlit cigarette. "Are you doing this for me?"

"No. It's for me." I swallowed hard. "I want to be thin in high school. Not like now."

Her face relaxed. "Sunnie, this will be the best decision of your life."

"I hope you're right." Now that I'd told her, I did feel a little better.

Mom went to the garbage can and rummaged through the cigarette butts, coffee grounds, and potato peelings before finding the fat camp application forms. She slid the papers out carefully, brushing them off over the sink and blotting them dry with a towel. "We can go to Boston Store tomorrow and buy a new swimsuit." She beamed. "By August you'll need a bikini."

"I hope not." I was horrified by the thought of my pink cottage cheese stomach revealed to the world.

Pop strode into the kitchen, opened the fridge, and took out the cloudy, unmarked bottle of homemade lingonberry beer that Uncle Arne had given him over Memorial Day.

"Guess what?" Mom was nearly breathless as she searched for a ballpoint pen. "Sunnie's going to the retreat after all."

"Fine." Pop took down a glass, poured some beer, and swallowed loudly, grimacing at the taste.

"Honestly Peter, pour that swill down the sink. It's nasty." Mom shook her head.

"It's not nasty. It's part of our heritage. You'd do well to show a bit more pride." Pop poured another half glass and waited for the dark sediment to settle. "Where is this retreat again?"

"Lake Horicon, Minnesota," Mom answered proudly.

"I suppose we'll be driving." Pop sipped the bittersweet liquid. "It costs gasoline to get there, you know."

After we finished the application forms, Mom sealed the envelope and leaned close to my ear. "I know I shouldn't do this," she said in a guilty whisper, "but we have to celebrate. Let's go out for ice cream. As a family."

43

"Ice cream?" My stomach rumbled. I couldn't even remember what ice cream tasted like, it had been so long. While Mom struggled to round up the family, I imagined ordering an extra large banana split with three cherries on top, double hot fudge, and ruffles of whipped cream sprayed from a can. This time the man in the paper hat behind the counter would hold his tongue and decide not to warn the fat girl about eating so much ice cream.

Grannie's bunions were sore and Max was grounded for using the Bunsen burner in his bedroom, but at last we were all assembled in the front hallway.

"Wait! Let me get a picture," Mom said as Max hung on to the door handle, anxious to leave. She hurried back with her camera and squeezed us together in a tight little bunch.

"I *was* studying for my chemistry final," Ingrid seethed behind me, grinding her jaw. I felt her hot breath against my hair.

"Everybody smile! Come on, Sunnie, give us the thousand watts!" As Mom snapped the photo the flashbulb popped, plunging my eyesight into a dazzling darkness where, for a split second, I remembered how ice cream tasted again.

CHAPTER THREE

The first days of June 1978 were the best of my life. After deciding to spend the summer at fat camp, I reasoned that I should eat whatever I wanted before I left. Every morning I jumped on a junk food merry-go-round full of French fries, Eskimo Pies, Little Debbies, Susie-Qs, Crunch Berries, and Sno-Cones. I shared egg roll with the Chans every afternoon and I never left the White Hen Pantry without a stash of Slim Jims, Strawberry Yoo-Hoo, and licorice Good-N-Plenty. I felt stronger and more confident than I had in months. I never once fainted; I never went to bed hungry. I did miss my lunch-hour meetings with Nurse Nellis, though. Sometimes when I passed her in the hall between classes, she sighed and gave me a sad little wave.

On June 9th my classmates and I sat on cold metal benches in the lunchroom, waiting to hear the winner of the banner design contest. Our eyes were glued to the raised platform where Principal Henderson and Miss Hill stood with a photographer from *The Milwaukee Journal* and a representative from Rambert Specialty Jams.

Emily and I locked arms and closed our eyes. "Let one of us win, let one of us win," we chanted.

"Is this thing on?" Principal Henderson's voice wavered over the lunchroom. I peeked through my eyelids as he shook the microphone. Miss Hill adjusted the metal stand, solving the problem.

Principal Henderson cleared his throat. "Thank you, Denise." Miss Hill nodded as her hands disappeared beneath her poncho and she stepped back in line.

"And a special thank-you to Rambert Specialty Jams for sponsoring this contest," he continued. "After careful consideration, the winner has been chosen. She is an eighth-grader in Miss Hill's art class." Principal Henderson unfurled a small roll of paper and tried to decipher it.

I tingled with anticipation. *Please let me win.* Emily's fingernails dug into my arm.

Meanwhile the lights go down on the Dorothy Chandler Pavilion. An enormous screen displays the climactic scene from Girl on the Lam *as Kristy McNichol runs into the loving embrace of her long-lost parents, played by Carol Burnett and Alan Alda. Tears flow like honey, on the screen and in the audience, where soft sniffles are disguised with coughs by the diamonded throng. The lights go up and the screen rises high into the rafters. At the podium below, a spotlight finds Jack Nicholson in a tuxedo waving the white envelope aloft. "And the winner for Best Director of a Feature Film goes to . . ." He tears the envelope and pulls out the card. That devilish smile. ". . . Wilma 'Sunnie' Sundstrom for* Girl on the Lam*!"*

"Sunnie! He called your name!"

I opened my eyes and looked straight into Emily's beet-red face.

"What?" My head started spinning.

"Wilma Sundstrom for her design, 'Truth and Humanity: The Pride of Truman School,'" Principal Henderson repeated. He surveyed the lunchroom from tiptoes, craning his neck. "Is Wilma here?"

Emily pulled me to my feet. "Oh my God! You'll totally share your jam, right?"

"Sure," I said, still stunned. My feet moved without me as I made my way down the narrow aisle between lunch tables.

"Hey Ten-Ton," Todd Wombat shouted. A spitball hit me in the back.

"Sundstrom," Ricky Rinaldi replied, centering another spitball just beneath Todd's. The crowd started chanting, "Ten-Ton. Sundstrom. Ten-Ton. Sundstrom."

I reached the stage and Principal Henderson helped me up the three steep steps. My tight denim jumper didn't allow much legroom.

I walked to the microphone expecting to deliver an impromptu speech but Miss Hill motioned me away. Instead she handed me a gold-paper certificate full of fancy writing. All I could read was "Wilma *Sun*strom." They'd left out the "d." I hoped I wouldn't have to forfeit the jam.

Principal Henderson unveiled a large reproduction of my design, which he handed to Miss Hill. The photographer started snapping pictures and I quickly handed Miss Hill the certificate so I could have the banner. I held the banner shoulder-high and centered over my stomach.

"Are these pictures really going to be in the Journal?" I asked the photographer.

He held the huge camera beside his head. "That's what they pay me for." He was a large, sweaty man with thick eyebrows and a bulbous lower lip. I didn't want to make him angry.

"It's an honor to be in your newspaper," I said quickly. He motioned me closer to Miss Hill, Principal Henderson, and the Rambert representative.

"*The Milwaukee Journal!*" My mind raced. "Pop might tape this picture to the fridge beside that cartoon of President Carter. And a lifetime supply of jam! Hope it's not orange marmalade, which nobody likes."

"C'mon kid, smile," the photographer implored as his camera clicked away, leaving the smell of burning sulfur wafting through the lunchroom.

I broadened my smile without parting my lips.

"At least *look* happy." The photographer sighed. "You just won a bunch of jam!"

I *was* happy. Overjoyed, in fact. But I couldn't explain to the photographer that if I smiled more, my face would look chubbier. Total strangers reading the paper might guess how fat I actually was, and that would spoil everything.

During study hall I was called to Principal Henderson's office so he could coach me on my commencement speech. "The Truman team is counting on you, Sundstrom." Principal Henderson stepped out from behind his desk and crossed his arms.

"Yes, Sir." I gazed at the souvenirs from his days as a star quarterback at the University of Wisconsin. Cartoon badgers in red-and-white sweaters fought for space between photos of a young Principal Henderson in shoulder pads with slicked-back hair and a granite jaw.

"Keep it brief. Ten minutes, tops." He began pacing. "Attack your point. Into the end zone. Leave them cheering in the stands." He squared his hands as if signaling a touchdown.

"I'll do my best," I promised, staring at the trophies in his locked glass case.

"The theme of your speech is 'School Spirit.'"

"School spirit, Sir?"

"Yep. School spirit. Run with that, Sundstrom, and see where it takes you." He arched his arm as if throwing a football, passing it confidently over my head.

Nurse Nancy hurried into the hallway just as I left Principal Henderson's office.

"Sunnie, hang on a minute. Congratulations on winning the contest." She pressed her throat, slightly breathless.

"Thanks, Nancy. I am pretty excited, I have to admit." I glanced through the doorway to Nancy's office. Jimmy McGuich lay on the green Naugahyde couch, moaning for his Mom. The damp cloth draped over his forehead glowed white in the darkened room. "What's wrong with him?" I asked.

Nancy looked over her shoulder. "Stomach flu. Or so he says. Me, I think it was too much candy." Nancy smiled as Jimmy moaned again.

"I miss our little meetings, kiddo." Nancy pretend-punched my arm, which stung more than she intended. Nancy didn't know her own strength. "But I'm glad you're not fainting anymore. What happened?"

"I'm spending the summer at fat camp, so I better eat now."

"Oh." She gave a sad little smile. "Well, you'll meet some nice kids there."

"I hope so," I replied. "At least I can start Central High skinny." I lowered my voice so Principal Henderson couldn't hear. "What have I missed on *Days*?"

Nancy gently shut the door on Jimmy and leaned close. "Marlena's twin sister was murdered by the Salem Strangler and the police think Don is guilty."

"No way! Does Marlena think Don's guilty?"

"She's still unconscious."

"Unconscious?"

"Uh huh. She's been in a coma since she heard the news..."

The spirit of a school is in its students. The spirit of a school is found in its students. The soul of school spirit is found . . . I was in my room writing my speech but I couldn't concentrate because of the noise from Ingrid's hi-fi, rising up through the heating vent.

I pushed my papers aside and went downstairs, fighting through the heavy gray haze of unfiltered cigarette smoke, past the beaded fringe curtain and bubbling lava lamps.

"Ingrid?" The cement block walls were covered with reproductions of Edvard Munch's *The Scream* and stills from *The Seventh Seal*, in which a knight of the Crusades plays chess with Death.

"Ingrid?" I asked. It was so dark and smoky I could only see a few feet.

"What do you want?" The maroon blanket stirred. A long, thin arm pushed away a hill of pillows and reached for the cigarette smoldering on the nightstand.

"Can you turn the music down?" I stepped closer to the bed.

"Why?" Ingrid rubbed her eyes as the cigarette found her mouth.

"Your music's too loud. I can't write my speech."

"Sorry. Wouldn't want to bother the 'scribe' at work." She blew a smoke ring that floated to the ceiling.

I looked at her shadowy face, searching for the sister I'd had two years earlier. When she was fourteen and I was eleven we shared a bedroom, playing Barbies all night in the Malibu Dream House and naming our future babies. Ingrid liked "Barnabas" and "Vincenzo." All my future sons, of course, were "Johnny."

She lowered the music, which I took as an invitation to sit down. "Ingrid, what's wrong?"

"Nothing." Her chin jutted forward in defiance.

"You're always in the basement," I said. "You never talk anymore."

She balanced the cigarette on her can of Tab. "Familial interaction is overrated. I'm preparing for the inevitable." She hooked her long pale hair behind her ears.

"The inevitable?" I asked.

She nodded. "This family is falling apart. Mom and Pop are incapable of honest communication. Their relationship can't last. And Max will wind up in jail."

I crossed my legs. "Grannie thinks he's plotting against the government."

Ingrid's eyes widened. "Grannie said that?"

"Uh huh."

Ingrid nodded her approval. "The old lady's more with-it than she seems." She clasped her hands behind her head and slid under the blankets. I lay down beside her, staring at the exposed-wire ceiling. Our elbows touched and we were quiet for a while. I felt her breathing, the steady rise and fall of her chest. The bass from the hi-fi vibrated the bed frame, entering my back.

"I'll miss you when you go to Sweden," I said at last.

"I can't wait to leave this stink-hole." She dug her heels into the mattress. I wanted Ingrid to miss me too. While I waited for her to say more, a soft plum seemed to ripen and die inside me.

"You really think Mom and Pop might get divorced?" I watched the lava lamps billowing waves of blood-red wax.

Ingrid took a deep breath. "Sunnie, just be prepared, OK?"

50

Then she yanked the blanket over her shoulder and curled up in a ball.

The night before graduation a series of storms tore through the state. Twelve dairy cows were electrocuted on a farm near Nekosha, and with the forecast calling for more rain, Mom feared they'd have to move our ceremonies inside to the multi-purpose room. She needn't have worried. Friday, June 16, 1978, was a gloriously warm and sunny day. I was up at five-thirty A.M. French-braiding my hair like Marie Osmond's. My cap-sleeve sundress felt tight in the bust and hips, but it would have to do. There were no more side stitches to let out.

I practiced my speech before the bathroom mirror. My focus was "school spirit" but I worked in a few lines about character: *The character you develop in junior high follows you the rest of your life.* I hoped my message wasn't too subtle: I wanted Todd and Ricky to feel guilty for being so mean since second grade.

Before I went down to the bus, I knocked on Grannie's door.

"Come in," came the faint reply.

Grannie was in her rocking chair, looking pale and rubbing her elbow. "What's wrong?" I asked, coming closer.

"I slept on my arm wrong. It's powerful sore." With a wan smile she held up her arm and let the loose skin sag. The sunlight through the draped window cast a fuzzy glow around her old plaid flannel bathrobe. Laid out on the bed was her powder-blue pantsuit and silver brooch.

"Will you be OK for the ceremony?" I straightened her outfit on the bed.

She nodded. "If they have to drag me from the back of a Buick, I'll be there." She pressed her hands on the rocking chair as if to stand, then thought better of it. "Wilma, open my night-stand drawer. There's something there for you."

I went to the nightstand and opened the drawer. At first I didn't see anything unusual, just a bottle of Milk of Magnesia, some loose antacids, a photo of Granddad Lassen and Grannie's 1903 Swedish prayer book and hymnal.

"Look deeper. It's in there," Grannie instructed. I moved the hymnal and found a small white cardboard box with "Marshall Field's" stamped on the cover.

"Is this it?" I showed her the box.

"Yes. Go on and open it."

I slipped off the cover to reveal a shiny silver charm bracelet resting delicately on a bed of cotton batting.

"No way!" I squealed. "It's the one I wanted for Christmas." I had circled the bracelet in Field's' Christmas catalog but Mom and Pop said no, the bracelet was too expensive for a twelve-year-old and it would take too long to collect enough charms to make me happy. They got me a transistor radio instead, then took the radio away when I played it at night, after *The Tonight Show* was over and I tuned in AM stations all the way from Sheboygan.

"Grannie, it's beautiful." I pinched the end of the chain-link bracelet and watched it glimmer in the muted sunlight. One charm was already on the bracelet, a tiny scroll with "Diploma" and "6-16-78" etched into the silver.

"Put it on me, please," I asked, rushing to Grannie's chair. I handed her the bracelet and she motioned my wrist closer. She squinted and strained, finally catching the eye in the clasp and securing the bracelet.

"It's just what I wanted." I leaned forward as if to kiss Grannie, then stopped. Our family didn't put much store in physical affection. Diseases were spread that way, along with the risk of spoiled children. Instead of hugs and kisses, we got lectures and inspections.

"You know Wilma, you might be the brightest child this family has ever produced." I wilted beneath Grannie's stern-eyed gaze. I didn't want a lecture now.

Grannie rocked back and forth, tapping the floor with her slippered heel. "Well, Lena's boy Lars was smart, until that horse kicked him in the noggin. And Anneke was studying law until she ran off with an Eye-talian. With your gift comes responsibility. Don't let your head be turned."

She was rocking faster now and the fire in her eyes bordered on anger. My lip trembled. "Be happy," I wanted to say. "This is a good day. Why do we have to be like you were in the Old Country?"

When Ingrid, Max, and I were little, Grannie told us bedtime stories about immigrating to America on a huge, crowded, foul-smelling ship. The bodies of those who died during the journey were tossed overboard before they started to smell, even the infants wrapped in gray linen, bound tight at their skulls and their round, chubby fists. "That's the stock you come from," Grannie would warn us. "Remember that. We don't indulge in weakness and tears."

"Now whatever you do, don't run off with an Eye-talian," Grannie insisted, shaking her finger. "Don't let your head be turned."

"I won't." I pinched the bracelet, pressing the charm deep into my thumb.

"Good. Now before you go, let me inspect you." I stood at attention as Grannie rose from her chair and placed her hand on my head.

"Getting taller, I see." She nodded with satisfaction, then she straightened my shoulders, pushing them back. "Don't stoop," she commanded. "Stand straight. Chest out. There's nothing wrong with being tall." Her pale, powdery eyes were intent and serious as I met her gaze.

She squeezed my elbows like ripe fruit. "Now, arms at your sides . . . "

"Sunnie, the bus is here," Mom interrupted, yelling up the stairs.

"Sorry, I gotta go." As I turned my elbows slipped from Grannie's grasp.

"Speak loudly during your speech," she called after me. "Some of the old folks don't hear so good." I grabbed my book bag and hurried from her room.

Mom waited at the bottom of the staircase, stretching open my jeans jacket and propping the front door with her foot. I slipped into the jacket and waved for the bus driver to wait.

"See you this afternoon," Mom yelled as I ran down the sidewalk. "Look for me in the crowd. I'll be wearing hot pink. No, wait!"

I stopped and turned around.

"I think they call it fuchsia now."

I climbed onto the bus, nodded my thanks to the driver for waiting, and took my seat beside Emily. She was dressed in a brown calico dress with a pointy beige collar. Her dark hair had been secured high in a rubber band, revealing the full width of her pale, almost luminous, forehead.

"You look nice, Sunnie," she said, admiring my yellow sundress. "Like a real grown-up today." She opened her book bag and grabbed her inhaler, stealing a few quick puffs that left a lingering medicinal smell.

"Thanks. So do you." The bus lurched to its next stop and Billy Bannion got on, pausing in the aisle beside Emily and me. "Look everybody, it's Fat Girl and Robin."

The whole bus erupted in laughter.

Billy sang, "Jingle bells, Fat Girl smells, Robin laid an egg. Fatmobile, lost its wheel and Commissioner lost his leg." Billy skipped to the back of the bus while Emily clutched her face.

"Don't worry." I rubbed her back. "Next year will be better."

"No, it won't." Emily quivered beneath my hand like an injured bird. "In high school there will just be more kids to make fun of us."

All morning I practiced my speech in my head, even while we collected report cards and signed yearbooks and Mrs. Tooley jumped back in horror when a grass snake planted by Eddie MacArthur slithered out from under her desk.

At 11 A.M. we were sent to the courtyard for commencement. The eighth-graders sat in metal chairs behind Principal Henderson on the stage while the sixth- and seventh-graders, along with the audience, sat in semi-circular rows in front. As we filed into our seats, I searched for the fleck of fuchsia that would be Mom, but it was impossible to find individual faces in the crowd.

54

"Welcome to Truman Junior High's fifty-second annual commencement," Principal Henderson began, standing tall at the podium. "We thank you for joining us here today." The sun burned Principal Henderson's bald spot, while the warm breeze fluttered his belted blue leisure suit.

The ceremony moved quickly as Principal Henderson spoke passionately about teamwork and how parents and teachers needed to "stay in the huddle" for the sake of the school. After the principal's speech, Mr. Johnson's first-period jazz band played the theme from *Peter Gunn*, and the Drama Club performed "Ease on Down the Road" from *The Wiz*. Loose straw from their scarecrow costumes still littered the stage as Principal Henderson introduced me to the crowd.

"Wilma Sundstrom, winner of Truman School's banner design contest sponsored by Rambert Specialty Jams, will honor us with a speech about school spirit." He turned to face me and clapped in an exaggerated gesture of applause. I was suddenly paralyzed, frozen to my seat.

I'm backstage in Johnny's green room, shaking with fear. I've downed three scotch-and-sodas as I stare into my empty glass, unable to face the crowd. My career will end right here, before I've even finished the sequel to Girl on the Lam. *A washed-up has-been at age thirteen. Don Rickles' stand-up routine is killing them; the audience's laughter torments me with a series of mild giggles punctuated by horsy guffaws.*

"What's wrong, kid?"

A figure in the doorway blocks the light. I look up into Johnny Carson's kind blue eyes. He's dressed in a beige suitcoat, tan slacks, and a wide white tie. His pancake make-up gives his round features a soft, orangy, unreal glow.

"I can't go out there, John. I'm just too nervous."

Johnny steps closer. I smell his latest cigarette and notice a nicotine stain on his thumb. "I get nervous too sometimes," he confides. "Always have, even as a kid doing magic shows back in Nebraska. Come on, I'll help you through it. Just focus on my eyes."

Johnny smiles a crinkly smile and offers his hand, leading me down the darkened corridor and into the hot, hazy light.

I took a deep breath and stood, swallowing hard. The folds of my nylon gown unfurled, draping me in waves of fabric, and the sunlight struck the tight French braid atop my head. I strode to the podium, adjusted the microphone, and cleared my throat. The world was silent for a blissful instant, waiting for me to speak.

"The spirit of a school is found in its students." My voice was strong and steady. "Truman School, when empty, is only bricks and mortar. But when filled with students, this old building comes to life . . . "

When the ceremony was over I felt exhilarated, free. I was happier than I'd ever been before, even happier than the day I received Johnny's autographed photo. I wondered if skinny girls felt this good all the time. I felt more generous and more forgiving than I could imagine. I even wanted to make peace with the Romulans, letting Todd and Ricky know that I forgave them, because my future was so much brighter than theirs. Clinging tightly to my diploma, I dove into the crowd, searching for Mom and Pop. I was approaching our neighbor Mrs. Koslowski when Nurse Nancy spotted me and hurried over.

"Sunnie, wait. I've been looking for you everywhere." She was panting, out of breath. Her misshapen sack dress was pulled to one side, exposing the strap of her bra.

"Hi, Nancy. Did you like my speech?"

"Yes. Sunnie, we need to talk." She lifted her hand, shading her tiny black eyes from the sun. Beads of sweat peppered her upper lip and her cheeks looked spotty.

"What's going on?" I felt my diploma dampen, getting sticky in my fist. "Where are my parents?"

Her eyes jumped everywhere, flitting from the parking lot to the gym to the courtyard and back again. Desperation tugged at the cords in her throat.

"Nancy?" My voice sounded tinny and faraway.

Nancy looked defeated as her heavy gaze settled on my shoulders. She took a deep breath and blew it out slowly. "There's no easy way to say this, Sunnie." The color drained from her face. "Your grandmother passed away this morning."

CHAPTER FOUR

Nurse Nellis and I wove through the satin-sashed-and-tasseled throng to the parking lot behind the school where her car was parked beneath the "Faculty Only" sign. She unlocked the door, slid beneath the steering wheel, and motioned for me to get in. Her car was a beige Cadillac; a long, sleek, fishtailing tank. It didn't just look like an old man's car, it smelled like one too, like stale tobacco and sweaty golf shoes.

"Sunnie?" Nancy pushed open the passenger door and I stepped back. There was something sleazy and unseemly about this car, as if something evil had happened in the back seat.

"Honey, get in. Your family's waiting." Nancy looked up at me, pleading, through the tinted window that splashed a blue-green wave across her face.

As I got into the Cadillac my plump bottom deflated the hot vinyl seat, releasing a foul odor that whispered of whiskey and gin. This must have been her husband's car, I realized. Bernard. Bernard who was five-foot-seven and had a limp. Bernard who bought Nancy an ironing board for their anniversary. I remembered that; I remembered every single thing anyone had ever told me. All the little details counted now that Nancy seemed to think that Grannie had died. Of course she hadn't died. I would know if something had happened to my own grandmother. *Nancy will be so embarrassed when she gets me home and realizes her mistake.*

Nancy turned the key and the radio exploded with the chorus of Captain and Tennille's "Muskrat Love."

"Sorry, sorry, sorry." Nancy flipped the dial to "off" as her neck blossomed in spots.

"Leave it on," I said. "That's my second most favorite song."

Nancy looked surprised.

"It would be my first favorite except I'm starting to like 'Afternoon Delight' a little bit better."

When we reached West Hadley Avenue, Pop's 1975 Oldsmobile Cutlass Supreme was parked in the driveway on an awkward angle, with the right front wheel flattening the grass. Behind Pop's car was Reverend Tobiassen's somber green sedan with a cross on the back bumper beneath the word "clergy." I wondered if Reverend Tobiassen had brought his new assistant, Pastor Rick, who had a neat Jesus beard and wore a leather bracelet.

Grannie admired Reverend Tobiassen because he came from the days when Lutherans weren't allowed to dance or to listen to fast music, but she disapproved of Pastor Rick because he chanted the liturgy and, she said, exhibited definite Methodist tendencies.

Rather than wait for Nancy to slide out from under the steering wheel I headed straight up the sidewalk to the house, letting myself in through the warped screen door. I couldn't wait to tell Grannie how many people clapped when I finished my speech.

"Grannie?" The screen door rattled shut behind me. I stopped in the foyer and absorbed the silence. The house had to be full of people but they made almost no sound. I stepped softly, arching my feet to cushion their impact. I felt like a cat burglar or a liquidy ghost. If no one saw me, this would not be real.

In the living room Pop stood with his back to the bookcase facing Reverend Tobiassen in his black suit coat and Uncle David, fresh from playing golf in his hot Madras pants and tangerine shirt. The men drank tiny glasses of Scotch that glowed in the low light and they spoke in low, somber, grown-up voices, pausing often and shaking their heads.

In the kitchen Pastor Rick, his beard flecked with summer auburn, sat at the Formica table in a narrow wedge between Ingrid and Max. Their two blond heads were cradled in Pastor Rick's armpits as if they were holding him aloft. Max's round face was red and blistered while Ingrid had two pink circles just beneath her eyes.

The doorbell rang and I knew that Nancy, huffing and puffing, had reached the front door. I wanted to get away before Pop invited her in. Nancy belonged to my life at Truman Junior High and having her here would upset some vital private balance.

Mom's dropping Grannie off at the Home for Aged Lutherans, I decided. *Grannie's canvas sack is stuffed with Bibles as she moves from room to room distributing the* Good News. *Her feet will ache when she comes home. I better get the Epsom salts.*

As I headed to the bathroom Aunt Ruth intercepted me, stepping heavily into the hall and letting the strings of beads dance closed behind her. "Oh Sunnie, come here," she pleaded. Wiry gray hairs escaped from her bun.

I shook my head. "No," I said. "No."

Aunt Ruth's arms opened wide, ready to fold me into her heavy embrace. "Come now, child. It's OK."

"No!" I turned and ran upstairs to Grannie's room. *If she is gone, and I'm not saying she is but if she is gone then she did not go quietly. There will be signs of a struggle: broken glass, torn curtains, a bloody club. The worst thing I have ever seen.*

I threw open Grannie's door. The room was so hot I couldn't breathe. I felt dizzy and had to hold on to the door. Grannie was not there but she had been, recently, and was soon to return. No one had died here, I was sure of that. The bright sun burned through the shabby lace curtain, making little heat rings rise and shine from every surface.

Laid out on the bed was Grannie's blue polyester pantsuit, neatly pressed, untouched since the morning. The cuffs and hems were as smooth as when I had straightened them. The pantsuit looked patient, even prayerful, ready to rise up and assume Grannie's familiar form.

I stepped to the nightstand. Grannie's Bible and Swedish hymnal were stacked beside a glass of water with her fingerprints still visible, the mark of something tightly-held, and with a lip-shaped pucker staining the rim. Several crumpled antacid wrappers were the only signs of anything amiss.

"Grannie? It's me. Wilma." My voice came out low in my throat and strangled, like I was talking underwater but didn't believe my words would reach the surface. I had given up hope of being heard.

Suddenly a soft little cry filled the room.

"Grannie?" I dropped to my knees and lifted the bedspread's dusty hem. Behind a single flat-soled dress shoe and a plastic L'eggs egg sat Grannie's cat Magda, curled up in a tight orange ball meowing.

"Come here, kitty, come on," I coaxed. Magda's eyes were two huge black pupils ringed with yellow. She meowed again.

"Come on, Magda."

The cat cried silently as her mouth opened, revealing jagged teeth and a pale triangular tongue. I crawled as far under the bed as my thick chest would let me but Magda's coarse fur remained just beyond reach.

I lay flat on the floor, defeated. *This cat has seen secrets she can never tell me,* I thought. *How can human beings understand anything?* My chin sank into the shag carpet and I felt my heart beating through the baseboard and into the living room below. If Pop, Reverend Tobiassen, and Uncle David looked up I knew they could hear it.

Magda began to howl.

I sat up. *Nothing in the world, not even a terrified old tabby cat, wants any of my love right now.*

I pulled a pillow off Grannie's bed, not the pillow she slept on but the other one, the one that always stayed cool and plump and straightened. I crossed my legs, spread the pillow in my lap, and rested my head.

Grannie will come back. I rocked back and forth. *If I wait long enough, she'll appear.* I thought about Jesus' friends who left him to suffer alone in the Garden of Gethsemane. *That's not me,* I promised myself. *I'm not like that. I'll stay right here until she returns.*

I thought back to third grade when, on a dare from Rusty McGuinness, I climbed Mr. Arkin's tree and fell, breaking my arm. Grannie was furious. "A crabapple tree can't support your weight," she insisted. "Any fool could see that just by looking."

Even so, she sat in a hard wooden chair beside my bed all night long, rousing me every hour. The doctors said I didn't have a concussion but Grannie wasn't convinced. After all, that's what doctors had said when cousin Lars got kicked in the head by a horse. He was fine at first. By the time brain damage set in, it was too late.

I had been settled into bed with a row of pillows along my side. More pillows propped up my arm, the pure white plaster cast glowing like neon. A damp cloth covered my forehead in case I became feverish.

"Wilma?" Grannie's voice rose from the darkness. When I didn't answer fast enough she waved the open bottle of smelling salts beneath my nose and I was instantly awake, my head spinning, smarting with stars.

"Can you hear me?" Grannie's pale blue eyes were wild in the darkness, deep with fear and caring.

"I hear you." My disembodied arm glowed, rising above the bedsheets.

"What's your name, child?"

"Wilma, W-I-L-M-A, Sundstrom, S-U-N-D-S-T-R-O-M," I answered softly.

"Where do you live?" Her voice was stern, commanding.

"11529 West Hadley Avenue; Wauwatosa, Wisconsin, USA." My head ached and my broken arm throbbed in time with my heart.

"Now repeat the Nicene Creed."

I tried to concentrate through my headache-and-aspirin haze. "We believe in one God, the Father, the Almighty, maker of heaven and earth, of all that is, seen and unseen. We believe in one Lord, Jesus Christ, the only Son of God, eternally begotten of the Father, God from God, Light from Light . . . " I stumbled. "God from God, Light from Light . . . " My voice trailed away.

I heard panic in Grannie's silence. "I better call the doctor."

"Wait," I insisted, trying to raise my hand. "I never remember all the words."

Grannie stroked her lip. "All right then. But next time you better remember at least as much as now."

"I will. Can I go back to bed?"

"Only for an hour." She replaced the sour washcloth on my forehead, cool in the middle but warmer where her hands had been. As I nestled into my cloud of pillows I felt ashamed to be so loved, ashamed to wallow in it, lost in the satisfaction of it all. Falling asleep, I felt a dull thud followed by an electric pain as my skin brushed the gauzy sock inside the plaster cast and I knew with certainty that the break in my arm was real and absolute, a long narrow crack that dove deep into the bone.

I can't say how long I stayed in Grannie's room but it must have been several hours. The room cooled as the hot sun retreated, its thick shaft of light narrowing and disappearing, compacting to a small spot behind the bed. Cars came and went, parking quietly, their doors slamming shut with respectful restraint. I heard voices downstairs and a brief clatter in the kitchen. Life was continuing but it was life at half-speed; life with the sound turned down.

I put the pillow aside and stood slowly, feeling my way around the foot of Grannie's bed. I was too scared to turn on the light. Even in the semi-darkness I saw the outline of Grannie's pantsuit and felt Magda still curled beneath the bed, her iridescent eyes searching and unblinking, watching the movement of my legs.

I went to the window and looked out towards the big blue water tower and the world beyond Wauwatosa. I guessed it was just after eight o'clock. Streaks of pale light drenched the distant sky, out where the concrete overpass of the interstate met the silvery back of a factory. I realized that our little family tragedy meant nothing to anyone else and our house, this four-bedroom white brick Colonial with black shutters in the middle of busy West Hadley Avenue, was all alone in the center of the world.

As I walked into the hall I saw that Mom and Pop's bedroom door was open. I stood there a few moments before going in. Light from the closet revealed the silhouette of Mom's body, fully clothed, curled on top of the bed. By the rhythm of her breathing I guessed she was awake.

"Mom?" I whispered.

There was no response.

"Mom?" I asked again.

"Uh huh," she croaked.

I didn't know what to say. "I'm home now."

"OK."

I stared into the deep abyss of the bed, not sure what to do. I sat down and slowly advanced until I was positioned behind Mom's back. She folded her arms and tucked in her chin. Her whole body was rigid with trying not to cry.

"Mom?" I asked softly, touching her back.

Her spine stiffened.

"It's going to be OK," I whispered, surprising myself. It wasn't going to be OK.

I stretched out in the narrow trench behind Mom, watching her shoulders rise and fall. I barely moved as she drifted into sleep, her breath coming slower now, without struggle. Suddenly she jerked forward and bolted upright. "Mama!" she called.

"It's OK." I tapped her shoulder. She turned and looked at me with eyes that were empty and stunned. Her mouth fell open but no sound came out.

"It's Sunnie." I tried to smile. "It's only me."

Her eyes narrowed, then tightened with recognition. "Oh," she moaned. She turned back to the wall, punched the pillow with her fist and buried her head. Her shoulders shook but still she did not cry.

I went down to the den where Pop sat quietly in his La-Z-Boy recliner, working the *TV Guide* crossword puzzle in his lap. He was still dressed in work clothes: a wide-lapeled navy blue suit with a white shirt and a broad blue tie, but his collar had been loosened and his tie was askew. He ate from a bowl of potato chips and between bites wiped his fingers on a paper napkin. I didn't want him to eat potato chips; not now, not ever. I could allow him his hunger, as long as it was hunger for bread or beer or meat or liquor, something masculine and appropriate to the moment. If my grandmother was gone, and that was still an "if" as far as I was concerned, then no one in this house could eat potato chips.

"Pop?" I asked.

"Uh huh."

"You should be with Mom."

He stiffened slightly but didn't look up. "Did she ask for me?"

"No."

We were both silent. Pop's eyes stayed level with the crossword puzzle. I could see the small photo of Bob Newhart in the middle and I was certain that either he, or his TV show, contained the crucial clue. I could tell that Pop wasn't reading because his eyelids didn't flicker. He was waiting for me to speak.

"Go talk to Mom," I said.

"Later. She wants to be alone."

"Did she tell you that?" I was shocked. I had never challenged my father. Pop's gaze stayed on the puzzle but now his eyelids darted quickly back and forth.

He wasn't going to move. I wished I could carry him up to Mom. He didn't look particularly heavy with his handsome face and perfectly parted hair, damped down close to his scalp but with the ends tossed off in loose, wild waves. He was all airy lightness now, now when I needed him to be heavy. I wanted him to be solid and substantial, a full-figured father, a lead-solid certainty, undoubtedly grave. I wanted Pop to be like Debbie Schneider's Dad. Hugo Schneider was a large, dark-eyed, olive-skinned man with a broad beer belly; a prosecuting attorney who locked people up for life. When he came to Career Day at Truman Junior High, he stood at the blackboard and said that a good lawyer was someone who did hunger and thirst after righteousness. After the talk Debbie clung to her father's side, linking her arm in his, beaming with pride. I wanted Mr. Schneider to be my father, just for today.

"You should be with Mom," I said again.

"I will," Pop answered, flipping through the *TV Guide*. "I've got to make a few phone calls first."

I couldn't watch *The Tonight Show* that night. Johnny felt far-away, hidden behind the screen in a hot blue maze of glowing tubes and wires. Even Ed's hearty laughter sounded forced and hollow. Johnny did Carnac the Magnificent but I didn't want him to be the mysterious visitor from the East. I wanted him to take off the plush turban and the glittery red cape, put aside his stack of white envelopes, and just be my friend.

I turned the TV off and padded down the stairs in darkness. There was a stack of papers on the kitchen table that I knew were for the funeral. Even in the moonlight I recognized a line of gold lettering and a simple black cross.

I opened the fridge and let the thin yellow light shine from my feet halfway up my nightgown. Suddenly I was famished, realizing I hadn't eaten since breakfast.

The fridge was packed with covered dishes, initialed in black marker pen, delivered by neighbors who had heard that Grannie died. I sorted through the Tupperware containers of Tuna Surprise, Sour Cream Tortilla Casserole, and Cool Whip Fruit Parfait. None of these sloppy concoctions held together with mayonnaise and cream of mushroom soup appealed to me. They looked too much like lotions. I guessed you could spread them over your skin to cool a sunburn or apply them with a pallet knife directly to your heart.

At the back of the fridge behind the Tupperware and a six-pack of Dr. Pepper I found a small glass pan. I pulled the pan forward and saw that it was a special little cake that Grannie had made just for me. In shaky red lettered icing she had written, *Skøl, Wilma!*, which meant Cheers, or Congratulations. She must have made the cake that morning, after I left for school. As I took the small pan from the fridge it felt so heavy that I had to hold it with both hands.

I cleared a spot at the table and sat down with the cake, cutting a small corner and lifting it to my mouth. The cake was rich and delicious with hints of a burnt-chocolate bitterness. I tasted the care that went into its creation. Between bites I tried to wipe my lips but the vanilla frosting left a buttery smear. *Grannie, if you were here, we would sit together and share this cake like a communion. I still have to tell you all about graduation.*

I cut into the second piece with surgical precision. I was determined to eat the whole thing. It would be a sin to leave anything, even a tiny morsel, behind.

Suddenly I imagined Reverend Tobiassen in his long purple Lenten robe standing before the kitchen table as if it were an altar, preparing to consecrate the graduation cake. "Jesus gave thanks, broke the bread, and gave it to His disciples saying, 'Take, eat, this is my body which is given for you,'" Reverend Tobiassen intoned. "Do this in remembrance of me."

Come, Grannie, and share the cake, I encouraged her, cutting another generous slice. *Together this will bring us peace.*

Reverend Tobiassen's somber voice filled the empty kitchen with the fifteen words I most longed to hear. "Having loved His own who were in the world," the reverend promised, "He loved them to the end."

CHAPTER FIVE

In keeping with our family's tradition, children were not allowed to attend Grannie's funeral at Crown of Thorns Lutheran Church. Instead Ingrid, Max, and I, along with our cousins Meg, Erik, Lucy, and Todd, waited on plastic chairs in the church's Sunday School annex until the service ended. Lucy told us how she planned to become a Lutheran nun and fly bush-plane missions to underprivileged children in Namibia.

"The Lord came to me in a vision once," Lucy's brother Todd wheezed between clogged tonsils. "He called me to minister to lepers and bums."

"Right. Like there are *so* many lepers in Sheboygan." Meg popped her gum.

"The Good Book says, 'The poor you will always have with you.'" Lucy pulled out a Chap-Stik and wound up its tiny translucent tip. "Anyway Father says Todd has to finish junior high before he can minister to anyone."

It was precisely things like calling the Bible the "Good Book" that made Lucy so grating. Meg had never liked Lucy and she seemed determined to pick a fight.

"You know, the undertakers put pennies on Grannie's eyes." Meg fanned her cheeks, suddenly breathless. "Before they put her in the coffin."

"We'll all be in a coffin someday." Ingrid sat across the room in a chair pressed against the wall. With her pale hair hidden beneath a black headscarf she looked years older and strangely

Rumanian. "Grannie's decaying body may feed the tree that eventually encloses our mortal remains."

Meg shook her head. "That attitude won't get you laid."

Meg's little brother Erik left his Matchbox cars on the floor and crawled closer to her, scuffing the knees of his suit. "Did they really put pennies on Grannie?" he asked.

Meg leaned forward, exposing her tiger-stripe training bra. "Yes. Otherwise her eyes might fly right open." Erik started to cry, and Max, who had been sniffling all morning, joined him.

"Shut up," I told Meg. "You're just mad because Grannie said you're easy." At fifteen Meg had already had three serious boyfriends, including one in the Navy. Uncle Karsten was ready to enroll Meg in reform school when her Navy boyfriend got transferred to Guam.

"For God's sake, keep Meg away from sailors," Grannie had warned. "During the war her type traded their virtue for stockings and Hershey bars."

"Sometimes they bury people who aren't really dead." Meg loosened her scarf, unveiling a mottled blue-and-pink hickey. "When they dig them up later they find scratch marks inside the coffin."

"'Tis a sin to speak unwell of the dead." Lucy traced a protective cross in the air while Todd nodded somberly. "We shall pray for your soul along with the soul of our grandmother."

From deep in the recesses of the church I heard Mildred Sorensen warm up the organ, three or four chords that rattled the whole building. Soon, very soon, the funeral would begin.

Ingrid lit a Virginia Slim.

"What about Todd's asthma?" Lucy asked. Todd provided an impromptu hacking cough.

"So open a window." Ingrid blew several smoke rings that obscured the poster above her head, a pastel depiction of Noah welcoming the dove back to his ark.

Suddenly Pastor Rick appeared in the doorway and cleared his throat. "Good morning, children," he said awkwardly.

Meg secretly tested her breath on her hand. "Hello, Pastor. It's a pleasure to see you again."

Pastor Rick smiled sadly. "Me too. I only wish we were meeting under happier circumstances." Pastor Rick looked handsome in his long robe and hand-embroidered stole. The cream-colored fabric set off both his increasing tan and the fiery red flecks in his beard. "I thought we could offer up a prayer before the service."

The annex walls were covered with cartoon shepherds and cotton ball sheep. *Not here, Pastor Rick,* I wanted to say. *Grannie's prayers should come from someplace better.*

As we gathered in a prayer circle, Max's tears turned to sobs. My brilliant brother suddenly looked like the nine-year-old child he really was. Pastor Rick embraced Max, nearly crushing Max's glasses. I envied Max being so close to the pastor's heart.

"Hey Champ, it's OK." Pastor Rick stroked the smooth strands of Max's hair that Pop had styled that morning. Watching him earlier, I had loved Pop again; loved his helpless struggle as he spit-combed Max's hair, chose a totally inappropriate dress for Mom to wear to the funeral, and prepared a hurried breakfast of Pop-Tarts and Tab. I regretted ever wishing that I had Debbie Schneider's father instead of my own.

Pastor Rick pulled Max's chair beside him while Meg sat at Rick's other side. I sat between Max and Eric while Ingrid kept her chair outside the circle. Pastor Rick bowed his head. "Dear Lord," he began, "we come to You today to remember Grannie Lassen, who left us to share in Your glory."

"Kyrie Elesion," Lucy chanted.

"Lord, hear our prayer," Todd replied, raising his hands.

Pastor Rick stopped, looked up, then quickly resumed. "We know from the words of Your Son, our Lord and Savior Jesus Christ, that all who mourn shall be comforted, all who grieve shall find peace . . ."

A frantic yet gentle "tap-tap-tap" opened my eyes mid-prayer. I looked beyond Pastor Rick's lowered head to a streak of red at the window. I let go of Max and Erik's hands and slipped from my seat.

". . . We ask for Your blessing in our time of sorrow, we entreat You to make our burden light . . . "

I tiptoed to the window. The red flash was a large cardinal with a twig in its beak, perched on the windowsill tapping the glass. I moved close enough to observe the cardinal's shiny black eyes, black-crested head and smooth, blood-red plumage. "Grannie," I whispered. My breath iced the glass, briefly obscuring the bird. I thought about the dove returning to Noah in the poster above Ingrid's head. Sometimes the most delicate creatures get stuck with the toughest jobs.

The wind rose, ruffling the cardinal's feathers. He bobbed and weaved on his tiny feet, balancing the twig. I pressed my palms against the glass as if to steady him but, startled, he flitted away. The twig tumbled from his beak and landed in the parking lot beside Gunderson Brothers' hearse, just as Grannie's plain pine coffin emerged from the hearse's dark, curtained hold. Pop, Uncle David, Uncle Karsten, and my cousin Bjorn, all dressed in black, took their places as pallbearers, standing straight-backed and solemn, the shortest of them Pop at an even six feet.

The men raised the coffin to their sides and then to their shoulders. Mom, Aunt Ruth, Aunt Ginger, and the other women shuffled behind the coffin as the men carried it up to the church. The concrete was wet from the recent rain and Uncle David slipped. His knees buckled and his silver hair disappeared behind the coffin's side. Pop, Uncle Karsten, and Bjorn staggered to pick up the sudden added weight, allowing Uncle David time to right himself.

When Uncle David reappeared his eyes were focused but his cheeks were red and puffed with shame. As Grannie's coffin dipped, then straightened, my own joints jackknifed in pain. I understood that all that remained of Grannie—silver hair, copper pennies, a broken ankle bone—was locked inside that wooden box now moving through the church's stained glass double doors.

I pressed my forehead to the window and the draft circled my skull like cold, skillful hands. Pastor Rick over my shoulder closed his prayer. Younger, softer voices murmured beneath

71

Pastor Rick's, holding him aloft like a tired swimmer. ". . . as we pray the prayer that Jesus taught us. 'Our Father, who art in heaven, hallowed be Thy name, Thy kingdom come, Thy will be done, on earth as it is in heaven . . . ' "

As we drove home from Grannie's burial a cold drizzle followed us out of the cemetery, through the fog-shrouded city and into the suburbs. When we reached our driveway, Pop parked the car and turned off the engine. I stared up at our house, afraid to break the strange stillness inside the car and admit that this, the five of us, was our whole family now and that we lived here where grief had come calling, had visited us at home.

Mom rubbed her thumb against the window, slashing the bright beads of condensation. "Look, someone left a plant." She pointed to a tall plant with yellow-green leaves positioned beside the back door. A notecard plastered to the flowerpot bled red-green ink in twirling ribbons down the concrete walk.

"That poor, poor plant." Mom's door sprung open and she hurried out, bustling on her wobbly heels while holding her coat's collar arched above her head. She grabbed the plant and held it tenderly in her arms. She pulled open the screen door, then pushed the wooden door, but it didn't budge. The rest of us climbed out of the car and zigzagged to the house, dodging raindrops.

"Hold on Christina, I've got the key," Pop called. Mom pushed harder, ramming the door with her shoulder.

We huddled against the back door away from the rain as Pop fumbled in his pockets. Mom's hot angry face was speckled with wet make-up.

"It's from Mrs. Gutknecht." Mom's bottom lip trembled as she held the flowerpot level with her abdomen. The plant's narrow, tubular stalk and thin curling leaves looked to me like a diagram of Mom's internal organs, rising from deep inside her body. She cradled the tender top shoots, shielding them from the rain. "Mrs. Gutknect. The one whose daughter died last year." Pop looked down as he turned the key and opened the door. I could tell by Mom's expression that she would never, ever forgive him.

That night my whole body ached with missing Grannie, and every room of the house echoed with her absence. When I closed my eyes expecting to see Grannie's face, I saw only Uncle David, slipping on the wet church step and disappearing behind the coffin.

I sneaked some M&Ms upstairs, along with a Kit Kat and a $100,000 Bar, and sat cross-legged on my bed, working on *Girl on the Lam*. I hadn't written a word since Grannie died, and I had left off at a key scene. Stormy and Eric were walking romantically along the banks of the River Seine. Eric had broken through Stormy's street-kid exterior but now he feared she would see his brain tumor scar and be disgusted by its ugliness.

"Eric turned and kissed Stormy square on the lips." *Destiny has brought these two wounded souls together,* I wrote for the voice-over. I wondered if Stormy should see fireworks as they kissed and if so, how I would write that into the script. Should it just be a sound effect, or did I actually have to *show* the explosions?

A soft knock at the door startled me. "Sunnie?" Mom whispered.

I quickly shifted my screenplay beneath the covers. "Come in," I said, pulling the blanket to my chin.

The door cracked open and Mom stepped inside, allowing the brief sliver of hallway light to disappear behind her. "I wondered if you were still up."

"Uh huh. I was just . . . thinking," I replied.

She nodded. "I can't sleep either." She was dressed in her nightgown and her pale, freckled skin was dusted with dark gritty powder. Her hair was flat on one side and dried tears stained a single cheek: she must have cried lying down. She rubbed her eye with a tightened fist, smearing the make-up nearly to her ear.

"I've got chocolate." I folded down the bedding to reveal a dish of M&Ms. Her face lit up as she shuffled to my bed. I pushed the loose-leaf pages of *Girl on the Lam* onto the floor and moved over. Mom's feet were cold as she slid in beside me. She propped up the pillow and slipped one arm behind her head. The other hand reached for the M&Ms.

We lay side by side, the tops of our heads just visible in the movie star mirror. "That space on your dresser." She raised her chin. "Something is missing."

I followed her gaze to the small ceramic pedestal between my seventh grade spelling bee certificate and my yellow ribbon for playing baritone at the 1977 state competition. "That's where Johnny's picture goes." I crunched a mouthful of candy. "Well, at least until the Romulans ripped it up."

"That picture meant a lot to you, didn't it?"

"More than anything."

"He'll send you another photo. I'm sure he will." For the first time in four days, my mother smiled.

I reached over and turned off the reading lamp, plunging the room into an utter and dazzling darkness. The darkness was so complete I couldn't believe that light had ever existed. I saw floating halos and something hurt behind my eyes. I heard the sweet secretive rustle of candy wrappers, muffled beneath the sheets.

"Sunnie, I promise I won't ever die," Mom whispered.

I swallowed hard. "You can't promise that. No one can."

"Yes, I can. I promise." Her breath was hot above the covers. "I'll never do to you what Mama did to me."

"OK. Whatever you say," I replied. In the dark recesses of the bedsheets Mom's fumbling fingers searched for, then found, the warm hollow of my hand.

CHAPTER SIX

Three days before fat camp Ingrid drove me to the bank downtown to deposit the five thousand dollars that Grannie had left me in her will. Mom was supposed to take me, but she was spending most of her time watching Phil Donahue, clutching the big plaid pillow and chain-smoking Virginia Slims.

Mom had grown tender in the twelve days since Grannie died and she now looked as pale and soft as an exotic fruit. Even a brief slash of sunlight escaping from the Venetian blinds could bruise her fragile skin. "Close the curtains," she'd say, holding up her freckled hand and squinting severely. "You're giving me a pain."

Mom's heart had softened too, allowing in great waves of sympathy for Phil Donahue's wronged guests. Once Mom wept for the career gal whose husband wore lingerie. "Underwear is underwear," I reasoned. "It's not that bad."

"No. Humiliation makes it painful." Mom pounded the pillow. "Phil's audience doesn't understand."

I waited until Ingrid had steered Mom's Ford LTD station wagon past 118th Street before I broached the subject.

"Should we do something about Mom?" I asked. Wind whipped through the open windows.

"Like what?" Ingrid nearly collided with a bicyclist. "Out of the way!" she shouted as the old man clutched his handlebars for dear life.

"I don't know. Tell someone, I guess." I braced myself as Ingrid screeched to a halt.

"What would we say? Our Mom watches Phil Donahue?" Ingrid tapped her cigarette out the window and bits of ash blew back inside.

"No. You know." I brushed the hot gray flecks from my lap. "About Mom. Missing Grannie."

"What's there to say?" Ingrid had been counting the days until she'd leave for Sweden. In a rare display of enthusiasm, she had taped Swedish flash cards to the furniture, in the cupboards, and on all the appliances. If I ever found myself in Sweden I could ask for a toaster, a fridge, or a colander.

"So with you gone, me and Pop and Max have to deal with this on our own?"

She sighed. "Welcome to the real world, kid."

Ingrid dropped me at the steel-and-stone entrance to Traders Guarantee and screeched back into traffic before I could say good-bye. Sweating in my long denim jumper, I hiked up the concrete steps and stumbled into the revolving glass door that spun me around and around before depositing me inside the bank's cold marble lobby. The lobby smelled like money, from the deep green carpeting to the rows of prim tellers to the rickety elevators with old-fashioned collapsing-cage doors and mother-of-pearl call panel buttons that glowed like milk-white jewels.

I introduced myself at the reception desk. "Mr. Peter Sundstrom, please," I asked in my best grown-up voice. "I'm his daughter."

The receptionist picked up her phone and punched in some numbers. A shiny placard on her desk announced that a brand new five-setting Proctor-Silex toaster was free to anyone opening an account this week. I was glad I'd come today: last week I'd have gotten a five-piece tool set, while next week's prize was a chef's apron and long-handled barbecue fork.

"Miss Sundstrom, your father will be down in a moment," the receptionist said. "Wait here."

I took a seat on one of the green velvet chairs arranged around the lobby. I had never been to Pop's bank without Ingrid and Max.

Every year we attended the employees' Christmas party, me in a red velvet dress handed down from Ingrid with the waist and sleeves mercifully released. At the party we were given little net sacks filled with gold-wrapped chocolate coins. The coins carried profiles of mens' heads and inscriptions like, "The Republic of Chocolate," "In Fudge We Trust," and "E Plurebus Eat 'em." Every year at least twelve people would say, "Don't spend those all in one place," and expect us to laugh.

The elevator rattled to a landing just beyond the lobby. Pop emerged from the shadow and bustled toward me, arm extended. "Sunnie, so good of you to come."

So good of me to come? Speechless, I shook Pop's hand. Did he suddenly think I was someone else- a fellow vice president of mortgage lending, perhaps? I turned to go up to Pop's office but he steered me instead to the tellers.

"A vice president's daughter shouldn't get special treatment." Pop chuckled. "We'll set up your account down here."

"Does a vice president's daughter get a free toaster?" I asked anxiously.

He stroked his chin. "Depends on how many are left."

We took our place in line behind an elderly lady with a vinyl purse and a clear plastic sack of pennies.

Pop folded his arms and rocked back on his heels. "I remember opening my first bank account." His eyes narrowed as he peered deep into his own past. "How much do you think I put in?"

We shuffled a few inches closer to the tall bank of tellers. "A hundred dollars?" I ventured.

"Hardly." Pop seemed pleased that I had guessed so incorrectly. "My first deposit was five dollars and thirty-three cents." He sighed deeply, releasing what sounded like real regret. "This was back in 1947, when folks understood the value of a dollar." For Pop, "the value of a dollar" was an important concept and, like many things in our lives, had a secret link to Communism. It was no doubt a result of Soviet influence that people didn't value the dollar as much as they once did.

77

"I earned that money on my paper route." Pop's eyes were lost in the 1940s as the old lady in front of us sagged beneath the weight of her collected pennies. "Other kids bought bikes or wagons or baseball cards but not me. You know why not?"

My mind flashed to photos I had seen of Pop as a child: toe-headed and gap-toothed with a bowl-shaped haircut and a tight fiddly collar.

"You were saving for your future?" I guessed.

"That's right." Pop deflated slightly at my correct guess. "It's possible that interest from my first deposit is still generating income today. The money I use for our mortgage, and food and clothing."

"That's pretty . . . important," I offered, for the sake of conversation. I wondered if Mom would let me keep the toaster in my room. After all, Max's room had a whole science lab complete with test tubes and an autoclave.

Pop surveyed the cold marble lobby of Traders Guarantee as if it were the gateway to a magical kingdom. "People say money doesn't buy happiness but it does, Sunnie. It does." His eyes blazed. "It buys food and medicine and education. Money makes the world go around and I'm not ashamed to say it."

Pop lurched forward, nearly trampling the elderly woman with the pennies as a new window opened up at the end of teller's row. "Come on, Sunnie. Looks like she's waiting for us."

It wasn't quite two o'clock when we finished setting up my new account. Pop kept my passbook and starter checks in his jacket pocket while I carried my new toaster, enjoying the unexpected bulk of its stapled cardboard box. I was supposed to go home with Pop at 5:30 but I sensed mild panic as he contemplated what to do with me for three-and-a-half hours. "How'd you like to watch your old man at work?" he asked with forced cheerfulness. "I'll show you how to research mortgage applications."

"Great," I replied, balancing the toaster on my shoulder. On the way up to Pop's office the elevator stopped on the tenth floor and a man got in. Pop introduced him as Ed Vicks and he looked exactly like Pop except he had dark hair and blue eyes. One floor later another man, Bob Rusch, got in and he could have been Pop and Ed's missing triplet. He was a few years older and wore glasses but like Pop and Ed he had neatly clipped hair and smooth, even features, dressed in a dark suit, white shirt, and solid-color tie. It occurred to me that every floor of Traders Guarantee was full of clean-shaven, square-jawed men in dark suits who looked just like Pop. I could go home with any one of them and no one would ever be the wiser.

"Hey Pete," Ed whispered, elbowing Pop as the elevator stopped on the 14th floor. "Tell Bob that joke. About the nun, the priest and the duck."

My throat narrowed with alarm. *My father does not tell jokes,* I wanted to say. *Not ever. Nothing is funny to him.*

Pop blushed. Color warmed his cheekbones and the tips of his ears. "I'm not sure I remember it . . . "

"Go on, it's a riot," Ed encouraged. "I tried to tell it to Bob here but you do better voices."

Voices? My father does *voices?* The only voice I'd heard, other than his everyday voice, was the angry voice he used when threatening to write to Comrade Brezhnev at the Kremlin.

"I don't know if it'd be appropriate." Pop's gaze landed on me. "Sunnie's thirteen and it's kind of a grown-up joke."

When we reached Pop's office he ushered me through a door with a plastic tab that read, "PETER SUNDSTROM, V/P MORT-GAGE LENDING." His office was small and stuffy, smelling of newsprint, stale doughnuts, and day-old coffee. His office reminded me of a motel room with its long metal desk, standard file cabinet, floor lamp, and coat stand. In front of Pop's desk were two small chairs where married couples sat and waited for Pop to approve or deny their dream of home ownership.

"Office, sweet office," Pop said, straightening his coat on the stand.

I took a seat and placed the toaster beside me. I had just settled in to read a copy of the "1978 Fiduciary Projections" pamphlet in tiny newsprint type when Pop was called into an emergency meeting.

Pop's face showed a mixture of surprise and relief. "Don't answer the phone if it rings," he said as he gathered a notepad and pen. "If you get thirsty, ask Sharon, the secretary, to show you the soda machine. There's change in the top drawer."

"I'll be fine," I said as he hurried from the office. As soon as Pop's footsteps disappeared down the carpeted hallway I plopped down in his padded chair and rolled back on its tiny wheels.

I was surprised to see photos arranged on Pop's desk. The closest photo was a black-and-white shot of Mom, dating back to high school. In the picture Mom was dressed in a twin set, pearls, and one of her beloved Pendleton skirts. Her hair was pulled back in a 1950s-style ponytail that exploded in curls above her shoulder. Her face was thinner, narrow through the cheeks and chin. It was true; she had only weighed 108 pounds junior year. Although she recalled this as the happiest time of her life, the photo hinted at sadness behind her eyes and revealed a downward tug to her smile.

I looked at last year's school pictures of Ingrid, Max, and me. In her photo Ingrid looked pale and severe, resenting her own traditional prettiness, while in my photo the strong lighting gave my forehead an oily glow.

I opened the top drawer of Pop's desk. Beneath the ruler, pencils, and spare change I found a stack of photos bound in a rubber band. I was scared to look; afraid of discovering Pop's double life, images of another family whom he loved more than us.

Instead the photos showed scenes of earlier times: Pop and his brother, Anders, as children in a wooden sled; Mom and Pop's 1960 Christmas as newlyweds, standing stiffly beside a knee-high, spindly tree; and Ingrid as a newborn, surprisingly plump, just home from the hospital.

I wondered if Pop leafed through the photos while talking on the phone or writing his quarterly reports. *Pop is forty,* I thought, *and has been working at Traders Guarantee since before Ingrid was born.* Every day he put on a dark suit, a white shirt, and a plain tie, and drove the same nine miles, parked in the same spot, and stepped through the same revolving glass door.

I felt a strange guilty grief for my father, a man who hid his sense of humor, a man who owned voices I had never heard. Maybe handsome Peter Sundstrom with his dollar-fifty haircut dreamed of another life somewhere else. A life where Communism wasn't an everyday threat and Leonid Brezhnev was friend, not foe. A life where he didn't have a broken-hearted wife and a fat teenage daughter. Grannie once told me that we could never earn the sacrifices others made for us. She meant her parents, coming over on a boat from Sweden, enduring that passage to give us all a better life, but I realized that the debt had been passed down through every generation, with no hope of future redemption.

Pop returned from his meeting just before five-thirty. "How did it go?" he asked. "Complete any major financial transactions?" He seemed almost jovial, maybe because his day spent entertaining me hadn't been so bad after all. "Next time we'll tour the vault," he promised. "The door lock alone weighs three hundred pounds." He straightened his notes, packed up his briefcase, and patted his jacket to show that my passbook and starter checks were safely stowed away.

The sun was still up as Pop's 1975 Oldsmobile Cutlass Supreme hunkered out of the employee-parking garage and onto Wisconsin Avenue. Traffic was heavy throughout downtown as idling exhaust fumes mixed with the heat off the sidewalks to create a thick yellow haze.

Nearly every other car was driven by a single clean-shaven man in a dark suit heading home to the suburbs. In another hour downtown Milwaukee would be a ghost town, returned to the custody of winos and whores, street preachers and bums, and lumbering city buses that lifted trash like hope before rudely blowing it back into the gutters.

When we reached the suburbs traffic thinned, splitting off in different directions as we made our way west with the sun burning low through the windshield, casting the recessed dashboard in dark shadow. Pop hadn't said a word since we left the bank but I could feel him change with every passing mile. His hands tightened on the steering wheel as he worked the muscles in his jaw. Resentment radiated from his skin as I imagined him mentally listing the million ways we had all disappointed him, and the million little hurts we still had in mind.

Glancing in the side view mirror, I could just make out the meager skyscrapers on Milwaukee's lakefront skyline. I imagined that Pop had left his other self back there in that land of lost fathers, a place where all the other middle-aged men gave their best selves like blood and came home, diminished, to their ungrateful families every evening. *We do this to him. We make him unhappy,* I thought. *Me, and the rest of the family. He likes the family in the photos in his desk drawer. He just doesn't like us for real.*

Pop's anger increased once we reached home. Mom was curled up in the den watching Merv Griffin as he flirted with Zha Zha Gabor and ignored Captain Steubing from *The Love Boat.* Mom hadn't made supper and Ingrid had gotten a speeding ticket.

"Why the hell were you going forty-five in a twenty zone?" Pop's face went from pink to crimson. "Do you realize how dangerous it is to speed?"

Ingrid shrugged. Her pale hair hung heavily over her eyes but for once her casual innocence seemed forced. "We're all just speeding towards our eventual deaths."

"So why am I paying thousands to send you to Sweden?" Pop shook the ticket. "Why not live out your miserable existence here?"

Before Ingrid could answer, a loud crash shook the floor above us. A split-second later Max came screaming into the kitchen. His glasses were askew with one of the lenses shattered like a windshield. Flecks of blood and pus stained Max's orange T-shirt and Pop paled at the sight.

"Jesus Christ, what happened?" Pop dropped the speeding ticket, grabbed Max's shoulders and lifted him clear off the ground.

"The-the-the-it-it-went . . . " Max couldn't catch his breath.

"Are you hurt, son? Are you hurt?" Pop searched Max's skinny, quivering body, looking for a wound.

Mom stumbled in from the den, rubbing her eyes. "What's all the noise?"

"My tadpoles," Max whimpered. "They exploded!" He burst into tears.

I couldn't believe it. Exploding tadpoles? Stuff like that only happened on TV. I ran upstairs. The scene in Max's room looked like something from a mad scientist movie. A goldfish bowl on Max's desk had shattered into daggers of glass, leaving only the round base still intact. A clear plastic tube snaked from the remains of the goldfish bowl to a glass beaker full of foamy yellow fluid. Another tube was attached to an extension cord with duct tape and plugged into the wall below Max's Chewbacca night-light. A huge puddle of gloppy green water dripped from Max's desk to the carpet below.

Pop, Mom, Ingrid, and Max entered the room behind me and stopped in awe. "What the hell were you doing?" Pop asked.

"An experiment." Max sniffled. "I wanted to see if an electrified saline solution would make my sea monkeys more active. I practiced on the tadpoles."

"Jesus." Mom gagged and ran to the bathroom, slamming the door.

As Pop and Max went to get cleaning supplies, Ingrid and I surveyed Max's desk. Not a single tadpole had survived the experiment. Tiny squirts of blood peppered the wallpaper between thick trails of yellow-green slime that, on closer inspection, contained tadpole heads, fins, and tiny tails, as transparent as Scotch tape. A damp haze filled the room with the odor of potting soil, rotten eggs, and Truman School fish filets.

Ingrid folded her narrow arms. "You've got to give our little brother credit." She nodded solemnly. "There's nothing he wouldn't try at least once."

Pop and Max returned with buckets and sponges. "I don't care what your mother thinks." Pop loosened his collar. "You are grounded until September."

Max's thin arms strained as his bucket sloshed its soapy contents onto the floor. He tilted his head, trying to see through his shattered lens. "Grounding has never been an effective disciplinary technique," he explained. "Doctor Spock himself has said . . ."

"Shut up and clean," Pop muttered, rolling up his sleeves.

Suddenly the doorbell rang. "I'll get it," I said. The bell rang three more times before I could answer it. "I'm coming, I'm coming," I yelled from the stairs.

When I pulled open the front door a large dark man was slouched on the doormat, clipboard in hand. He was sweating around the stretched neck of his T-shirt and he wore a menacing five o'clock shadow. An embroidered red patch on his chest said "MARCEL" in surprisingly delicate lettering.

"I'm looking for a," he glanced down at the clipboard, "Wilma Sand Storm."

"You mean Sundstrom?" I scratched my head.

"Sand storm, sun storm, rain storm, wind storm. I ain't here for the weather report."

"I'm Wilma Sundstrom. You're looking for me." I joined Marcel on the top step. He smelled strangely of stewed fruit, a mixture of salty human sweat and sweet ripe berries.

"Sign this." He pushed the battered clipboard into my hand. Clipped to the front was a single sheet of white paper.

"What is this?" The paper was covered with faint black type.

"Your contract." Marcel wiped his blackened fingers on his apron.

"My contract?" I noticed a large "X" at the bottom, waiting for my signature.

Marcel waved to a big white truck parked in front of our house. "Hey Louie, this here's the place," he shouted, cupping his hands to his mouth. As Marcel stepped aside I saw that the truck had RAMBERT SPECIALTY JAMS, WAUWATOSA, WISC. painted on its side in old-fashioned black lettering.

Rambert Jams. The banner design contest. My lifetime supply! So much had happened in the last few weeks that I had forgotten all about it.

"Is it all for me?" I asked, scribbling my name beside the "X."

Marcel started back to the truck and I hurried to catch up. I searched my mind for places to store my windfall of jam. The garage? The attic? That weird little corner under the staircase where we kept the yardstick and dustpans? No, too many blind white spiders there that never saw the light of day.

I was breathless when I reached the truck. Louie, a small, balding man, had the back doors open and was stacking wooden flats in Marcel's bulging arms. "If you pull up to the garage," I panted, "we can unload there."

"Naw. I can make it." Marcel hiked the flats to his beefy shoulder.

"What about the rest?" I asked.

"This is it." He strode up the driveway to the house.

"That's it?" I struggled to keep pace and did some quick figuring. Each wooden flat contained five rows. Each of the rows held five jars of jam. There were five flats balanced on Marcel's shoulder. "But that's only one-hundred-and-twenty-five jars of jam," I said. "I won a lifetime supply."

Marcel pressed the flats against the house as I opened the door. "Read the fine print," he said. "Clause 7.5 (b)."

I pulled the contract from the front pocket of my denim jumper. I couldn't read the fine print, even as Marcel underlined the clause with his stubby finger. "It says you will receive a shipment of one hundred twenty-five jars of Rambert Jam on or before July first of every year for a period of ten years, commencing in the year of our Lord nineteen-seventy-eight."

"Oh." This was less jam than I had expected for a "lifetime supply." Still, looking at the glass jars stacked as high as my hip, I couldn't help but feel a little blessed.

"What's happening up there?" Marcel nodded to the noise above our heads.

"Some tadpoles exploded," I explained. "Pop's mad and Mom's addicted to Phil Donahue. Grannie died and Ingrid is leaving. I'm going to fat camp to start high school skinny."

"Jeez, Kid." Marcel shook his head. "You've got quite a life."

After Marcel and Louie left I phoned Emily and Jerry and asked them to bring over some bread and milk. Meanwhile I released my new Proctor-Silex toaster from its box, blew off the cardboard dust, unwound the kinked extension cord, and polished the aluminum siding with my sleeve. This was, without doubt, a beautiful toaster.

I toasted the last slices of rye bread left in the fridge. The first piece tasted like burning plastic but the next one came out just fine. I sampled all five toaster settings and was impressed by the distinct levels of doneness. Setting number three was the best, leaving the toast an intense golden brown. The whole kitchen filled with the sturdy smell of baking bread.

I set up a sandwich assembly line along the kitchen counter, complete with margarine, peanut butter, and several jars of my brand new jam. I plunged a knife into the Old-Fashioned Strawberry and Rhubarb Preserves and listened to Pop upstairs cleaning Max's room.

"My wife won't cook dinner," he said, slapping the sponge against the wall. "My daughters. Cost me a fortune." *Slap.* "With their fat camps, their speeding tickets, their study abroad." *Slap.* "And my only son. Is criminally insane. Might as well move to the USSR."

Even the worst moments of life hold a little sweetness, I told myself. I sampled a spoonful of Patriotic Concord Grape and knew in an instant what New England must taste like. *I'll take the sweetness, wherever it finds me. Grannie had such faith in me, but she didn't live to see my prize. Every day takes me further and further away from her, until one day I might not remember her at all.*

I set aside several jars of jam, Bursting Black Raspberry for Emily because strawberries gave her hives, and Sugar-Free Fresh Apricot for Jerry, on account of his diabetes. The rhythm of Pop's sponge slapping the wall became a kind of dance and I imagined rivulets of dirty brown water rushing down the wallpaper. "You'd never get away with this," he seethed. "In the Gulag. Comrade. I promise."

I closed my eyes and imagined Emily and Jerry walking home with my gifts of jam. Their heavy-laden arms would labor under the weight of so much golden richness as the summer sun dipped behind the horizon and I would know for certain that I had done at least one good thing. All around me I felt a great tenderness withheld, even as I hoped my suffering had not been forgotten.

CHAPTER SEVEN

In the final week before fat camp Mom spent even more time in the den, smoking Virginia Slims and drinking RC Cola. In addition to *Phil Donahue, Merv Griffin,* and *Dinah Shore,* she added *The Price Is Right, The New High Rollers,* and *Match Game '78* to her daily viewing schedule.

"They make all the answers sound so dirty." She tossed the plaid headrest against the wall. I wanted to review the Summer Slim-Down Packing List with her but she wasn't interested. "I've never trusted Richard Dawson. Or Gene Rayburn either, for that matter," she said. "Richard Dawson looks shifty and Gene Rayburn has dishonest eyes."

"That's OK." I skimmed the list. "There are only a few things left anyway."

That afternoon I walked to the White Hen Pantry to pick up the last of my supplies, say good-bye to Mr. Chan, and purchase perhaps the final Klondike Bar of my whole entire life. I hoped the July issue of *Hollywood* had arrived, with the cover story promised last month, exposing Tinseltown's new breed of bad boys including Jeff Conaway and Ryan O'Neal.

Mr. Chan helped me gather the tongue depressors, suntan lotion, masking tape, and twine that I needed for camp. "Must be for jail break." He held up the tape and the twine. "Make rope, throw over wall."

When Mrs. Chan heard I was leaving, she hurried over with an impromptu picnic lunch. The shop was not very busy, just a few surly Central High kids on skateboards bumming cigarettes and drinking Mountain Dew, so Mrs. Chan and I spread newspapers over the card table in back and unpacked the little clay pots of pepper sauce and aromatic mustard.

"Sunnie, in honor of you leaving, we have special meal." Mrs. Chan lit a small white candle and I blushed, anticipating my first hot meal since Grannie died.

Mr. Chan rang up a sale of Hershey bars and Kotex, then joined us in back. Together we feasted on fresh egg rolls, fried pastry pockets and crab Rangoon beneath the single bare light bulb, surrounded by cardboard boxes and mildewy mops.

"This is delicious." I sucked the meat off a spicy chicken wing. "I wish the flavor would last all summer."

"Send child away to lose weight." Mrs. Chan, a large woman in a vast floral muumuu, shook her head. "Never hear of such a thing."

"I just hope it works." I sipped my green tea. "I can't come home fat."

"You not fat. You healthy." Mr. Chan scooped another mound of shiny white rice onto my plate. "You find boyfriend who like healthy girl, you be happy." He winked at Mrs. Chan.

As I prepared to leave Mrs. Chan embraced me firmly and kissed me, military-style, on either cheek. The aroma of lavender and talcum powder seemed to explode from every creased fold of her body.

"Sunnie, you are lovely girl. No matter what size." She smiled and held me at arm's length. I trembled, fearing she would say "only inner beauty matters," or that I had a "beautiful heart." These were expressions of lowered expectations that no fat girl ever wanted to hear, but instead Mrs. Chan gave me a little bamboo-paper scroll with a column of Chinese characters.

"Thank you. It's beautiful." I touched the fine black-ink figures.

"It says, 'Good luck and safe journey.'" She offered a slight bow. "To keep you on your trip."

I suddenly felt smart and sophisticated. I bet I'd be the only girl at fat camp with grown-up Chinese friends.

"Send us postcard from road," Mr. Chan called as I left with my camp supplies, my good luck scroll, and the new issue of *Hollywood*. My throat narrowed as Mr. and Mrs. Chan stood side by side, stiff as Red Army soldiers, saluting me from beneath the White Hen Pantry's orange-and-white cloth awning.

As I turned the corner of 116th Street onto Hadley Avenue, I saw Max sitting outside with his head down and his skinny arms holding his knees.

I ran down the block to him. "What's wrong?"

Max squinted into the sun. "Mom and Pop had a big fight." He looked pale and stricken. "Mom's not coming with us tomorrow."

I sat beside him, leaning forward to catch my breath. "Why isn't Mom coming?"

Max shrugged. "She wants some time alone."

"What did Pop say?"

Max took off his new glasses and rubbed his eyes. "He said that if Mom stays home, Ingrid and I should too. Then he left."

"So just me and Pop are going to Minnesota?" I shivered, even in the late afternoon's hazy heat. I couldn't imagine two days in the car with only Pop and the radio for company.

"Come with us." I nudged Max. "You can sit in front." Max threw up if he sat too long in the back of a moving vehicle. Grannie said he inherited the sensitive Lassen stomach from Grandpa's brother Henrik, tossed from the Danish Army for chronic vomiting during the wars for Schleswig-Holstein.

"Sunnie, don't you get it?" Max's eyes filled with tears. "Pop might never come home at all."

Seven o'clock rolled around and there was still no sign of Pop. I sat with Emily and Jerry on Emily's back step, tossing pebbles and tracing our names in the dirt. Jerry turned his Magic-8 Ball over and over, looking for a positive response. Beyond the wooden fence, happy splashing sounds came from the Marzettis' swimming pool, where I was forbidden to swim because Tony Marzetti had athlete's foot and Mom was convinced he was contagious.

"Dad wants me to transfer to Mary Queen of Heaven this fall." Emily flicked a pebble with her whittled stick. "So I can't date until I'm eighteen."

"At least it's a good school." I erased my name in the dirt and drew a circle. "MQH girls get into the best colleges."

"That's 'cuz no one gets into MQH girls." Jerry nudged Emily, throwing her into a fit of giggles that didn't stop until she blew her nose.

"That's so gross!" she cried, stuffing her Kleenex back into her sleeve.

Jerry set down the Magic-8 Ball and picked at a yellow scab on his wrist.

"Oh Jerry, don't." Emily softly batted his arm. "You'll get an infection with your diabetes."

"It's OK so long as I wash my hands good afterwards." Since school let out Jerry had been swimming every day at the county pool, where the sun burned his nose and peppered his cheeks with freckles. He had grown tall and firm in just a few weeks.

"Magic-8 Ball, will Emily be the most excellent girl at MQH?" Jerry grabbed the ball and shook it vigorously. The phrase, "It is likely" floated to the top.

Emily and I laughed but Jerry's mood suddenly darkened.

"What's wrong?" Emily touched his hand.

"My Dad's talking about going back to Ohio." Jerry sighed. "To be regional vice president in Upper Sandusky."

As I leaned back the cold concrete step sent a toothache-chill up my spine. I put one arm around Emily and the other around Jerry. "It'll be different when I'm home from camp," I said. "If you guys are gone I'll have no friends."

Emily poked me in the ribs. "You'll be pretty and skinny and popular. You won't need us anymore."

I pulled Jerry and Emily closer. "I'll need you guys forever. Together since kindergarten. Together for life."

Jerry shook the Magic 8-Ball. "Will we be friends forever?" he asked. He steadied the ball while we waited for an answer. "Not certain. Ask later," came the reply.

That night I packed an old Army duffel bag and my Hello Kitty backpack. I couldn't decide whether to bring my Johnny Carson scrapbook. Right after I started the scrapbook in 1972 Johnny divorced his second wife, Joanne, and married his third wife, Joanna. After Johnny's divorce I removed all images of Joanne from my scrapbook, lifting her out with an X-Acto knife and pasting her over with photos of Ed McMahon.

I'll leave the scrapbook home, I decided after I re-glued a loose picture of Johnny with his lawyer, "Bombastic" Bushkin. *At camp it could fall into the lake, be eaten by bears, or get covered with calamine lotion. It's safer here.*

The ten o'clock news ended and *The Tonight Show* began. Johnny stepped out to a roar of applause. "It was so hot in Burbank today . . . " Johnny plunged his hands in his pockets and rocked back on his heels.

"How hot was it?" the audience responded.

"It was so hot, people were hiding beneath Orson Welles just to get some shade."

I touched Johnny on the screen. "Don't have too many good shows when I'm gone," I warned. "Do Floyd Turbo and Art Fern, but save Aunt Blabby and 'Stump the Band' for when I get home."

It was past midnight when I bid good-bye to Grannie's bedroom. Pop still hadn't come home and the house was eerily quiet. Slowly I worked my way around the room, letting my fingers linger over the lampshade, the padded fabric jewelry box, and Grannie's old-fashioned alarm clock.

I slid open the closet and filled my lungs with the scent of Grannie's clothing, the dust of pressed powder and hints of lemon verbena. I missed the way she scolded Mom, I missed the steady creak of her rocking chair. I missed the way she asked about *Girl on the Lam.*

I reached Grannie's nightstand. The glass of water was still there, along with the crumpled antacid wrappers. The level of water had dipped a little, but otherwise nothing had changed. I wondered if the glass would still be here when I came home in

August. If all went as planned I would be a fraction of my former self by then; a silhouette, a shadow, down by a good twenty pounds.

"I'm leaving for fat camp tomorrow, Grannie," I said aloud. "I don't know what will happen there. I don't know what will happen when I get home. Mostly I just want you to be proud."

Suddenly I heard the back door open. Pop was home. I tried to gauge his mood by the noise he made. He opened and closed the fridge, dropped his shoes in the foyer, and tossed his keys in the ceramic pot. His actions sounded ordinary, not angry or embarrassed or remorseful, even the heavy trudge of his footsteps as he came up to bed, muttering beneath his breath.

Pop entered his bedroom and Mom said something, but I couldn't make out what. I held my breath and waited for shouting or an argument or even the icky sound of them making up, but there was nothing, only a deeper, darker silence, a silence as steady as death, as I left Grannie's bedroom and slipped back down the hallway to my own.

"Come on Sunnie, rise and shine." Pop's voice sliced through my dream. I burrowed into my pillow, clinging to images of Johnny and me in the Lipton Classic Celebrity Tennis Match.

"Sunnie. We gotta get going."

I squinted at the clock. "But it's only five A.M.," I croaked.

"Gotta hit the road by seven to make good time." There was never much traffic out of Milwaukee on a Saturday morning, but Pop got anxious if we didn't stick to a certain schedule.

"Are you really up?"

I looked at Pop in his short-sleeve shirt and cotton slacks. Even casually dressed Pop seemed ready to work, prepared to stop at a moment's notice should a rogue mortgage application float through the car's open window. "I'm up," I answered, covering my head with the pillow. "I'll be ready on time."

It was decided that Pop, Max, and I would drive to Minnesota while Mom and Ingrid stayed home. Even with all of Pop's nervous planning, 11:15 A.M. found us still packing Mom's green station wagon. Ingrid fixed us a big Thermos of coffee and wedged it between the front seats. I tapped Ingrid's shoulder.

"Farvel," I said, then added "Adjø," holding my lips in what I hoped was the proper position.

"What's that?" She sounded irritated.

"Swedish." My chest deflated. "Isn't it? For good-bye?"

She yawned. "Your accent needs work."

"Sorry." I pulled Ingrid closer. "Keep an eye on Mom," I whispered. "You know."

"I'll do what I can. But don't expect any miracles."

Mom came outside in her tattered robe and threadbare slippers to survey our preparations. She reached into the back seat and opened the insulated cooler.

"Soda and chips?" she asked. "That's gonna make a mess."

"We can't stop for meals every fifteen minutes," Pop replied. "We've already got time to make up."

"Whatever." Mom hugged me. "Be good, Sunnie. Wish I'd had this opportunity when I was young." She looked at me wistfully. "Don't get too skinny now," she warned. "I don't want my daughter disappearing."

I climbed in and buckled my seatbelt while Max settled into the "way-back" where he'd arranged some blankets as a fort. Pop limited Max to an hour in back; then we had to change seats because of Max's nervous stomach. As we backed down the driveway, Ingrid yawned again. Mom in her threadbare robe looked shipwrecked, marooned on a tiny island within her own life.

Pop drove down Hadley Avenue towards 118th Street. As we neared Emily's house she and Jerry burst through the front door and ran down the lawn. Jerry held up a cardboard sign that said, "See U in August!" The back said, "Thanks for the Jam!"

I stuck my arm out the window and waved. "Bye!" I yelled. "See you in seven weeks!"

At the intersection I turned in my seat. I could see Emily sobbing as Jerry stroked her back. He removed her glasses and rocked her in his arms. *They're falling in love,* I realized. *I've lost them both, whether Jerry moves to Ohio or Emily goes to Catholic school.*

94

By the time Hadley Avenue turned into Southward Boulevard, I was more alone than I had been when we pulled out of the driveway, only ten minutes before.

Once past the city limits the countryside revealed a steady stream of dairy farms with tall silos, broad wooden barns, and proud country churches with whitewashed sides and high pointy steeples. The rolling farmland was dotted with thousands of black-and-white Holsteins huddled close in conversation or sacked out in the sun, their round slack udders a naughty shade of pink beneath them.

When we reached Madison we headed northwest, entering a landscape of hills and valleys, apple orchards, and fields of corn that had kept the promise of knee-high by the Fourth of July.

"We should take a family vacation," I said. "To Disneyland. And Knott's Berry Farm too."

"A berry farm?" Pop scoffed. "Look around you."

"What?" I asked.

"There are farms everywhere. Lots of them grow berries. They just don't charge an arm and a leg to visit."

I ignored Pop's attitude. "Going to California would be my dream come true."

Pop eased off the gas and an eighteen-wheeler overtook us. "You might want to aim a little lower," he said. "Like summer camp in Minnesota."

"What do you mean?"

"Sunnie, I don't know if we'll have any more vacations. As a family." Pop clutched the steering wheel.

"Why not?"

He took a deep breath. "There might be some changes when you get home."

At Eau Claire we headed west into the setting sun. The Brewers-Yankees game that had followed us from Tomah remained strong through the middle innings but now, as we approached Minnesota, the signal began to fade.

"Pop, drive slower." My voice sounded strange, breaking the silence that had been filled with only radio.

"Why?" he asked. We were on the open highway with few other cars around.

"Because Yount is up in the bottom of the ninth. He's facing Goose Gossage."

"I see." As Pop eased off the accelerator the station wagon sputtered into a lower gear. The sudden lack of wind resistance heightened every knock and ping of the old Ford engine.

The score was 5-4 Yankees, and Gossage had been untouchable. I held my breath as Yount singled on the very first pitch. "Come on," I whispered, fingers crossed. Don Money struck out on a failed bunt attempt but Yount reached second on a wild pitch.

"Scoring position," I offered hopefully.

Sal Bando fanned on three straight fastballs.

"Two out," Pop warned.

"I know." The signal wavered as we crested a hill. I strained to hear Larry Hisle's last at-bat. It was a race to see if our car could beat the gathering darkness and hold on long enough to catch the final out. Somewhere over the horizon the lights of the Twin Cities blinked on and Pop, in silent understanding, slowed the station wagon to a crawl.

Strike one.

Strike two.

I leaned forward, clasping my hands over the dashboard. Hisle hit the next pitch into the right field bleachers for a two-run home run.

"Yes!" It was over. The Brewers had won. We kept listening until the last cheer faded away and other cars surrounding us turned on their headlights one by one.

"Thanks, Pop," I said.

"Don't mention it."

I tuned the radio dial to a Minneapolis station and found another game, the Twins against the White Sox at Comiskey. It was only the top of the fourth but I clicked the radio off.

"Not interested in the Twins-Sox?" Pop sounded surprised.

"Nope." I shivered as the silence inside the car seemed to mirror my own emptiness. I couldn't explain that Chicago seemed unimaginably distant; unreachable from here. I realized that there were places that existed inside of me, but also places that existed outside of me and without my knowledge. Behind me now, by hundreds of miles and becoming more distant every minute, was our house on Hadley Avenue. I could see Mom sitting alone in the den, the cool blue light of the TV shining on her silent tears, and also Grannie's room, where dust gathered in the corners and the glass of water still stood beside her prayer book and the Swedish hymnal. Ahead lay my summer at fat camp with the twin pains of hunger and humiliation and the acres and acres of my own pale pudgy skin, but beside me was America on every side, a huge country there for the taking, a bold raw beauty rough and untouched.

Looking out my window, I watched a steady stream of cars all heading somewhere. The noise of the Twins-Sox game still echoed in my head, but even so I couldn't quite fathom Chicago itself; I couldn't picture it as a place inside my head. Like everything happening at the house on Hadley Avenue, Chicago felt so far behind me now; so vast and so lost.

CHAPTER EIGHT

Pop, Max, and I spent the night at a cheap motel just outside the Twin Cities, where our room was so close to the highway that passing semis and eighteen-wheelers rattled everything in the room, including the hollow ice cubes in the insulated bucket, the black-and-white TV bolted to the floor, and the antiseptic bathroom soaps wrapped in paper jackets.

Pop roused us at five the next morning and we headed north through Clearwater, Sauk Rapids, and Little Falls. Once we passed Brainerd the woods grew thicker, seeming to close in on our car. As we negotiated groves of pencil-thin birch trees shedding curls of paper-white bark, I felt I'd entered a more natural and more elemental place. We passed small-town shops selling moccasins and deer meat and I pictured Indians crouched behind the trees with bows and arrows, ready to exact revenge for centuries of white man oppression.

The Summer Slim-Down Retreat was based at Camp Muknawanago, about four miles from town on the shores of Lake Horicon. The area's only other inhabitants lived across the lake at Camp Pentecost, a Bible camp for evangelical teenage boys.

We entered the campgrounds beneath the thick sign that had CAMP MUKNAWANAGO burned into the wood, and were greeted by rows of cars parked side-by-side in the gravel parking lot and overflowing onto the stubby grass. Brightly-colored banners on metal poles proclaimed, "Healthy Girls Are Happy!," "Believe It and You'll Be It!," and "Fit 4 Life!" Close to the lake's rocky shore stood the big wooden A-frame lodge that served as camp headquarters, housing the dining hall, offices, and infirmary.

"We could have made better time." Parking in the grass between two Buick LeSabres, Pop consulted his watch and frowned. "There was no reason for two bathroom breaks in less than forty-five minutes. No reason at all."

"Sorry, Pop." Max's small voice rose from the back seat. "That third Sonic burger did me in. I think the mayonnaise was rancid. Mayonnaise must be kept below forty-five degrees in order to maintain its chemical consistency."

"Whatever." Pop took my duffel bag from the way-back while I grabbed my Hello Kitty backpack and we trekked across the open field to a series of picnic table registration stations.

"Shoulda been here at nine," Pop muttered. "We'll be in line all afternoon."

As we worked through the long lines, paying tuition and dropping off consent forms, I was amazed by the number of overweight girls all around me. Girls were short and tall, aged eleven to nineteen, ranging from simply chubby to seriously obese. *Is this how other people see me?* I wondered. My camp mates looked nothing like the long-legged bikini-clad girls from the brochure.

"Open your luggage," the counselor at Station #7 demanded. "Contraband search." She was a tall, square-shouldered woman in khaki shorts, a red neckerchief, and a serious squint.

Pop withdrew my duffel bag from the counselor's reach. "At summer camp?" he protested.

"Rules are rules." She folded her fleshy arms. "No drugs, tobacco, edibles, perishables, or firearms."

"And who are you—the Stasi?" Pop challenged.

The counselor's squint got deeper.

"The East German secret police," Pop muttered, relinquishing my luggage at last.

Pop's defending me, I thought with pride. *That's never happened before.* The counselor unzipped my duffel bag and rifled through, pulling out items for closer inspection. She snickered at my *Hollywood* magazines but stuffed them back inside and slapped "INSPECTED" stickers on my luggage.

"Thank God they check for firearms," Pop said as we walked away. "I'd hate to see one of these girls go and shoot the place up."

After receiving my CAMP MUKNAWANAGO T-shirt, size XXL, and my photo ID card, we reached the final station, which handled cabin assignments. "You're in Oneida," the counselor said, circling the location on a little black-and-white map. Oneida was situated on the lake's western edge. "Take a flashlight when you use the latrines, even during the day," she warned. "Last summer we lost two Oneidans to a wild ky-ote."

"Thanks," I said and hoped she was kidding.

Pop, Max, and I followed a sandy trail past the A-frame lodge and along the lakeshore to Oneida. Along the way were several small, sturdy cabins, all named for Indian tribes and filling up quickly with excitable girls.

It was quieter at Oneida's secluded location on the edge of the campground. The cabin was musty, dark, and rustic, built of rough-hewn logs and without electricity. The furniture consisted of two metal bunk beds with green foam mattresses and two wooden cupboards with mirrors inside, some wire hangers, and two drawers. Wooden pegs lined the walls while a straw broom balanced in the corner.

"I'm living *here* for seven weeks?" I plopped down on a bottom bunk. "It's *Little House on the Prairie* without Willie Olson." The cabin smelled swampy yet medicinal, a combination of wet sneakers, sunscreen, and bug spray. In the distance bullfrogs croaked and horseflies buzzed while crickets sharpened their tune. I wondered how I'd ever sleep with all the racket.

Pop looked shocked. "So the cabin's . . . basic." He scratched his chin. "You'll be out having fun all day anyway."

Max clung to Pop's side. "But what about when it rains?" he asked.

Pop pushed him aside. "Then they'll hang out in the big cabin up front." Pop opened one of the wooden cupboards and the handle came off in his hand. Frustrated, he struggled to screw it back in.

My throat tightened as I realized that Pop and Max would be leaving me all alone in this damp, smelly cabin with total strangers, hundreds of miles from home and with limited food for the next seven weeks. *It's my own fault,* I thought. *I hate every Klondike Bar, every Dorito, every Three Musketeers bar I've ever eaten. I'm thirteen and I've already ruined my whole entire life.*

I stood, stretched, and looked at my watch. It was almost two o'clock. "You guys better get going." I tried to sound nonchalant even as tears pinched my eyes. "You'll hit Minneapolis by eight if you make good time."

Pop looked relieved. Max pushed up his glasses and wrapped his arms around my waist. "Be careful, Sunnie," he warned, his voice disappearing in my T-shirt. "Swim with a buddy. Don't scratch your mosquito bites. Look out for bees."

I stroked Max's white-blonde hair and remembered envying Max as Pastor Rick embraced him on the morning of Grannie's funeral. Max was closer now than he'd ever been to my own heart. "Take care of stuff at home," I told him. "But don't touch my room."

Pop stepped forward and opened his arms. "All right then," he said, clearing his throat. "Guess this is good-bye." For a moment I panicked, afraid Pop might hug me for the first time in my life, but instead he made an awkward ducking lunge and tapped my shoulder.

"Drive safe, you guys," I said, leading Pop and Max down the cabin steps. "Say 'hi' to Mom and Ingrid."

As they set off down the sandy path, Max turned and walked backwards, twirling his finger like an imaginary mosquito. "Don't scratch the bites!" he motioned, slapping his arm.

"Don't worry, I won't," I shouted back, cupping my hands.

A moment later Pop and Max disappeared among the maple, oak, and evergreen trees that lined the path back to the lodge. I glanced into Oneida and decided to use the bathroom before unpacking. I had needed to pee ever since we passed an A&W Root Beer stand in Bemidji, but we'd already stopped twice for Max's stomach and I didn't want to cost us more time.

According to the map, a latrine was located about three hundred yards due north of Oneida. Remembering the counselor's warning about coyotes, I put on my whistle, grabbed my flashlight, and trekked through the dense, leafy woods.

I smelled the latrine before I could see it, the air ripe with a putrid decaying odor. When the latrine finally came into view it resembled an outhouse from the Yosemite Sam cartoon, a narrow wooden shed with a cloud of insects around its roof and around the cutout crescent moon on its front door. The grass around the latrine was stunted to a straw-like fuzz. *Oh my God,* I thought. *Grizzly Adams never had it this bad.*

I held my breath and opened the door. A wooden bench with three evenly-spaced seats stretched the length of the latrine wall while the soil floor was slick with mud, grass, and toilet paper slime.

As the door closed behind me the walls began to move. The walls were covered with huge hairy black spiders, four or five deep, crawling over each other with arched, delicate, needle-thin legs. I pulled down my pants and peed as quickly as I could without opening my eyes or taking a breath.

I ran out of the latrine and into a clearing where I collected my thoughts. *Pop and Max are gone.* I rubbed my burning eyes. *This is my bathroom for the next seven weeks.* I swallowed hard. *Even if I go home skinny, Grannie still won't be there.* Tears streamed down my cheeks, attracting mosquitoes and confusing the bees that hoped the liquid on my face was sweet, not salty, and certainly not as bitter as it seemed to me. *I'll never see my whole family together ever again.*

Another camper had reached Oneida while I was gone and as I entered the cabin she strode toward me, extending a hand. "Fifi Berkower from Brooklyn," she said.

As we shook I admired her long, manicured nails. "Wilma Sundstrom from Milwaukee," I replied, "but everybody calls me Sunnie."

"Nice to meet 'cha, Sunnie." Fifi was fourteen, about my height and weight with olive skin and dark hair that exploded in a mass of corkscrew curls. She had hazel eyes and dazzling dimples. I desperately wondered if she was Jewish but felt afraid to ask.

"Oh my gawd, I'm glad you're here," she said. "This is my first time to fly-over land." She pronounced "land" like "l-ehhh-nd."

She was unpacking on a bottom bunk so I moved my duffel to the top. "Fly-over land?" I asked.

"Yeh. What we fly over from New Yaww-k to L.A. I always wondered what was down here." She hung some expensive-looking clothes in one of the cupboards. "This is such an adven-chah! I gotta lose a few, know what I mean?" She slapped her hip, clad in brand-new Calvin Kleins. I was so jealous—Mom wouldn't let me or even Ingrid get Calvins because she said they'd be a message to boys that we were easy.

"Want a cancer stick?" Fifi pulled out a pack of Merit Lights then held up her hand. "Wait—don't tell me. You wholesome Midwest kids don't smoke."

"How'd you sneak those past the counselors?" I asked, noticing that all her luggage had "INSPECTED" stickers.

"Honey, there are always ways." She rubbed her fingertips with her thumb, which I guessed implied a bribe. Before I could ask more we were interrupted by a knock on the open door.

"You must be at the wrong place," Fifi said, sizing up the new girl. "This is a fat camp and honey, you've got yourself a figure."

Standing in the doorway was a light-skinned black girl with round cheeks and almond-shaped eyes. Fifi was right; the girl didn't appear more than ten pounds overweight.

"Hi, I'm Sunnie," I said, guiding the new girl into the cabin. "I'm from Milwaukee. Fifi here's from Brooklyn."

"Cherise Norton," the girl whispered in a voice as soft as her handshake. "I'm thirteen. From Chicago's south side." Cherise was dressed in jeans and a denim jacket with a denim purse over her shoulder. Her luggage too was denim and she wore cowboy boots with a wide leather belt.

While we were getting to know Cherise the last of our cabin-mates arrived. Harriet Wells was sixteen, from Topeka, and weighed over two hundred pounds.

"This is my third tour of duty," Harriet sighed, heaving her huge suitcase on the bunk beneath Cherise. "Since 1975 I've gained sixty-seven pounds. Last summer I was named 'Camper of the Year.' What a load of crap." Harriet's light brown hair was short and spiky and she had dark liner around her deep-set, world-weary green eyes. Her nose was small and pointy while her tiny teeth were crooked, giving her face a pinched and uncertain expression.

"If it's so bad, why do you keep coming back?" Fifi extended the pack of Merit Lights and Harriet gratefully withdrew one.

"My folks want me out of the house." Harriet leaned over Fifi's lighter and squinted. "I embarrass them."

Harriet popped open her suitcase. "In case you wondered, I do have a boyfriend." She rummaged through some neatly-folded clothing, all of which was black. "His name is Lyle. He's six-three, good-looking, and hung like a race horse." She pulled out a framed photo and passed it around. I was anxious to see what "hung like a race horse" meant, but when my turn came I saw only a thin, angular young man with a sharp crewcut and pock-marked skin.

"He looks nice," Cherise said softly, rubbing the frame.

"He satisfies me, if you get my drift." Harriet drew a lungful of smoke and considered our blank faces. "Don't tell me I got placed in a cabin full of Virgin Marys."

No one responded.

"Has *any* of y'all ever been laid?"

There was another long pause. "Last summer I slow-danced with a guy at my cousin's bar mitzvah," Fifi braved. "His name was Ira Lipshutz and he kept fingering my bra."

Harriet rolled her tiny eyes. "Seems I've got my work cut out for me. Girls, prepare for your education." Harriet reached into her suitcase and pulled out a stash of *Playgirl* magazines, trashy romance novels, and a paperback copy of *Our Bodies, Our*

Selves. Like Fifi, Harriet must have known secrets for passing inspection.

"Oh my Gawd!" Fifi screamed. "This is like, so significant!" She grabbed a *Playgirl* and flipped through the pages of naked cowboys in neckerchiefs and chaps. "I was totally absent the week we had anatomy."

Cherise grabbed a well-thumbed paperback romance and held it close to her face, shielding her dark eyes, leaving me with *Our Bodies, Our Selves*. I opened to a diagram of an Asian-looking baby squished upside down in a birth canal. I closed the book and glanced over Fifi's shoulder.

"Wowser!" She held up a full-page color glossy of a fireman wearing only a helmet, suspenders, and a belt. "Guess he's not Jewish." She pointed to a long, pink-sleeved column of skin between the man's legs. This looked nothing like my only frame of reference, Jerry Junkett's wang-doodle, which he'd shown me once after losing two out of three in rock-paper-scissors.

"Yeah," I laughed, having no idea what Fifi meant. "Guess he's not Lutheran either." Fifi looked at me strangely. Harriet was right. I, at least, was in serious need of an education.

We were still surveying Harriet's secret porno stash when the three-chimed bell summoned us to dinner. Harriet showed us a shortcut through the woods that led directly to the lodge. Even though it was still light out, Fifi kept her flashlight focused on the trail in front of us, searching for the glowing yellow eyes of a raccoon, possum, or fox. "What the hell is that?" A cotton-tailed rabbit bounced across the trail and scurried under the brush.

"Only a rabbit," I reassured her. "They don't bite."

"Rabbit? More like a rat," she insisted. "I see them all the time on the subway going uptown."

"Why would rats go uptown?" I asked.

"Very funny, Milwaukee," she said. "Let's see who's laughing when they end up in our bunks, tearing our eyes out with their sharp little clawww-wahs."

Camp Muknawanago's dining hall was warm and homey, designed like an old hunting lodge with a high-beamed ceiling and a stone fireplace with deer and elk heads mounted above the mantle. The dining tables were arranged in rows with a counselor at either end and six campers on each side. The food was served family-style from long-handled spoons in large copper pots. Tall tin pitchers provided fresh, ice-cold water.

Dinner that first night consisted of a grilled chicken breast with wild rice, steamed broccoli, and fresh strawberries for dessert. Second helpings were forbidden but at least the food was tasty and well prepared. As we went around the table introducing ourselves, I found myself thinking, *I've dreaded coming here ever since Mom first saw the ad in* Family Circle. *But it might not be so bad after all.*

"My name is Sunnie Sundstrom and I'm from Milwaukee," I said proudly when my turn came. "I love Johnny Carson and I'm writing a screenplay called *Girl on the Lam.*"

After dinner a skinny girl in her early twenties with wire-rimmed glasses and permed yellow hair stepped to the front of the dining hall and cleared her throat. "Hello, everyone," she said in a thin, reedy voice. "My name is Pierce and I'm second in command here at the Slim-Down Retreat. It's my pleasure to introduce your head counselor, Randall-Anne Murphy."

There were a few half-hearted claps as Randall-Anne strode to the fireplace. "Welcome, girls," she said in a husky voice. "For the next seven weeks you will work harder than you've ever worked in your lives." Randall-Anne was about five-eleven with square shoulders, a flat chest, and broad hips. Far from skinny, she was solidly built with muscular legs and arms. Her dark brown hair was clipped short and her sun-creased face was somewhere between twenty-five and forty-five years old.

"Here you will learn the basics of weight loss and weight maintenance and go home, on average, thirty-five pounds lighter than you are today."

Randall-Anne paced the floor as she lay down the ground rules. Dressed in khaki shorts and a khaki shirt with the sleeves rolled up to her biceps, she was the image of a drill sergeant. Around her neck she wore a knotted red bandana and a big silver whistle at the end of a braided lanyard.

"You stuff yourselves. You watch too much TV. You're lazy." Randall-Anne squared herself and faced the assembly, fists on hips. "We're going to change all that. Mercy is for sissies. We'll work your lard butts hard."

"'Mercy is for sissies,'" I whispered to Cherise. "They should hang *that* on a banner out front."

Randall-Anne swiveled and her eyes honed in on me. "What did you say?"

"Nothing." I shrank in my seat.

She pivoted to face Cherise. "And what did you say?"

"She didn't," I offered quickly. "It was just me."

"Your friend can answer for herself," Randall-Anne insisted, taking two steps closer. "What did *you* say?"

Cherise opened her mouth but nothing came out. Instead she started to sob.

"OK, both of you. Give me ten. Now," Randall-Anne barked.

"Ten?" My voice squeaked.

Randall-Anne beckoned us out of our seats. Cherise and I walked, shaking, up to the fireplace.

"Drop and give me ten," Randall-Anne ordered, indicating push-ups. "Now. Before I make it twenty." I got down on the floor, nose to the wood, and began doing push-ups, my eyes level with Randall-Anne's Army boots. My stomach churned and I thought I might throw up. I could only complete six push-ups before my arms sagged beneath my body's weight, while Cherise, still weeping, finished all ten. Cherise and I stood, brushing off our clothes.

Randall-Anne whipped a small spiral notebook and pen from her back pocket. "Ten demerits each for talking during an assembly." She licked the pen's tip. "Names?"

"Wilma Sundstrom," I whispered.

"Cherise Norton." Cherise whispered too.

Randall-Anne scribbled a note and slipped the notebook back in her pocket. "Twenty demerits means probation," she explained. "Fifty demerits—automatic expulsion."

As Cherise turned back to the table, Randall-Anne grasped my arm and squeezed tightly. "I've got my eye on you, Sundstrom," she said. "If there's one thing I hate, it's a fat girl with attitude."

After the assembly Fifi, Cherise, Harriet, and I took the shortcut through the woods back to Oneida with Fifi and Harriet leading the way. Harriet stopped and looked back at me. "Randall-Anne is just a bitch, Sunnie," she said, the tip of her cigarette glowing orange in the darkness. "She once gave out five demerits 'cause someone looked at her cross-eyed. I think she's just frustrated, sexually-speaking."

I appreciated Harriet trying to cheer me up. "I can't believe I already got in trouble," I said. "Ten more demerits and I'll be on probation."

"Chalk it up to experience," Harriet said. "Hey, knock it off!" She turned towards Fifi. Fifi's flashlight beam traced nervous circles along our path, jumping up to explore the snap of a twig and every cricket's chirp or buzz. "You're making me dizzy."

"I'm scared," Fifi confided. "Cougars can smell me 'cause I'm havin' my period."

"Forget cougars. *Lions* smell blood," Harriet insisted, stubbing out her cigarette in the smoldering brush.

"It's not cougars or lions," I said. "You're thinking of sharks. And there are no sharks in Lake Horicon."

Cherise had hung back several paces so I stopped and waited for her to catch up. "I'm really sorry," I whispered in her ear. "I got you in trouble."

She dabbed her eyes with her denim sleeve. "I don't blame you," she sniffled. "Randall-Anne is just one nasty lady."

"Still, I'm gonna keep my big mouth shut from now on." We fell into step side by side and I linked my arm with Cherise's. "So, Cubs or White Sox?" I asked, hoping she was a baseball fan.

"Sox, of course!" she protested. "I'm Southside through and through. But Ron LeFlore of the Tigers is some hot property!"

"He's all right but he's no Paul Molitor," I said and laughed. As our feet crunched the fallen leaves and Cherise's arm pressed against mine, I realized I had never in my life touched a black person before.

Back at Oneida it was only nine o'clock but there was nothing else to do except prepare for bed in our close, damp, musty quarters. Outside it was pitch black and noisy, the darkness of the night sky emphasizing the whirl of wind through the treetops and the distant, despairing cry of loons.

"Sure is dark out there," Fifi said softly. She sat cross-legged on her bunk, braiding her hair.

"Uh huh," Cherise replied, rubbing cocoa butter into her elbows and filling the cabin with a sweet delicious beachy smell. "I thought there'd be more stars."

"That's for sure." Suddenly we were awkward and self-conscious, with none of the easy conversation from earlier in the day.

"Wake me if one of y'all needs to pee." Harriet balanced a flashlight in her lap and unwrapped hard candies while she wrote to Lyle. "Rumor has it last year an Oneidan got eaten by bears."

"Really? I heard it was a ky-ote," Fifi said. "Whatever a ky-ote may be."

I lay back on the thin mattress that smelled like mold and held the transistor radio to my ear. I could only tune in two stations. One was AM country music while the other had a preacher screaming that all non-believers were headed straight to hell. I turned the station quickly, hoping Fifi couldn't hear. I'd known her less than a day but already I felt protective towards her faith.

"I miss my Daddy." Cherise's voice was muffled by the sheet. "Tucking me in and kissing me good night."

Fifi took a deep breath and released it slowly. "Seven weeks is like forev-ah."

Harriet stopped writing. "I'm imaginin' Lyle holding me in his big ol' arms right now."

In a moment all three girls were crying. I cleared my throat. "So, do you guys watch late-night TV, like *The Tonight Show?*"

Cherise blew her nose. "My Mama and Daddy watch it," she said. "I hear them laughing from my room."

"I watch sometimes on Fridays," Fifi added softly. "I'm allowed to stay up late when there's no school."

"I watch it every night," I said. "It's my favorite show of all time." I paused, then took the plunge. "It was so boring at Camp Muknawanago today . . . "

Fifi caught on right away. "How boring was it?" she asked.

"It was so boring that the spiders jumped into the latrines just for a change of scenery."

Fifi laughed while Harriet and Cherise giggled.

"Do another one." Fifi sat upright and straightened her sheets.

"It was so boring today . . . " I paused. Years of watching Johnny had taught me the importance of timing in stand-up comedy.

"How boring was it?" all three girls asked in unison.

"It was so boring that Randall-Anne gave herself ten demerits just to stay busy."

My impromptu monologue continued for a good twenty minutes. I wasn't hilarious; I wasn't close to Johnny territory, but I made my cabinmates laugh, and took their minds off being homesick for at least a little while. Hearing them laugh made my spirit soar. I wondered if Johnny felt this good every night.

"President Carter declared Camp Muknawanago a federal disaster area today." I paused. "When Randall-Anne found out, she gave the President a hundred demerits and made him do twenty-five push-ups for Congress."

"In a related story, Randall-Anne Murphy is now on death row," Fifi added in a mock-newscaster voice.

My giggling shook the bunk bed's thin metal frame. "Yeah," I added. "But Randall-Anne's lawyer, Pierce, plans to file an appeal."

CHAPTER NINE

I woke the next morning to Randall-Anne bellowing just outside my window. "Out of bed, Oneida!" she screamed. "Anyone not out here in five minutes gets five demerits!"

I squinted at my watch. "It's five-o-seven," I croaked. "In the morning." The others stirred as I rubbed my eyes.

Randall-Anne's voice volleyed into the distance as she roused the surrounding cabins. "Out of bed, girls! Let's go, go, go!"

I threw on my Camp Muknawanago T-shirt and khaki shorts. My shoes weren't even tied as I stumbled out of Oneida and into the path of a large girl from Chippewa who nearly bowled me over with her meaty elbows. The air was so cold that the grass glistened and I could see my own breath.

Randall-Anne jogged back toward Oneida, pumping her knees high and hard as her big silver whistle bounced madly on its lanyard. "All right, run! Run! Run!"

As I sprinted past Iroquois, its four inhabitants tumbled out looking equally rattled. Girls from Bad River, Munsee-Stockbridge, and Ho-Chunk joined the formation and soon the entire Slim-Down Retreat was huffing and puffing in the cold morning air.

Fifi approached and matched her pace with mine. "Oh my gawd," she panted. "I cannot do this every freakin' day!"

"Maybe we'll get used to it," I said breathlessly. "It should be easier by the end of camp."

"I'll be dead by then," she replied. "At least I'm hoping."

"If I don't pee I'll explode," I said. "Join me in the bushes?"

"Sunnie, don't." Fifi pulled my sleeve. "If you get caught, more demerits."

I had no choice. "I'll only take a minute," I promised. "Meet you by the lake." I slowed down, checked for counselors, and ducked into the heavy brush along the path. I slipped behind a tree, checked for poison ivy, and pulled down my shorts, bending forward so I wouldn't wet myself. The wonderful relief was short-lived.

"Identify yourself!" a voice ordered from the path. I pulled up my shorts and moved in front of the tree, holding up my hands like in the movies.

"Wilma Sundstrom," I yelled, "but people call me Sunnie."

"Sundstrom? Didn't you get demerits last night?" It was Pierce, Randall-Anne's assistant with her pointy nose and permed hair, clutching a clipboard.

"Yep. Ten demerits." I felt strangely proud of my newfound rebel status. "I spoke up during an assembly."

"Well, congratulations. You now have ten more demerits." She scribbled on her clipboard. "You're already on probation and it's only day two."

"But I really had to pee." I stepped over the moss and rocks to reach Pierce's side. "I couldn't wait, you know?"

"A likely story." Pierce squinted, looking deeply disappointed. "Come on before you miss any more exercises." Pierce guided me back toward the lakefront.

"So Pierce . . . May I call you Pierce?" I struggled to match her head-down, determined pace.

"You can call me Pierce." Her voice was flat, expressionless.

"Is that your first name or your last?"

I didn't think she'd answer. "Middle," she snapped. "Not that it's any business of yours."

I nearly tripped over the logs and stones that marred the path. "So Pierce, where are you from?"

"Pierre. South Dakota."

"Pierce from Pierre," I said. "Interesting."

She stopped and turned around. "Why is that interesting?"

"Just that it's two guys' names, I guess."

When we reached the thin crescent of oil-colored sand separating the lake from the woods, the other campers were already aligned in military formation, doing calisthenics. Pierce motioned for me to join in, so I began the routine of jumping jacks followed by push-ups, sit-ups, leg-kicks, and deep-knee thrusts. By the time we reached the cool-down stretch my whole body hurt.

"We went easy on you today," Randall-Anne announced through her megaphone, her voice reaching across Lake Horicon. "Tomorrow the real work-outs begin."

As Pierce and Randall-Anne marched us back to the lodge I weaved through the line of sweat-soaked girls until I found Fifi.

"You almost gave me a heart attack," she said, slipping out of her NYU sweatshirt and fanning her face. "I thought you got eaten by beh-rrs."

"Better," I said. "Ten more demerits."

"Shit!" Her hazel eyes widened. "You can't get expelled and leave me alone in fly-over l-ehh-nd."

"I've never been in trouble before," I admitted. "I won our 4-H Club's Good Citizenship Award three years in a row." I didn't tell Fifi that being a bad girl for the first time in my life was actually kind of fun.

"Gawd, I could eat a horse," Fifi confided as we were shepherded into the dining room. "What the hell is that?" Fifi pointed to what looked like a livestock scale in front of the fireplace.

I clutched Fifi's elbow as we fell into a single-file line. "They're going to weigh us!" I whispered. "In public, no less!"

Fifi shook her head. "This is worse than singing solo at Jewish Day Camp."

I wasn't the heaviest girl at camp but still my stomach churned. To me a scale was like a coiled snake or a loaded gun. The red needle resting quietly at zero was actually a poison arrow, ready to shoot to the heavens in public response to my weight.

Fifi and I inched forward as one by one Randall-Anne motioned each girl onto the scale and announced her weight while Pierce recorded the numbers on a chart.

113

"I won't listen to yours if you don't listen to mine," Fifi offered, extending her hand.

"Deal," I said quickly, sealing it with a shake. "Let's keep one tiny shred of our dignity."

"Atkinson, Tara," Randall-Anne boomed, her voice rising to the rafters. "One-eighty-seven. Friedman, Sharon. One-forty-four. Gomez, Theresa. One-ninety-six . . . "

As the girls walked past us to the dining tables I recognized their expressions—eyes cast downward, cheeks hot with shame. I'd seen that look so many times on my own face in the bathroom mirror.

When my turn came my hands shook and my stomach was in knots. All I remembered of my at-home pre-scale preparation was emptying my lungs. *That's stupid,* I thought. *Air doesn't weigh anything.*

"Sundstrom comma Wilma," Randall-Anne commanded. When I moved too slowly she grabbed my arm and yanked me onto the scale. The needle jumped to 190, fell to 160, then quivered between 165 and 185 before stopping on 176.

"Sundstrom comma Wilma, one-seven-six," Randall-Anne called out like a bingo number. Dutifully Pierce wrote the figure on the wall chart with her black marker pen. "Next."

"That's wrong," I sputtered. "A few weeks ago I was one-sixty-one." Speaking caused the scale's needle to quiver, threatening me with an even less accurate 177.

"Next," Randall-Anne insisted as she pulled me off the scale. I didn't weight 176 pounds but now every girl at camp, excluding Fifi, who had indeed closed her eyes and covered her ears, believed that I did.

When I reached our table I plopped down beside Harriet and across from Cherise. I hated Cherise a little for weighing only 133 pounds. I decided that Harriet, at 204, made a more appropriate friend.

"I bet they rig the scales to weigh heavier," I said. "Then gradually turn them back to tell our parents how much we lost."

"A conspiracy theorist." Harriet nodded. "I like that, kid."

As the final girls were weighed, recorded, and sent to their seats, the kitchen crew barreled into the dining room wheeling metal carts. Trails of steam curled up to the high-beamed ceiling as the workers went down the narrow aisles dishing out food. I didn't think I'd ever been so hungry. When my turn came at last a large woman in a black hairnet and tattooed arms handed me a plastic bowl filled with a gray, lumpy, glue-like substance.

"What is this?" I asked Harriet.

"They call it 'health porridge.'" Harriet took her own bowl and nodded thanks. "Better known as gruel."

I poked it with my spoon. "What's in it?"

"High-fiber oats and protein with soy milk," Harriet explained. "Bon appétit."

I took a spoonful and could barely swallow. The porridge tasted like scalded oatmeal with a vegetably-minerally baby-food aftertaste. I washed it down with our only beverage, a bitter powdered orange drink with a white film floating on its surface.

"I don't get it." I shook my glass and watched the sediment settle. "Last night supper was good. What happened?"

Harriet rolled her tiny eyes. "Of course last night was good. They don't serve the real stuff until all the parents are safely out of screaming distance." Harriet glanced over her shoulder, then reached into her pocket and pulled out three little packets of sugar, tore them open and sprinkled them over her porridge, stirring quickly with her spoon. "You think breakfast is bad, just wait until lunch."

After breakfast and a brief morning assembly, I was ready for the day's first educational session on "Calories: The Building Blocks of Fat." Instead Pierce took me aside and led me to Randall-Anne's private office beyond the kitchen, between the laundry room and the infirmary.

Randall-Anne's office was spacious but surprisingly messy, filled with loose files, hastily pinned wall charts, and stacks of twigs that had been partially whittled and then set aside. *Probably did those with her teeth,* I decided.

Randall-Anne sat writing in a ledger at her big wooden desk. Her lanyard and whistle were curled up beside her. "Sundstrom comma Wilma," she said, looking up.

"Call me Sunnie." I approached with my head held high.

"Sundstrom comma Wilma." Randall-Anne glared. "You're officially on probation. Ten demerits last night and another ten this morning. I don't know if a camper has ever reached probation so quickly."

I smiled shyly. "It's just a gift," I replied.

"Cute," she said. "Very cute. Let's see how cute it is when you're up to your elbows in ex-cretia." She made a note in her ledger, then underlined it several times. "One week of latrine duty." She paused. "You're excused."

"Oh boy, you are *so* lucky," Pierce confided as she took me to the supply room and fitted me with rubber gloves, a bucket, a sponge, and a long-handled toilet brush. "She showed you mercy."

"What's worse than a week of latrine duty?" I asked, juggling my sudden armful of cleaning supplies.

"*Two* weeks of latrine duty," Pierce replied. "That's standard for probation."

Pierce demonstrated how to mix the bleach-and-water solution and then took me to the first bank of latrines, closest to the lodge. She showed me how to prop open the door, scrub every surface, then pour the bleach solution in a circular pattern down the hole, being careful it didn't splash back in my face. Between latrines I would have to return to the lodge, mix more solution, and refill the bucket. Pierce handed me a map and circled the six additional outhouses located around the campgrounds.

"But this will take all morning," I said, figuring the number of latrines and the distance back to the lodge.

"That's the idea," she explained, pushing up her glasses. "You'll need to hurry if you want to finish by lunch."

"I'm calling a lawyer," I complained. "Child labor was outlawed by the Geneva Convention."

"Look at it this way." Pierce smirked. "You'll burn more calories than you would sitting in a morning session."

The first latrine was horrible. I ended up chasing huge spiders with my sponge and watching their legs curl and sizzle in response to the burning bleach solution. My neck and shoulders ached from carrying the heavy bucket back and forth. But after a while I relaxed and began to enjoy the clean fresh swimming-pool smell of the bleach solution. The bright yellow rubber gloves extended almost to my elbows and my hair was pulled back tightly in a rubber band, leaving stars of sweat around my scalp. It felt good to be really working, for once.

The morning had started out cold but by eleven the sun was shining and it was 75 degrees with a slight breeze. Birds were chirping and the woods felt heavy with wild scents and distant voices. I liked being alone. My hands were cleaning latrines, but my mind was on Johnny and neither Randall-Anne nor anyone else could take that away.

"Tell us, Sunnie, is it true you attended fat camp as a teen and cleaned the outhouses?" Johnny's brow furrows as he folds his arms and leans forward on his desk. Charo, on my right, giggles at the mention of outhouses, accidentally tickling me with her feather boa.

I pick up the Guest #2 mug and delicately sip my apple juice. "Yes, John, that's true," I answer, crossing my legs. "I wasn't always the glamorous and successful 105-pound director you see before you today . . . "

Even while scrubbing the deeply gross latrines I sensed that everything that happened to me, every element of my life, was part of a bigger picture; something I could pull and bend and use. Like clay between my fingers, my personal raw material could be changed into something great. *When I'm telling this story to Johnny and to the world, the spiders will be bigger and more poisonous; the latrines deeper and more dangerous, and Randall-Anne's meanness will be more extreme. Whatever happens to me belongs to me and to me alone. I am my own creation; my own small work of art.*

I finished the latrines just before lunch. I washed up quickly, then hurried to the dining hall. Just as Harriet had promised, the meal was dreadful: a lump of dry meat, well-done and shot through with sinews, a single anemic leaf of iceberg lettuce, a scoop of pinkish cottage cheese, and to drink, that powdered orange juice.

As I sat between Cherise and Fifi I was pleased to see that my morning exploits had already earned me a reputation. "Did you really go to Randall-Anne's office?" a pale, pudgy girl from Oklahoma asked, her eyes wide and excited. "And is it true she keeps a goat's penis on her wall?"

"No, but she does have a bunch of lanyards representing all the girls she's expelled from camp," I lied. "She pinned my name up, pointed her finger, and said I would be next."

I had been wrong in thinking that my story would change by the time I visited *The Tonight Show*. The morning's latrine-cleaning story had already changed; had grown more vibrant and more dramatic by twelve-thirty that same afternoon.

"One of the spiders in the latrine near Cherokee, I swear, it was the size of my hand," I said. "It had to be a black widow because it had stripes down its back and really pointy legs, so I flicked it into the latrine and threw down a whole bucket of bleach right on top of it . . . "

Back at Oneida that night Cherise held a flashlight overhead as Harriet read to us from *Amber in Eden*, the first step in our sexual education.

"He took her in his arms and kissed her deeply." Harriet read quickly, her voice soft and urgent. "His throbbing manhood, engorged with blood and with racing, mad desire, ached for the sweet release only she could provide. Lady Alana opened herself to Lord Willoughby, ready to admit his lance of fire, to swallow the sword that would split her maidenhood and accept the precious wounding that would mark her out as his forever."

"Do grown-ups really *do* that stuff?" I wondered as I slid beneath my scratchy blanket. What about Joanna Carson? Did she

118

admit Johnny's lance of fire? I hoped not. What about Mom and Pop, or even Nurse Nellis and her late husband, the limping, bad-gifting Bernard? All the talk about sword swallowing and precious wounding made me nervous. If sex was good, why would it hurt?

"Ick," Fifi proclaimed, kicking her sheets. "I'll take a chocolate milkshake any day."

"Sounds great," I replied, "just give me a load of barbecued ribs to go with it."

Harriet closed the book and Cherise snapped off the flashlight, plunging the cabin into an utter darkness that amplified our breathing, made our voices soft and close.

"There's this great Italian restaurant in Topeka." Harriet spoke slowly, drawing out the words. "Spaghetti and meatballs, baked ziti, stuffed green peppers, four-cheese lasagna. In summer, gelato and home-made cannoli."

My mouth watered. After our meager evening meal of dried beef and steamed spinach I was hungry enough to cry. "What do you guys hate most about being fat?" I asked carefully.

No one replied at first and I knew that this was the magic question. We were at a Summer Slim-Down Retreat. A sign in the dining hall boasted that over six collective tons had been shed since the camp opened in 1963. We would be attending daily sessions on exercise, cutting calories, and portion control, but even with all that, no one ever actually talked about being fat.

"The clothes." Fifi rolled over and punched her pillow. "All those great outfits that'll never fit. Being a size sixteen in a size two world."

Harriet spoke next. "It's not how people look at me." Her voice was brave, defensive. "But how they look at Lyle. Like they're saying, 'You're a tall, nice-lookin' guy. *She's* the best you could do?'" Harriet started to cry.

"One time my sister and me were roller skating and we stopped by this little cart to get some cotton candy," Cherise whispered. "I had money from Granddad and I was treating me and Anita. Some man we didn't even know walked past us and said,

'That's right, girls, just keep on a-eatin'.' Me and Anita stuck all that cotton candy directly in the trash."

Now it was my turn. My heart was racing as I opened my mouth. "There's these two boys at school I call the Romulans." My voice shook. "Mostly they call me 'Ten Ton' but one day, I don't know why, they started calling me 'the Heifer.' They followed me from class to class and mooed."

The noises of the night took over, the buzzing locusts, and the crackle of tiny animals burrowing through the woods. We were all alone with our thoughts, with the solitary shame we each secretly harbored. Harriet drew back her tears and reached beneath her pillow, taking a handful of hard candies and fingering the shiny wrappers.

"What's that noise?" Fifi sat upright, poised and aware.

"Just some candies," Harriet replied, her mouth full.

"No, not that. Outside. Listen."

I heard some rustling, like a possum or a squirrel. Then, suddenly, the sound increased in speed and insistence, like footsteps moving closer.

"Hey. Anybody in there?" came a deep voice.

We centered our flashlights on the window in a single powerful beam. "Who goes there?" Fifi called out.

I wasn't worried. Girls from other cabins were said to visit at night, bumming cigarettes or asking for tampons.

"Men from Camp Pentecost, come to share the Good News," a voice replied.

"Boys! Rape! Help!" Harriet screamed, scrambling to find her whistle.

"Not so fast," Fifi implored. "What if they're cute?"

Fifi slid out of her bottom bunk, flashlight in hand, and slowly opened the door. "Can we help you?" she asked, voice steady. We trained our flashlights on the open doorway where four young male faces appeared, blanched white as ghosts and blinking madly.

The tall boy in back pulled off his baseball cap. "Sorry to trouble you young ladies," he said. "Hope we didn't wake you."

Fifi whisked off her headscarf, unleashing a torrent of long dark curls. "Oh, you didn't wake us," she said, fluffing her hair. "We were just talking."

"We like talking too," the boy replied. "About the loving sacrifice made by our Lord and Savior, Jesus Christ." The boys flashed well-worn leather Bibles, the gold-inlaid covers catching and reflecting the flashlights' single beam.

If Fifi was disappointed by the boys' religious affiliation, she didn't show it. "Come on in," she offered, "and make yourselves at home."

In a matter of moments all eight of us were sitting cross-legged on the cabin floor getting acquainted. The boys' names were Daniel, Asher Gideon, Bucky, and Ted. They were forbidden to leave Camp Pentecost without permission, but their higher calling was to preach the gospel so they stole two canoes and rowed across Lake Horicon to spread the good news.

Ted, the tall, serious one, was seventeen. Bucky was fifteen, almost as tall, and had wild red curls, while Asher Gideon and Daniel, the smaller boys, were both fourteen. Daniel was pale and thin with white-blonde hair, while Asher Gideon had wavy jet-black hair, a stocky build, and the beginnings of a mustache. Asher Gideon was the cutest, it seemed to me, and clearly had the fewest pimples. I just hoped he was at least five-foot-three.

None of the boys smoked or drank caffeine, but we managed to find, at the bottom of Harriet's huge suitcase, a dented can of 7-Up and a lint-covered orange that we sectioned and ate, each taking a single slice.

"Thank you Ma'am, that's mighty generous," redheaded Bucky said, cupping Harriet's hand. "Wherever two or more of you are gathered in His name the Lord is watching, even as we speak." Cherise pulled her robe a little tighter.

We bowed our heads as Ted, the group's clear leader, said a prayer, punctuated by Bucky's enthusiastic, and seemingly unplanned, Amens. Daniel, who had a big voice for such a small, pale boy, sang "Kumbaya," and we linked arms and swayed.

It didn't take long for us to pair up, in the mysterious way these things usually happen. Redheaded Bucky went off with Harriet, while Fifi took the tall, straight-faced Ted. Cherise connected with pale little Daniel. That left me with Asher Gideon, whose full name, I learned, was Asher Gideon Zephaniah McNamara, and who, based on my standing next to him, was about five-foot-six.

"That's a lot of names for one boy," I offered as he and I sat on two stones in a clearing behind Oneida.

"Asher, Gideon, and Zephaniah are Old Testament names," he explained in his soft Southern drawl. "McNamara is Irish, County Down to be exact, but we left there in the 1840s and for five generations have lived outside of Murfreesboro, Tennessee. I aim to be a preacher. My Daddy is a preacher, my Grand-Daddy is a preacher, and my Great-Grand-Daddy before him all were preachers."

"Wow," I marveled. "Your family must be super-religious."

"Naw, I wouldn't say that," he replied. "We're just lucky to have seen the Lord's light."

Asher's Momma taught the third grade and his younger sisters were Rachel, Naomi, and Ruth. He loved the St. Louis Cardinals, Led Zeppelin, fried chicken, and Ne-Hi, but most of all Asher Gideon loved the Lord. The Lord was with him always; the Lord informed his every thought.

"Is it OK if I pray with you, Wilma?" he asked anxiously. "Tonight, on this very spot?"

"Sure," I answered, caught off-guard. When we were introduced I had said, "call me 'Sunnie,'" but when he said "Wilma" it felt just right.

"Thank you, Wilma." He nodded solemnly. "For letting me pray with you." He cleared his throat, then reached over and took my hand. I wondered if he could tell that I'd never held hands with a boy before, never even touched a boy outside of kissing Bobby Hickey after gym class. Asher Gideon had small powerful hands; callused, I guessed, from swinging a baseball bat. Beneath the skin I felt the secretive movement of tendons, muscles, and blood vessels; the promise of something very much alive. My own skin grew hot from the contact.

122

"Dear Lord, thank You for gracing us with Your presence this evening, as we meet new friends and, hopefully, bring them to the fullness of Your love . . . "

It was hard to get a good look at Asher Gideon with only the moonlight above. He had a few freckles across his forehead and a round, slightly upturned nose below which sprouted the beginning of a little black mustache. One thing I knew for sure—at home a boy this cute would never even say hello.

"Thank You for Your gracious gifts, Oh Lord. Amen and amen."

"Amen," I echoed. We were still holding hands. "You speak like a real preacher," I said. "You must practice lots." My palms started to sweat.

"Thank you kindly." Even in the darkness he appeared to blush. "Twice a week I'm youth minister . . . " He stopped and dropped my hand. It fell heavily, brushing against the big cold rock.

"Hey Ash, we gotta go." Bucky came into the clearing straightening his clothes. Even in the low light his bright smile was visible as a flash of white teeth.

"Can't we stay a piece longer?" Asher Gideon's deep voice sounded higher, until he cleared his throat. "There's still more ministering to do."

"Nope. Ted says we hafta go now." As Bucky ran his hand through his wild red curls, I wondered where Harriet was and if her next letter to Lyle would mention anything about the boys.

I expected Asher Gideon to follow Bucky back to their canoes, but instead he offered to escort me back to Oneida. "I'll make my own way," I said. "Your friends are waiting."

"I couldn't do that," he replied. "A gentleman always sees a lady home." Using his flashlight to guide the way, Asher Gideon helped me onto the path and led me through the brush with his hand pressed to the small of my back. When we reached Oneida we shook hands to say good night.

"Good-bye, Asher Gideon Zephaniah McNamara," I said softly. "It was a pleasure to meet you."

"Good-bye, Miss Wilma. The pleasure's all mine."

I didn't ask if he planned to visit again because I was already certain that the answer was yes.

123

Back inside Oneida the cabin buzzed with energy as Harriet, Fifi, and even shy Cherise talked about the boys. "Ted was the cutest." Fifi crossed her legs and bunched up her pillow. "Handsome, even, with those cheekbones and that jaw-wah."

"Ted's all right, but Bucky has the biggest package," Harriet argued. "And you know redheads—they're red all over, if you get my drift."

"But Daniel has the cutest buns!" Cherise giggled, hiding her face in a pillow.

"Sunnie, you're awful quiet. What about the dashing Asher Gideon?" Harriet looked up from her bottom bunk.

"He's nice," I said, climbing to the top and slipping under the covers. "Super nice, that's all."

The others groaned at my lack of intimate detail, but I refused to say more as I held myself tightly, trying not to shiver, even though the night was warm and close.

I closed my eyes and imagined the boys paddling back to Camp Pentecost knowing that they have sinned, taking a canoe without permission, but they were sinning to save souls; canoeing for the greater good.

The moonlight over the lake will be cool and muted and the night so still that even the mosquitoes seem to sleep. An owl cries in the distance as a lone wolf unleashes a sorrowful howl. The only breaks in Lake Horicon's glassy surface come from the hand-carved tip of the narrow canoe.

I imagine taking a place behind Asher Gideon, opening my legs and wrapping my arms around his torso. Muscles tighten in his shoulders and sides; I sense the solid stability of his lower spine. Pressing against his back, I feel the firm curve of ribs around his fragile lungs and listen to his breathing, to the steady beating of his heart, thumping through his body and into my own. Each measured stroke of the long wooden paddle—left right, left right, left right—pushes the canoe forward, gliding on a knife-line back to Asher Gideon's campground where we will dock, with confidence, in the warm bosom of the Lord.

CHAPTER TEN

Asher Gideon visited the following night, and then again a few nights after that. At first all four boys made the trip, but eventually only Asher Gideon and Daniel came to see me and Cherise, secretly paddling their hand-hewn canoe across Lake Horicon and docking in the cove just north of camp.

During the days between Asher Gideon's visits, life at the Slim-Down Retreat fell into a predictable pattern of dreadful meals, calisthenics, and arts and crafts. My favorite project involved making sit-upons, squares of colored plastic stuffed with newspaper and stitched with twine. A nervous girl named Carla from New York vomited on her sit-upon, allowing the session leader a perfect opportunity to demonstrate the easy clean-up; a few sweeps with a damp cloth and you're done.

Meanwhile, I had fallen in love with Asher Gideon. I was certain we'd get married, and I contemplated life as a preacher's wife in Murfreesboro. I'd bear a houseful of Biblical children, direct the church choir, host Stone Soup Sundays, and sew my own dresses from surplus cloth. I would sit among the faithful and stare up at my husband as he preached hellfire and damnation and the word of the Lord. *But what about Johnny?* I sometimes worried. *How can I be Mrs. Asher Gideon McNamara* and *the jet-setting director of feature films?* For the first time ever, my future felt threatened. I wondered if this was how dreams die. I remembered Nurse Nellis' warning: "Tall, romantic, and passionate. A woman has to suffer for that kind of love . . . "

When Asher Gideon next visited he brought me a bouquet of dandelions and three-leaf clover; just ordinary weeds, but special because they'd come from his side of Lake Horicon.

"They're beautiful," I said, placing the bouquet on my pillow, where the raw green odor would seep into the fabric and comfort me while I slept.

I grabbed two cans of Mr. Pibb that I'd traded an issue of *Hollywood* for on the camp's black market and together Asher Gideon and I hiked to a sheltered cove north of the campgrounds, where we collapsed softly in the sand.

"It's a beautiful night," I said, catching my breath.

"Sure is." Asher Gideon sidled closer to me, beneath a row of weeping willows that cast long shadows over our heads. I clasped my elbows and shivered. "Cold?" he asked.

I nodded.

"Can't have that." He draped his satin baseball jacket over my shoulders.

"Thanks." I traced the canvas patch that said "Murfreesboro Blue Bombers." I pictured Asher Gideon tapping the ground with a Louisville Slugger as he stepped to the plate. "Do you say a prayer when you go up to hit?" I asked.

His shy smile flashed in the semi-darkness. "Each and ev'ry tiiiime," he drawled.

"So you must be hitting a thousand."

He laughed. "Nope. But three-ninety-nine ain't bad."

"That's for sure." I looked up at the sky, which was purple and black with tiny stars shining like pinpricks in a gauzy fabric.

"What do y'all think about the stars?" Asher Gideon asked, glancing up.

"Stars are possibilities," I replied. "Stars remind me what I want to be someday." In sixth grade we'd taken a field trip to the Adler Planetarium in Chicago and when we stopped for lunch at McDonald's, Shannon Atkinson vomited all over the life-sized Mayor McCheese. Mrs. Rice declared the entire day a disaster, while back on the bus Todd and Ricky called me "The Ass-teroid," saying I was as big as a planetary body and fat enough for moons to orbit. I was surprised I still remembered some of what I'd learned that day.

"Stars are made of gas that burns out eventually," I explained. "We catch their dying light, shining brightest just before the end." I paused. "After I die, I want people to see *Girl on the Lam* and remember me, Sunnie Sundstrom, the girl who created it."

I felt a surge of pride, but Asher Gideon remained quiet. I leaned close to his shadowy face. "Does that sound crazy?" I asked.

"Not a'tall," he whispered, shaking his head. "It's just dif-f'rent for me."

"How do the stars look to you?"

He took a deep breath and released it. "Like the Lord's hand-iwork. He made the stars, just like He made us and everything else, for His pleasure. He tossed up those stars like a handful of dust. That's how powerful, how almighty He is."

Asher Gideon's fingers fumbled over his little black mus-tache. His devotion touched and humbled me; made me want to weep. "Asher Gideon, can I ask you something?"

"Shoot."

I swallowed hard. "Do you like me?"

"'Course." He cleared his throat. "You're a fine young lady."

"Would you like me better skinny?"

"I dunno." He scratched his head. "Do you *want* to be skinny?"

"That's what I'm here for," I replied. I suddenly wondered if he knew that Camp Muknawanago was a weight-loss camp. Surely he'd noticed that Fifi, Cherise, Harriet, and I were all over-weight.

"The question is still, do you *want* to be skinny?" He traced a circle in the sand.

"I'm not sure," I admitted. "Sometimes I want to be really skinny, bones-sticking-out skinny, on-the-verge-of-collapsing skinny. Other times I just want to lose a few pounds. And some-times I like myself the way I am."

Asher Gideon turned and knelt before me, grasping my knees. His gray-green eyes flashed, even in the darkness. "Jesus loves you, Wilma," he said roughly, touching my face. "Just the way you are."

His closeness, the fire in his eyes, the touch of his hand, made me lean forward and kiss Asher Gideon right on the lips.

Surprised, he let out a little squeal and tipped backwards in the sand, landing flat on his bottom.

"Sorry," I said quickly, grasping his hand and pulling him up. As he came forward his mouth met mine and we kissed again, longer this time. I felt the tough bristle of his little mustache and the hot thrust of his tongue. I slipped my arms around him and tried to call up advice from *Amber in Eden*, but Asher Gideon jerked away.

"Stop," he insisted, breathing fast and hard.

"What's wrong?"

"This is sinnin'." His face looked hot and angry. "Get thee behind me, Satan. Get thee behind."

My heart deflated and I thought I would cry. "Sorry," I mumbled. I assumed he was disgusted by my fatness, which he hadn't completely appreciated until he held me, all of me, in his arms.

"Hey, it's not your fault." He softened a little and stroked my cheek. "But we aren't married, and Elder Fredericks says that even kissin' is a sin for unmarrieds."

"Oh." I straightened my T-shirt and shorts. I hated Elder Fredericks, whoever he was. *Amber in Eden* offered no advice on this situation. "What should we do now?" I asked.

Asher Gideon jumped to his feet. "Clear our minds of impure thoughts," he said decisively. "Pray for forgiveness."

"All right," I replied. I followed Asher Gideon to the soft sand fringing the lakefront, where we knelt and clasped our hands beneath our chins. It felt good and shivery to be so close, skin to skin, huddled under our shared umbrella of shame.

"Oh Heavenly Father, forgive us." Asher Gideon's voice was deep and anguished. "We ask, as Your children, that You look upon us with Your supreme kindness and wash away our unclean deeds . . ."

"Amen," I whispered periodically. "Have mercy and amen." I imagined crossing my fingers behind my back. I didn't want to anger God, but I was convinced that there was no sin in kissing Asher Gideon.

When we finished praying we stood and brushed the sand from our clothing, then walked quietly back to Oneida. I walked slightly behind, eyeing the sit-upon in Asher Gideon's back pocket. I thought about those Sunday School pictures of Adam and Eve after the fall; Eve's long hair covering her breasts, and Adam's small, but strategic, fig leaf. *Maybe that is us,* I admitted to myself. *Maybe we went too far and now know more than we should. Shame and knowledge; well, at least there's knowledge. I can be satisfied with that.*

I returned Asher Gideon's jacket and he handed me the sit-upon. In the distance Cherise and Daniel were silhouetted beside a massive oak tree, kissing a tender good-bye. Clearly Daniel's religious convictions weren't as intense as Asher Gideon's.

"Come back soon," I said, offering Asher Gideon a handshake.

"You know it," he replied, pulling me into a grown-up embrace whose sadness and regret lingered long after we parted.

I had tears in my eyes as I stepped back into the cabin.

"How was lover-boy? Smooch, smooch, smooch?" Harriet smacked her lips and kissed her bunched-up pillow.

"Shut up," I said. "It's not like that." Harriet's hair was done up in tiny pink rollers. Fifi was dry-shaving her legs and the whole cabin smelled of nail polish, hair spray, and hot wax.

As I climbed to my top bunk, Cherise stepped through the door sobbing. "What's wrong?" Harriet leaned forward, excited. "Did he touch you down there?"

"No." Cherise blew her nose. "I'm in love. How can I tell Mama and Daddy that I love a white boy?"

"Do you think they'll be mad?" Fifi asked.

"Uh huh." Cherise stepped into her long flannel nightgown, still sniffling. "They might be."

I shifted beneath my sheets and positioned the bouquet of weeds beside my head. "Your parents won't mind," I offered. "If they see that you and Daniel are truly in love."

I recalled a recent episode of *Fantasy Island* in which a brown-skinned native girl from Mr. Roarke's island fell for Parker Stevenson. The girl's father put a hex on Parker, but love conquered all and in the end they were married to the music of ukuleles.

"What matters is that you and Daniel love and respect each other," I explained, summarizing Mr. Roarke's advice.

"But what if that's not enough?" Cherise asked.

"I don't know," I replied, stroking a dandelion. "I only know I would die if I couldn't see Asher Gideon again. I would totally, totally die."

An entire week passed with no visits from the boys. "Maybe they got tired from all that prayer and volleyball," Cherise said, sounding unconvinced as we stood shivering at the cove, staring across Lake Horicon for any sign of a small pilfered canoe.

"Or maybe they got caught taking a canoe and punished," I offered.

"Maybe." Cherise buried her chin in her denim jacket. "Do you think Daniel stopping coming 'cause I'm black?"

"When did you tell him?" I asked.

She flashed a quick smile, then turned serious. "What if they went home?"

"They would have said good-bye first. I'm sure of that." I couldn't share with Cherise my deepest fear: that Asher Gideon had confessed our kiss to Elder Fredericks and was now burning in his religion's hell, complete with flames, pitchforks, and little red men.

Sent to hell for kissing a fat girl, I thought. *He deserves better. If I'd been skinny, it might have been worthwhile.*

I cleared my throat. "Cherise, what if we went over there to find out?"

Her eyes widened. "Steal a canoe?"

"Not steal. Just borrow."

"I don't know . . . "

"Come on. Please. It's not that far. And we wouldn't stay long. Just ask what happened, then come back."

130

"What if we get caught?"

"We won't. I promise."

She looked down, toeing the ground.

"Cherise, ask yourself. We've only got four more weeks of camp. Can you go home without knowing what happened?"

She shook her head. "No. That would just 'bout drive me crazy."

"OK. Then let's do it. Let's go tonight."

Enlisting Fifi and Harriet's help was no easy task, but by 10:30 P.M. we were walking in total darkness to the dock, carrying our shoes. We didn't dare speak or use flashlights as we tiptoed past the other cabins. Ojibwa was playing "Light as a feather," while Menominee girls were giggling and smoking pot.

The wind, which had been quiet all day, picked up speed, scattering leaves like hurried footsteps.

"Don't go," Fifi pleaded. "It's gonna rain. Go tomorrow."

Cherise and I exchanged glances. "No," I said. "We gotta go now."

"All right," Fifi said. "But when you end up at the bottom of Lake Horicon, don't say I didn't warn you."

We mounted the dock, which was covered with a thick, foul-smelling algae. Fifi, prepared for everything, used a barrette to pick the lock on the supply shed and Cherise and I quickly outfitted ourselves with paddles and life jackets.

Fifi and Harriet untied the last in the row of canoes stored upside down along the dock. As Fifi and Harriet steadied the canoe I climbed in and Cherise settled in behind me.

"Don't stay too long." Fifi splashed into the shallow water and steered us away from the dock. "Be back by twelve. Our flashlights will guide you back in."

"Thanks, guys," I said, dipping my paddle into the water. "We owe you big time."

"Just give lover-boy a smooch smooch smooch," Harriet called after us. "But make sure you use protection!"

As we paddled away from the dock, small waves lapped the canoe's rounded hull. With the wind behind us I figured we could cross the lake in twenty minutes.

"I'm scared," Cherise admitted. "What if Daniel doesn't like me anymore?"

"I'm sure he still likes you." I paused to catch my breath. "And if he doesn't, isn't it better to know?"

"Yes." She stroked left, then right, then left again. "I s'pose so."

Our initial progress was slowed by the slimy, cooked-spinach plant life on the bottom of the lake, but once we got further out we picked up speed and fell into a smooth, even rhythm. Cherise began to hum, then broke out singing in a strong soprano voice, "Amazing Grace."

Before she had finished the second verse the wind rose up and teased my hair. Seconds later the first raindrops struck my arms.

"Damn it." I paddled faster and motioned for Cherise to keep up. I thought we could beat the storm to the other side, but we weren't yet halfway across. Then the rain turned to little missiles, popping on the water like shrapnel.

I looked over my shoulder through the raindrops and saw the frantic flashlight beam as Fifi signaled us to return.

"Sunnie! Go back!" Cherise called out.

Before I could answer a wind gust caught the canoe and drove the bow high in the air. My stomach clenched as we bottomed out and veered wildly to the side. Electricity prickled up and down my arms as the first bolt of lightning divided the sky.

"Paddle!" I yelled to Cherise. "Just paddle!"

The smell of sulfur filled the air as a million little tentacles entered my body. Pain knifed through my arms and shoulders as I paddled harder. Between thunderclaps came Cherise's voice behind me, clarified by terror. "Our Father, who art in heaven . . . "

Lightning lit up the sky and I saw Fifi clearly, knee-deep in water, pelted by rain, frantically waving us in. "Come on!" I screamed to Cherise. "We're almost there!"

"SUNNIE!"

The canoe rose and tipped in mid-air, dumping me out. As I splashed down, the canoe caught me between the shoulders, knocking me breathless. The life jacket held me upright as wave after wave crashed over my head. Trails of seaweed strangled my legs as I tried to kick free. "Cherise!" I screamed. "Cherise!"

Something grabbed my arm and spun me around in the water. It was Fifi, her face a white mask of terror shown clear by lightning. "I've got you," she yelled, circling my neck and tugging me free.

"Cherise!" I yelled. "Cherise!"

Fifi held me tightly, dragging me to shore. I tried to stand, but my legs collapsed beneath me. My face landed in the damp, gritty sand and I vomited black water. My skin froze and my whole body shook with tremors. The last thing I saw before blacking out was Harriet, Randall-Anne, and Pierce, rushing toward the dock, limbs flashing like skeletons dancing on the sand.

I woke up in the infirmary, covered by a stiff blanket and sheets that reeked of bleach. My head ached and my eyes burned, but I was alive. I was definitely alive. I looked at the poster of a bulging heart and other muscles and the rows of glass jars filled with cotton balls, Q-Tips, and tongue depressors.

Why did we have to bring our own tongue depressors? I wondered. *They have a million of them here.* My stomach sank as I realized that Cherise had to be dead. *God, don't let me live if I've killed her,* I prayed.

I had visions of her funeral, a somber black family gathering around an open casket, and her mother singing "Amazing Grace" in a clear soprano voice as beautiful as Cherise's had been. Little Anita looks down at her dead sister and remembers the cruel man and the cotton candy and feels that pain all over again, as fresh as the first time, only worse now, knowing that no one will ever hurt her big sister again. Then Cherise's Daddy, a tall, proud man in a long dark coat, weeps into his white handkerchief, remembering how he always kissed his little girl good-night and now can only kiss her one last time.

Suddenly the camp nurse, a squat, square-shouldered woman in a white uniform and paper cap, walked in. "You're up," she announced. She strode to the cot and touched my forehead, evaluating me with coldly clinical hands.

"Cherise?" My heart was pounding and I could barely breathe.

"At the hospital but fine." The nurse's cold gray eyes narrowed. "No thanks to you."

Tears of relief filled my throat. "What happened?"

"The canoe knocked her unconscious. The vest saved her life. She's got a broken arm, some cuts and bruises. They're releasing her later today."

"Does she hate me?" I tried to sit up but fell back, dizzy.

The nurse looked surprised. "I have no idea." She paused. "That's the least of your concerns."

I rubbed my temples. My eyes felt swollen and tender while my arms were covered with long red bruises. My stomach burned like a bag of boiling acid. "Am I going to be OK?" I asked.

"You'll live," she replied. "Now get dressed. Randall-Anne wants to see you."

I noticed the Camp Muknawanago T-shirt and khaki shorts folded neatly on the end of my cot. After the nurse left I dressed, glimpsing myself in the steel sink across the room. I walked over for a closer look. I had a four-inch gash on my forehead and a black eye that went from eyebrow to cheekbone.

Good, I thought. *I want to look as terrible as I feel. They believed I was a bad girl until finally I became one.*

From the window I could see the archery range, where a dozen square-bottomed girls stood aligned with bows and arrows, pulling their strong arms back and releasing in unison. The sky momentarily darkened as the clutch of arrows blocked out the sun. *I'm finished,* I thought, feeling a heaviness in my chest. *No matter what happens, a part of me is already far away from here.*

I drank three Dixie cups of water from the big steel sink and once my stomach and head had settled, I stepped across the hall to Randall-Anne's office. She was reading at her desk, forehead deeply furrowed, chin pressed to her fists. "Sundstrom comma Wilma," she announced, looking up. "How are you now?"

"Fine," I lied.

"Well, I'm not fine." She swiveled in her seat. "I'm not fine with campers stealing a canoe and paddling across the lake in the middle of the night. The police could arrest you, you know."

"We didn't steal the canoe," I said. "We planned to bring it back."

"Well, the hull is cracked and it has to be replaced." She tapped a pen on her desk blotter. "Those canoes were handmade by juvenile delinquents on the Red Lake Reservation. A single canoe takes six months to construct."

"Sorry about that," I mumbled.

"Do you know what the punishment is for canoeing without permission?" she asked.

I wondered if anyone had ever even stolen a canoe before. "A million demerits?" I ventured.

"One *hundred* demerits," she replied. "You are officially expelled from the Summer Slim-Down Retreat." She uncapped the pen. "Your family is aware of the situation. You will be leaving on the bus tomorrow morning." She scribbled a note in her ledger. "You're the first camper to be expelled since 1965." She fixed me in an icy stare. "And that girl, I'll have you know, joined the Manson Family and ended up on death row."

"My parents can't pick me up?" My voice squeaked.

"No. You're taking the bus."

I panicked, wondering what had happened. No matter what I'd done I couldn't imagine Mom and Pop not picking me up. *They've separated,* I thought. *Pop moved out and Mom's scared to drive alone.* I pictured Pop in an efficiency off the highway, the kind of place with a hot plate in every room and vending machines in the hallway dispensing discolored pastries and crackers and cheese. *They're waiting to tell me until I get home.* I imagined them sitting me down in the den, waiting for the beaded curtain to stop swaying before saying, "Sunnie, this isn't easy for any of us, but there've been some changes while you were away."

This is all Grannie's fault. I left Randall-Anne's office and my sore eyes filled with tears. *If she hadn't died, none of this would have happened.*

After Randall-Anne's dismissal I spent the rest of the day in the infirmary. I had nothing to eat until the nurse brought me a metal tray with a plate of cold sticky noodles, a watery red sauce, and a hard green pear for dessert. It didn't matter because I had no appetite. After the other girls returned from the evening assembly, Pierce took me back to the cabin, where I was allowed to pack my things and spend my final night at Oneida.

I was nervous as I walked up the cabin's short wooden steps, afraid that Cherise blamed me for what had happened, but as soon as I entered she ran into my arms and started crying. "Daniel," she sobbed. "I'll never see him again."

"I know." I stroked her back, careful not to jostle the big plaster cast that immobilized her arm, bird-like, away from her side.

Fifi and Harriet had prepared a going-away party for me and for Cherise, whose parents were on the way from Chicago. Fifi's bottom bunk was covered with black market treasures and going-away gifts: candy, gum, magazines, two cans of Pabst Blue Ribbon beer, contraband Fritos, *Amber in Eden*, and a pile of cash totaling almost $250 that the girls had collected in my name.

"You're kind of a hero around here," Fifi admitted. "They'll be talking about you for years to come."

I don't want to be a hero. I just want to be a camper. I want to stay here with my friends.

"Thanks, guys." The threadbare money felt thin as linen beneath my thumb. "I don't know what to say."

A soft, steady drizzle pelted the cabin's wooden roof and the evening's blue mood was matched by the music from my transistor radio. We took turns slow-dancing, closing our eyes and pretending to be held and guided by our missing boys. Procol Harem's "A Whiter Shade of Pale," my third favorite song in the world, came on and I felt, in the one-armed embrace of Cherise, Asher Gideon drawing me close and breathing in my ear. I started to cry and Fifi rushed to comfort me, pouring beer over my trembling lip, then patting it dry with her sleeve.

"Don't cry," she said, stroking my back. "You did something brave, going across the lake to find your boy."

"But I didn't find him."

She shrugged. "At least you tried."

"If Asher Gideon comes back . . . " I stumbled. "Tell him what happened. Give him my address and have him write me. If he comes back . . . "

"Of course, Sun." She smiled. "He'll be real impressed, dontcha' know?"

As I packed my meager belongings they seemed very small indeed—just my camp ID card, my clothes, my toothbrush, my sit-upon, Harriet's book, and the Chinese scroll from Mrs. Chan. We used Harriet's marker pen to sign Cherise's cast, the fresh plaster dazzling white against her bruised brown skin.

Harriet had written, "Remember the girl in the city, remember the girl in the town, remember the girl who spoiled your cast by writing upside down." I wrote in block letters near her wrist, "CHERISE: U R 2 GOOD 2 B 4-GOTTEN," then hoped that didn't sound childish. Jerry Junkett had written that in my year-book after sixth grade and it still brought me hope, two years later.

"We'll keep in touch," I promised Cherise, patting her good hand. "Chicago and Milwaukee are close. We'll visit often. And we'll call."

"Sure thing," Cherise agreed, but we both knew in our hearts that it wouldn't happen. Although only ninety miles apart, we lived in different worlds. We would never see or hear from each other ever again, and these bittersweet few moments were the last we'd ever spend together.

"Christmas cards!" she said suddenly, her dark eyes flashing. "We'll exchange Christmas cards."

"Of course," I answered. "Each and every year."

CHAPTER ELEVEN

The following morning Pierce and I were at Horicon's Big
Blue Bus depot by, according to her military precision
Timex, "o-five-hundred-hours" for the 6:15 A.M. bus to Mil-
waukee via Minneapolis, scheduled to arrive at 7:20 P.M.

"Home in time for a late supper," Pierce said as she pulled
open the depot's greasy glass door. "Maybe they'll save you some
of that fattening grub."

"At least I'll be eating real food," I replied, guiding the duffel
bag with my foot. "No more morning gruel."

The Big Blue Bus Company, founded in the early 1970s, had
had its biggest year in 1976, inspiring it to re-christen its silver-
and-neon-blue fleet with Bicentennial names like "Prairie
Schooner," "Manifest Destiny," and "Westward Ho!" But following that great patriotic rush to see America, Big Blue's business had declined steadily and by 1978 the only people who still
seemed to be riding were sailors on leave, church social groups,
and girls thrown out of fat camp like me.

The Horicon depot was a narrow glass storefront wedged
between Larry's Bait-N-Tackle, where worms were selling for a
dollar a pound, and Jensen's Authentic Chinese Carry-Out, where
Pork Chop Suey was the special of the day. Inside, the depot
offered an RC Cola machine with a hand-penciled "OUT OF
ORDER" sign, a warped ticket counter manned by a bleary-eyed
agent, and a large luggage scale. My first impulse upon seeing the
scale was to climb on board and prove that during the previous

three weeks I had lost more than the measly seven pounds that the Retreat's livestock scale gave me credit for.

"Sit there." Pierce pointed to a chair. "Be quiet and don't move."

"Yes, Sir," I replied with a brisk salute.

After Pierce bought my ticket and sat beside me in the row of plastic chairs, she reached over and pressed a large yellow sticker to my chest.

"What's this?" I asked, irritated. I looked down and read "UNESCORTED MINOR" in big black letters.

"So you don't get lost," she explained. "The driver can keep an eye on you."

"I can take care of myself," I insisted.

"Oh yeah? Well, you've done a stellar job so far."

Having arrived so early, there was little for me to do but stare out the grease-smeared window or up at the depot's single decoration, a faded poster of Minnie Pearl performing at the Grand Old Opry. I would have been happy reading Harriet's gift of *Amber in Eden* with the most educational passages underlined, but Pierce couldn't resist getting in a few final jabs.

"You screwed up big time, Sundstrom." She stretched her skinny arms, popping both shoulders.

"Oh really?" I reached into my backpack for some gum.

"Yep." She yawned, patting her mouth. "Coulda turned your entire life around."

I bristled at her suggestion that my 'entire life' needed turning around. After all, I was a straight-A student who'd won a truckload of jam.

"High school would be so different if you were slimmer."

"Different how?" I asked.

She squinted. "No one would know you used to be fat."

"Is that so?" I challenged. "What makes you such an expert?"

"This." Glancing up at Minnie Pearl, Pierce reached into her denim jacket, slipped out a photo, and pressed it to my hand like contraband candy.

I looked down at the tattered Polaroid of a heavy girl in a sheer white blouse with a tight perm and thick, black-framed glasses. It was Pierce, sixty or seventy pounds ago. "So this is you." I nodded in admiration.

"I first came to Camp Muknawanago back in 1971," she confessed. "That was me then."

I compared the photograph to Pierce's now-streamline face. The present-day Pierce had defiant eyes and a tight, narrow jaw, but something quivered behind her bravado. This photo was her reminder, her battle scar, the thing that kept her honest when a slice of coconut cream pie or a chocolate éclair cried out to be eaten. All of Pierce's humiliations were written on this picture, as clearly as if written on her skin.

Suddenly the depot door swung open and in waddled a pregnant young woman, pale hair braided to her waist, with five little boys in tow. "Dwight David! Stop hitting your brother," she insisted, swatting one boy's wrist. "John Quincy! Hands out of your pants!"

Even with the sudden commotion, the room's energy stayed focused on the photo in my hand, as if all of Pierce's pain were centered on this unsmiling version of her earlier self. I gave back the photo and she slipped it into her jacket.

"You could have had a picture like this too." She tapped her pocket triumphantly.

"Big deal." I pushed the duffel bag beneath my feet. "I'm going to Hollywood someday to meet Johnny Carson and direct feature films."

Now it was my turn to be vulnerable. With the photograph safely stowed, Pierce returned to the offense.

"If you say so," she sniffed. "But have you ever asked yourself how many fat girls get famous?"

"I haven't counted."

"None." Her smile revealed two rows of tiny teeth. "But everybody needs a dream. To go to Hollywood someday. Even if it never comes true."

As I blinked my black eye ached, retreating deep into the damaged socket. Pierce had gotten the best of me, but it wasn't over yet. *Damn you,* I thought. *And your ugly little Polaroid too.*

I could leave for Hollywood this very afternoon. As I thought it, the possibility became real. Go to California. Watch Johnny tape *The Tonight Show,* and maybe even get another autographed photo. Why not? Who would stop me? *I'll do it,* I decided. *I'm not just a stupid fat girl who stole a canoe. I'm Sunnie Sundstrom, writer and director of feature films.*

The Big Blue Bus—rusty, dented-roofed, and decorated with large peeling decals of Old Faithful and Sacajewea—rolled up to the Horicon depot at precisely 6:10 A.M. I grabbed my Hello Kitty backpack and duffel bag and climbed on board, moving down the narrow center aisle and glancing out the window only long enough to see Pierce smile condescendingly and then, a final dagger, pat the photo near her heart.

So what? I thought, taking a window seat. *I'm riding this bus all the way to California while you, Pierce, spend the rest of the summer doing calisthenics.*

"Yeah, 'mornin', folks. Welcome aboard. The name's Omar. Your driver." The scratchy voice came over the loudspeaker as we pulled out of the parking lot. After a mile or two Horicon's Main Street widened into a two-lane highway, leaving the town's few buildings behind, rising from the dewy earth like cardboard cutouts.

". . . due to arrive Minneapolis at eleven-thirty; how 'bout them Twins . . . "

Besides me, the other passengers were an old woman with a gray beehive hairdo sitting right up front, a baby-faced sailor sprawled out on the long back seat, and the young mother whose five sons were swinging, monkey-like, hand over hand along the luggage racks.

"Smoking in the back seats only; no alcohol, no loud radios. . . ." Omar droned on monotonously until one of the little boys shrieked, then fell on his brother's head. "Missus, mind that child," Omar warned without raising his voice, simply adding a footnote to his well-practiced spiel.

The scenery was a magical dance of thick forests, rushing streams, and sun-dappled lakes as we drove south through small Minnesota towns advertising moccasins and Paul Bunyan memorabilia. I was running away; I had already decided it, but I kept that knowledge at bay for fear of ruining the plan, or worse, changing my mind. I didn't get nervous; I just pretended I was an ordinary passenger to Minneapolis, no different from the beehive lady and the sleeping sailor. *Pierce is wrong,* I told myself, scrunching my backpack against the window. *Fat girls* can *get famous too.*

The bus' on-board toilet thrilled me, even though the bright blue chemicals bounced dangerously close to my bottom with every bump in the road. This was the first toilet I'd used in three weeks and I almost cried over its spider-free luxury. The bathroom also had a mirror and an aluminum spit-sink like in the dentist's office, but when I pressed the sink's handle, only stale vacuumed air came out. A metal bracket above the sink held moist towelettes, tampons, and maxi-pads. I stuffed my pockets with sanitary supplies, just in case. *This is a real adventure, and you never know what's gonna come in handy. Why, my period could arrive at any time; even while I'm sitting in the audience watching Johnny.*

We reached Minneapolis on schedule at 11:30 A.M. I took a deep breath, grabbed my luggage, and got off the bus just behind the beehive hairdo lady, but my bright yellow tag caught the driver's eye.

"Hang on, where are you goin', young lady?" He held my arm and stared.

"Home. Just to Milwaukee," I sputtered as the sleepy sailor ducked out of line behind me.

The driver nodded. "That bus leaves from door number four. Wait inside until they call first boarding."

"Thanks," I replied, hurrying into the depot that was filled with heavy-set men in camouflage, excited high school kids, and poor families on summer vacation. Announcements droned overhead as I walked past vending machines dispensing hot water disguised as coffee or chicken soup. Beyond the vending machines was a row of little black-and-white TVs where, for a quarter, you could watch fifteen minutes of *Phil Donahue*.

I stopped first at the ladies' room, where I peeled off my "UNESCORTED MINOR" tag and dropped it in the trash when no one was looking. *Stormy would be proud,* I thought as I washed my hands and adjusted my luggage. *Of course when Stormy escapes from international drug smugglers in* Girl on the Lam, *she has to perform a dangerous, high-speed maneuver on skis.*

Back in the lounge, I took a handful of maps from a metal dispenser, then glimpsed a newspaper draped over a chair. I suddenly realized that I'd had no contact with the outside world for three weeks. *So many things must have happened since then,* I thought. The Tonight Show *has been on fifteen times, which means Johnny has welcomed forty-five guests that I know nothing about.* For the first time since I hatched my plan, I felt scared. *What if I go all the way to California and Johnny isn't there? What if it's a "Best of Carson" night, or worse, Johnny's guest host is that scary Robert Goulet?*

I looked at my watch. I could still get on the bus to Milwaukee and be home by 7:20 P.M. No one would ever know what I almost did. *But go home and do what?* I thought. Face the wrath of Mom and Pop? First, they'd sit me down and reveal their separation, and then they'd sign me up for the "D Club" at Crown of Thorns, a prayer circle/support group for kids whose parents were divorcing. Central High was starting in four weeks with Emily and Jerry either gone or in love and me all alone and still weighing 169 pounds.

My life is hopeless, I decided. *Thrown out of fat camp. I've got nowhere else to go. At least if I meet Johnny, I'll have one nice thing to remember until I die, and dying itself won't be so bad, because in heaven I'll be skinny and I'll get to see Grannie again.*

After convincing the Minneapolis ticket agent that I really was seventeen and had lost my driver's license to a pickpocket, I bought a one-way ticket to Los Angeles and climbed aboard the creaking "Continental Divide" with about twenty other passengers, mostly elderly women and sleepy-eyed college kids.

"Welcome aboard," announced the driver, a more dynamic type than Omar had been. "This here is the twelve-thirty Continental Divide from Minneapolis, due to arrive in Des Moines at five-thirty this even-ning. If y'all are headin' north, you're on the wrong bus."

The sun burned brightly overhead as we headed south on Interstate 35. I had a row of two seats to myself so I curled up, opened *Amber in Eden*, and let the words lull me to sleep. *Lady Alana lay back, heaving, beads of moisture collecting between her pendulant breasts. "Lord Willoughby," she sighed, reaching for his hand. "Do me the honor of ravishing me once more with your potent sword of flesh . . ."*

I woke up at a quarter to four just as we crossed from Minnesota into Iowa's endless acres of corn and wheat, rippling like ribbons of yellow and green, with distant farmhouses dotting the landscape like bright red exclamation marks.

Johnny was born in Corning, Iowa, in 1925, I thought. I knew a lot about Johnny from research I had done in Mr. Matusak's social studies class. We were supposed to write about an "American Innovator." Mr. Matusak suggested I write about George Washington Carver, but I managed to convince him that "by revolutionizing late-night television and the talk show format itself, Johnny Carson represents a true American Innovator."

The temperature rose as we continued further south until thirty miles outside of Ames, where the air conditioner quit completely. Heat and hostility built up quickly in the metallic silver-and-blue bus, creating a symphony of bad smells ranging from gym socks and sweaty armpits to garlic and chicken soup. A baby in seat sixteen screamed bloody murder while a pair of old ladies played a hostile game of poker, bitterly wagering nickels and dimes as their cigarette smoke rose above the upholstered bucket seats.

The bus became more crowded with every small rural stop and soon there wasn't a single empty seat left. I had to share my row with an old woman, oddly bundled up in the heat, knitting a long, beige, shapeless sweater. She hummed "What Wondrous Love Is This" over and over and every time she began a new row of stitches she accidentally jabbed me with her knitting needle. "Mighty sorry," she'd say. "Pardon me."

"All right already," I said for the dozenth time, squishing closer to the window, hopefully out of the needle's pointy reach.

By five-thirty the day's excitement had worn off completely. I was hot and hungry; my neck was sore and my limbs ached. Even the periodic trips to the on-board bathroom were losing their appeal, particularly since the bathroom's condition deteriorated by the mile.

We reached Des Moines at 6:45 P.M. and I had an hour's wait before the bus to Omaha. Des Moines didn't have its own Big Blue Bus depot. Instead, the stop was inside Daisy Mae's, a truck stop restaurant along the interstate. I climbed out of the bus and stretched my arms and legs, eager to taste my first real food in weeks.

I followed the other passengers inside and sat down on one of the restaurant's red vinyl stools. In front of me was a Lucite case filled with homemade apple pie, carrot cake, and a thick slab of gingerbread just begging for ruffles of whipped cream. I reached for the laminated menu, layered with greasy fingerprints distinct enough to help solve crimes.

"What kin I getcha, honey?" The waitress, chewing a thick wad of gum, posed her stubby pencil above a pad.

I skimmed the list of skirt steaks, Denver omelets, and mushroom burgers. "A tuna melt with fries, Cole slaw, and a chocolate shake," I said. "Wait—make that a large chocolate shake."

"Your family joinin' ya fer supper?" she asked.

"Nope." I tried not to panic and give my age away. "I'm on my own this trip." I folded my Hello Kitty backpack at my feet, hoping the waitress hadn't seen it. "Visiting my aunt and uncle."

She didn't look convinced, but she nodded and walked away.

Along the lunch counter, wire baskets held little packets of sugar, salt, pepper, and non-dairy creamer. I was stuffing Hello Kitty with supplies when someone tapped my shoulder.

"Excuse me, Miss."

I spun around, nearly knocking into a burly older man in a white shirt stained yellow at the underarms.

"May I borrow your ketchup?" He was tall and olive-skinned with thinning, greased-back hair.

"Sure." I handed him the half-empty bottle of Heinz crusted brown around the cap.

"Thank you kindly," he said, offering a bow.

"No problem." I noticed that there were ketchup bottles at every table.

The waitress delivered my tuna melt in a red plastic basket and the first bites were disappointing. The cheese had melted clear and oily while the bun was damp and fishy, as if the tuna hadn't been drained. The fries were greasy and underdone. At least the shake was good, made from ice cream, whole milk, and thick chocolate syrup. I drank the whole thing quickly, even the dregs from the cold metal canister that the waitress left beside my plate. The shake made my stomach hurt, but it was a good hurt, the hurt of something expanding, growing bigger and more generous, allowing more to come in. *It won't take long to gain back those seven pounds,* I thought sadly, tracing condensation down the side of the cold metal canister. *Not long at all.*

"Bus one-one-seven, the Forty-Ninth Parallel, boarding now," came a tired voice over the loudspeaker. I took a final spoonful of bitter Cole slaw and wondered how much to tip the waitress. I'd never tipped someone before. My dinner cost $3.87. I tucked a five-dollar bill beneath the plastic basket, hoping that would cover it.

The Des Moines night air was hot and still with a warm prairie smell as I stood in line to board the 49th Parallel. The burly older man from the restaurant stepped out of line and waited for me to reach him.

146

"Thanks again for the ketchup." His smile revealed two rows of stained, stubby teeth. He had a wrinkled face and dark squinty eyes, fish eyes that reminded me of a dying thing caught in a net.

"That's OK." I hiked the backpack over my shoulder and reached for my duffel.

"Here- let me help you." He grabbed the bag and climbed the narrow steps behind me, wheezing. I stopped halfway down the bus and tossed my backpack on an open window seat.

"Overhead?" He indicated the duffel bag.

"Yes," I replied.

He forced the bag into the overhead rack.

"Thanks," I said as he took a handkerchief from his pocket and mopped his sweaty brow.

"Don't mention it." He extended his hand. "Arthur Burton."

I didn't want to shake the hand that had held the damp handkerchief. "Nice to meet you, Mr. Burton." I kept my hands on the seat.

"Please, call me Arthur. And you are?"

"Sunnie," I replied warily.

His dark fish eyes glazed over. "Young gal like you traveling all alone?"

My mind raced and I wished he'd go away. "Not for long," I said lightly. "I'm meeting my aunt and uncle."

"You don't say." He leaned on the armrest.

A bunch of passengers bottlenecking behind him struggled to squeeze past. "Excuse me, puh-leeeze," a man whined.

"Oops. Sorry," he apologized, face reddening. "See you later, Sunnie. Have a nice trip."

He ambled back and took a seat across from the on-board bathroom, then reached down and loosened his shoes. *I should have been nicer*, I thought, settling in. *Probably just an old guy wanting to chat.*

The 49th Parallel rolled out of Des Moines heading west towards Omaha with the slowly setting sun drenching the sky in shades of lavender, pink, and tangerine. The horizon was smooth and level, except for explosive tufts of soybean, alfalfa, and corn. The scenery was beautiful, but I couldn't get comfortable in my tiny bucket seat with my elbow pressed against the sharp metal window vent that alternated shooting streams of burning hot and ice cold air.

I looked at my watch. Seven-twenty P.M. and "Horatio Alger" would just be pulling into Milwaukee, lumbering up the little hill at the corner of 6th and Michigan. Mom, Pop, Ingrid, and Max would be standing at the depot, huddled close, watching passengers climb down the narrow steps one by one. At first they would be excited; Max would hold up a little sign saying, "Welcome Home, Sunnie," while Mom and Ingrid would bob and squint, anxious to see how thin I'd become.

Once half the passengers are disbursed, Mom would get nervous. "She should be off by now," she would say, wringing her hands.

"Don't worry." Pop would strain to see on tiptoes. "She's got to be there."

The final rider disembarks and I am nowhere in sight. Mom would grab the driver by his blue lapels. "Where is my daughter—Sunnie?" Her voice would be quick, insistent. "Where is Wilma? Wilma Sundstrom—she's tall with blonde hair . . ."

Ingrid and Max would try to calm her as Pop runs to the police. "Sunnie!" Mom would scream, her face dissolving in hot, frightened tears. "I want my baby! Please find my baby now!"

I sat up and rubbed my eyes. The bus was dark except for the little reading light above my head, still illuminated. In the window I saw the reflection of my face, like a hollow skull with black holes for my eyes and mouth. "Stop the bus," I whimpered to the empty seat beside me. The wheels clattered over some stones and I thought the tires would explode. "Stop right here." I started crying and couldn't catch my breath. *I have to get off. I can't do this to my family. I'm only thirteen and I want to go home.*

CHAPTER TWELVE

W e passed through Nebraska's eastern half in total darkness, to the tuneless whistle of air through the bus' massive wheels, while the highway itself remained uniformly smooth, flat, and quiet, mile after endless mile. I slept off and on, but never more than twenty minutes at a time. I stopped crying and settled into a manageable sadness like the gentle melancholy of rainy days and foggy nights. I didn't think about Mom, Pop, Ingrid, or Max. I kept that part of my mind dark, like a room with the lights turned off. *They'll see me soon enough,* I reasoned. *After I meet Johnny I'll call Mom and Pop and go home. Everything will be just like before: my movie-star mirror, my big brassy baritone, the kitchen filled with my prize-winning jam.*

It was around one in the morning when, bored and lonely, I went up to talk with the driver. He was a serious, straight-backed, gray-mustached little man whose Western shirt and cowboy boots didn't quite fit his insurance-agent face.

"Don't you get tired?" I asked, peering into the curved yellow pools cast by the bus' headlights. Watching the highway disappear beneath the bus' wheels reminded me that we were racing headlong into total darkness at seventy miles an hour and if we crashed, help, if there was any, would only come from far away.

"Tired? Sometimes," the driver admitted, pushing back his cap. "But I got my CB here, and thoughts of home."

"Where's home?" I asked.

"Kansas City. I've got this route as far as Denver, then I'm driving 'The Unsinkable Molly Brown' to KC." As he glanced back, light caught the liquidy whites of his eyes. "The name's Marvin Mitchell. Been driving buses for twenty-seven years."

"I'm Sunnie and I'm heading to L.A." I liked how that sounded, "Ell-ay," rolling off my lips.

"Been out there before?"

"Nope," I replied. "It's my first time."

"Oh Sunnie, you're gonna love it." Marvin shook his head. "The sun always shines and oranges grow everywhere. You can just reach up and grab one for lunch. And the palm trees, so pretty, like paradise on earth."

A crackle from the CB radio startled us both. "Breaker one-nine, breaker one-nine, smokey up ahead," said a scratchy male voice. "Do you copy, double M's?"

"In September we change routes and I'm hoping to get Denver to L.A. at least twice a month." Marvin grabbed the radio hand-piece and clicked it close to his mustache. "Yeah, ten-four good buddy, Double M's here, what's your forty?" He clicked the mike again, waiting for a response.

I listened as Marvin talked to the other driver, who was thirty miles ahead of us on I-80 and warning of a semi that had jack-knifed, spilling tons of feed. While Marvin talked I pictured his stately palms swaying in the California breeze. Then I imagined Johnny Carson in his little white Corvette, driving beneath those same trees every day and not even noticing them anymore as he thinks about Angie Dickinson, the monologue, and tomorrow night's guests. I guessed that even late-night talk show hosts and long-haul bus drivers harbored secret dreams they dared not broadcast, even in the quiet middle of the night.

I walked back to the bathroom. Arthur Burton was asleep with his fingers laced across his belly. He snored, deepening his wrinkles and working his jaw. Marvin and I were the only two people on the bus still awake, and I trembled with a newfound sense of responsibility. If we crashed right now, who else could account for the truth of this journey?

At three-thirty A.M. something metallic rattled off the bus' rear. We swerved, slowed, then picked up speed. "Sorry, folks," Marvin announced calmly. "Looks like we got some mechanical problems, but don't worry, we'll stop as soon as possible."

Marvin steered us safely to our next scheduled stop in North Platte, Nebraska, about twelve miles away. The forty other passengers rubbed their eyes, stretched their limbs, and smacked their lips as they struggled to wake up.

North Platte's Big Blue Bus depot was located just off Interstate 80, next to the Fort Cody Trading Post, a souvenir shop and museum designed like an old wooden fort and overseen by an enormous cut-out of Buffalo Bill Cody that dominated the low prairie skyline. The bus depot had closed for the night, but the front door was unlocked. "Lucky that the door was open," I told Marvin as he ferried us inside, waving his arms like a crossing guard.

"Lucky?" He shrugged. "No one ever locks this place up." Marvin found some blankets in a storage closet and handed them out judiciously, favoring women and children. Most people curled up in the rows of plastic chairs and covered themselves with jackets and blankets beneath a large poster advertising the Buffalo Bill Ranch State Historical Park. On the poster Buffalo Bill had Lee Majors' piercing blue eyes, a white goatee, and flowing silver hair. I watched as Arthur Burton, his tiny eyes swollen to slash marks, shuffled past the poster and flopped into a chair with his jaw sagging open.

Afraid to sleep among so many strangers, I sat on the linoleum floor behind the wire postcard racks and near the bathroom with my back to the wall. I took out my map and shone my flashlight on Nebraska, on the town of Norfolk, where Johnny had grown up. Facts from that old social studies report surfaced again. Johnny's dad Homer worked for the electric company. Johnny graduated from Norfolk High in 1943 and after serving in the Navy in World War II, earned a degree from the University of Nebraska.

I shivered, rubbing my arms. Did it even matter that I knew these things? Was Johnny Carson, the *real* Johnny Carson, an actual human being, or was he just another TV character like Gilligan and Mrs. Howell, Alice on *The Brady Bunch*, or Tootie from *The Facts of Life*?

No. I shook my head. *Johnny is real. He has to be. He's real and I'll see him soon.* I bowed my head, fighting off sleep. I wished I were back in my top bunk at Oneida, listening to Fifi, Harriet, and Cherise sleeping deeply, breathing steadily beneath the snap of crickets and the distant cry of loons. I ached to be back at Oneida, but I hardly thought about Asher Gideon at all. *That's the strange thing about leaving someplace,* I decided. *You never know what you're going to miss until it's gone.*

The depot opened at six the next morning, welcoming bright-eyed passengers for all destinations north to Bismarck. Two mechanics arrived from Grand Island and got to work right away, removing almost the entire front and back ends of the bus: hubcaps, tires, axles, pistons, and spark plugs. Marvin supervised the repairs with intense interest and offered periodic updates to those of us stuck in the lounge. "We'll be back on the road by noon," he announced with certainty at 9 A.M. "These fellas are working their tails off."

At two P.M. Marvin, looking sheepish, cap in hand, revealed that the mechanics had sent for a replacement part from Hastings and we'd be stuck at least until early evening. Everyone groaned.

"Next time I'm taking the train," a middle-aged man muttered. "It's worth a couple extra bucks." Our group of forty dwindled as several demanded their money back while others hopped on buses going anywhere, desperate to leave North Platte.

I spent hours sitting in the lounge staring out the depot window at the Pennzoil station, the High Lights Club, and the Motel 6 across the interstate. I watched Big Blue Buses pull up in front and heard the siren song of destinations such as Gothenburg, Cozad, Thedford, and McCook, then watched those same buses leaving, knowing that none of them could bring me even one inch closer to Johnny.

"Hey pretty lady."

I turned and looked up into the broad fleshy face of Arthur Burton. "Hi," I replied.

"Mind if I sit down?" One hand was on the chair back while the other held a brown paper bag.

"Go ahead."

He sat down, opened the bag, and took out a ham sandwich wrapped in wax paper, a pack of Twinkies, a Hostess Cherry Pie, and two cans of 7-Up. "Would you share this with me?" he asked. "I can't eat it all myself."

The depot's two decrepit vending machines had been empty since nine A.M. and with nothing else to eat, I was famished. "Where'd you get that?" I asked, mouth watering.

"There's a gas station across the highway." He grimaced as he straightened his knee. "My joints are killing me. Got injured in the war." He handed me half the sandwich and a can of 7-Up.

"Which war?" I bit into the sandwich and even though the bread was stale and the ham rubbery, it was the most delicious thing I'd ever eaten.

"Dubya-dubya-two," he replied. "Omaha Beach."

"Wow." I pulled the tab off the 7-Up and took a big swig. "You must be a hero and all."

His eyes narrowed and he shook his head. "Naw. Just a survivor."

I felt sorry for him, a damaged old man who had served his country, now reduced to riding a Big Blue Bus. "So where are you going?" I asked.

"Denver," he answered, stuffing the sandwich in his mouth. "To see Delia and my grandbaby, Trina."

"Mmmm." As my stomach filled, I felt friendlier. "How old's the baby?"

He reached into his pocket and took out a creased photo of a curly-haired baby. "Eight months old last week," he replied proudly.

"Beautiful," I said, admiring the photo.

"I'm only sorry Dolores passed before Trina was born." He winced and his skin reddened as he stifled a cough.

"Was Dolores your wife?" I asked carefully.

He nodded, running a hand through his oily hair. "Married forty years before the cancer took her. We didn't have Delia there until later in life." His lower lip trembled.

"I'm sorry," I said. "My Grannie died in June." I looked at baby Trina in the photo. She would never know her own grandmother except through pictures and other people's words. I felt lucky I'd had my Grannie for thirteen years.

Arthur Burton's dead fish eyes surprised me, rising soft and kind. "My condolences," he said. "Betcha miss her lots."

"Uh huh." I nodded. "But I've hardly been home since she died."

Maybe it was the lack of sleep, the loneliness of the journey, or the generosity of the thin ham sandwich, but I told Arthur all about Grannie, about camp, about Asher Gideon. He talked about Delores, who'd been a nurse, and his daughter Delia, whose dream was to do taxes for H & R Block.

Time passed quickly and I was sorry I'd originally found him creepy. *He's just a sad old man who misses his family,* I decided. *This could be like in* Girl on the Lam, *when Stormy befriends a hobo who's really Giles Van Dam, her parents' former butler working undercover to investigate their mysterious deaths.*

At six P.M. Marvin announced in a whisper that the replacement part from Hastings would not arrive after all, due to a mix-up in Omaha. "But don't worry," he added quickly. "Big Blue is sending another bus to take you all to Denver." He paused. "That bus will be here by eight tomorrow morning."

A chorus of dispirited boos reached the depot's rafters. Even the Buffalo Bill Cody poster appeared angry, revealing a fiery glint in the Lee Majors-blue eyes.

Arthur sighed heavily and repositioned his damaged knee. "Sunnie, how 'bout we rent us a car and drive to Denver tonight?"

"Drive to Denver?" I tried not to choke on the Hostess Cherry Pie.

"Sure. We could be there by morning." His dead fish eyes sparked to life. "Delia'll make us a big Western breakfast, then I'll drop you at the bus to California."

"I don't know." I glanced around the lounge. "I've already got my ticket to L.A."

He shrugged. "Well, you think about it. I'm going into town to find me a rental car."

As Arthur hobbled out of the depot I wasn't sure what to do. I actually kind of missed him after he was gone, and I couldn't imagine spending another long night on the cold depot floor. Still, everything I'd learned in school told me never to accept a ride from a stranger. *But Arthur's not really a stranger,* I thought. *I know his name, where he's from, and what he did in the war.*

When it got to be 8:00 P.M. and there was still no sign of Arthur, I wondered if he'd found some other way to Denver, but suddenly he appeared, sweaty and smiling, revealing his stubby brown teeth.

"I found a nice little ride," he announced, mopping his forehead. "A Ford Fairmont. Will I have the pleasure of your company as far as Denver?"

"Thanks, but no," I said, staring at the floor. "I should just take the bus. My aunt and uncle are waiting."

"I understand," he said gently. "Beware of strangers and all that?" He chuckled. "We raised Delia the same way." He scanned the lounge. "Will you at least join me for dinner? I passed a heap of nice restaurants on the way."

I glanced at the empty snack wrappers on the seat beside me. With the vending machines empty there'd be nothing more to eat until tomorrow morning at the earliest. "Sure," I said. "Sounds great."

I followed Arthur to the rental car in the dusty lot behind the depot. The sun was just setting behind the cutout Bill Cody and the hot night air smelled strongly of manure.

"It's gonna rain," Arthur announced, drawing in a deep, wheezing breath. "Can't smell it yet, but I feel it in my bones."

I hung on to my backpack as Arthur threw my duffel bag in the trunk and closed it with a metallic "clack" that echoed in my head. We climbed into the car and followed U.S. 83 as it turned into Dewey Street leading downtown. We drove at least a mile, passing dozens of restaurants along the way.

155

"Yep," Arthur said with a deep sigh, "my old joints are more accurate than any weather report."

When we ran out of street at the Union Pacific Railroad, Arthur crossed over a block and headed back through town on Jeffers Street. Again the same string of restaurants passed by outside the window. I clutched my backpack uneasily, fingering the soft tip of Hello Kitty's ear.

"You look beautiful tonight," Arthur said, idling at a red light and clearing his throat.

"Thanks." My voice sounded small. "But I know I'm not pretty."

"Of course you're pretty." His knee cracked loudly as he shifted in his seat.

"Pretty? Yeah, pretty fat," I said, trying to laugh.

"Not fat. Voluptuous." He coughed into his tightened fist. "You ever hear of Jayne Mansfield?"

"Nope." I had, but for some reason I said I hadn't.

"A movie star from the fifties. She's passed on now, but she was a real beaut. A full-figured gal. Like you."

Arthur seemed different now since we'd left the depot; nervous, distracted, with his fleshy hand pressing hard on the stick shift, turning his knuckles white. "In olden days, they appreciated such loveliness."

My stomach churned and I hoped we'd stop soon. "Look, there's an Arthur Treacher's Original Fish and Chips." I pointed to the tall yellow-and-black sign rising high above the street. "We could eat there."

He coughed, struggling to cut the heavy phlegm. "Let's find something classier. You deserve the best."

"Hamburger and fries are OK." My hands were shaking. "Look, there's a Howard Johnson's." The powder-blue-and-orange sign slid past in a blur. "And an A & W Root Beer right behind."

He crouched over the steering wheel.

"Look- a Shoney's Big Boy," I said. "And International House of Pancakes. They do great buttermilk pancakes, and all those flavored syrups."

156

He didn't respond.

"I sure would like to stop there, Mr. Burton."

"Please, call me Arthur." The forced lightness in his voice scared me even more. He came up close behind a dark Dodge Pinto, then pressed hard on the horn. "Aren't we friends?"

The Fort Cody Trading Post and the big cutout of Buffalo Bill loomed on the horizon. The last rays of daylight outlined the rim of Bill's hat and the tip of his rifle.

As we approached the bus depot once more I hoped that Arthur would just drop me off, but instead he made a U-turn at the Motel 6 and continued back towards the ever-darker downtown. "Sunnie, do you have a boyfriend?"

"No." I swallowed hard.

"No? A lovely girl like you?"

"I stay focused on school."

"Uh huh." He tapped the steering wheel. "Does your boyfriend mess you around?"

"No." I clutched my backpack so tightly that my fingertips turned numb.

"C'mon, Sunnie. I want to help you. Your boyfriend gave you that black eye, right?"

"No!" I said loudly, watching restaurants and motels and auto supply shops fly past.

"Then how'd it happen?" He turned in his seat to face me and his eyes were all pupil; no color or light. "Your father knocks you around so you ran away?"

He was breathing fast and I was ready to cry. "I told you I got hit with a canoe," I stammered. "That's all."

"You know what makes me sick?"

I was speechless, frozen to my seat.

"Men who don't respect their women. Don't treat them like they should."

I let go of my backpack and felt for the cool metal handle of the door. As we approached the Union Pacific rail yard once more he again turned and headed back south towards the interstate.

"If you were my girl I'd shower you with chocolate and roses. Something special every day." His forehead beaded with sweat. A thick blood vessel in his temple turned and pulsed.

"Let's stop here." I slipped my fingers around the door handle, gauging its resistance. "Ma Kettle's Soup Spoon looks good."

The car barreled through a yellow light.

"Where are we going?"

He didn't answer. I guessed that we were heading out of town, towards the empty prairie, away from civilization. Ahead was Fort Cody and beyond that, open grassland. Once past the city limits I'd be back in the no-man's land that I'd watched slip by from the bus' window. Out there I'd be completely at the mercy of Arthur Burton's dead fish eyes and trembling hands. I felt a cold sickness and wanted to vomit. I prayed to God, to Grannie, to Asher Gideon, to Johnny Carson, to everything that had ever been good or holy in my life.

As we approached the next intersection he slowed the car to a crawl, waiting for the light to turn. Traffic built up behind us. His hand inched across the gearbox. "Sunnie . . ."

"NO!" I screamed, popping the door handle. He slammed on the brakes and grabbed my backpack but I wrestled it away as the door flew open.

I swung my legs free just as the car jerked forward. The movement forced the door back, gashing my forearm and tearing my sleeve. A car shot past me in the right lane, almost knocking me down. I stumbled to the curb as the light turned green. I turned to see Arthur stuck in a mass of honking traffic, his passenger door still ajar.

I turned and ran as fast as I could, parallel to Jeffers along residential streets and alleyways until I reached a Clark Oil station at the junction of B Street and Willow. I had run six or seven blocks and was so winded I could barely breathe. I kept thinking that Arthur was right behind me, ready to grab me again.

The ladies' restroom behind the gas station was unlocked. I rushed inside and bolted the door behind me, sinking to a heap on the urine-stained floor. My body shook as blood trickled down my arm. *Oh my God, oh my God,* I whispered. *I'm alive. I'm alive.* I got to my knees and vomited violently in the toilet bowl that had no seat. A fluorescent light buzzed over my head, flickering unevenly. In the corner, dead flies clung like seeds to a curled yellow insect strip. I held my face and cried. *Stupid,* I told myself. *I deserved it. I should have known he didn't like me for me. Nobody wants to be friends with a fat girl.*

I went to the sink and tried to wash up, dabbing my face with paper towels and rinsing vomit from my hair. Between the cut on my forehead, my black eye, and now a gash on my arm, I looked like I'd been in an explosion.

My duffel bag, I suddenly thought. *It's still in the car.* I started crying again. My clothes, my sit-upon, and my Chinese scroll were in that bag. All I had left was my backpack with underwear, my toothbrush, and some cash.

I sank to the floor again, crossing my legs and holding my face, avoiding the bruises and wounds.

Johnny, you better be worth it. I rocked back and forth. *Worth all this and more. Thrown out of fat camp, scaring my parents half to death, nearly getting killed by an ugly old sex maniac. Johnny, if you're not worth it I'll just have to kill myself.*

I suddenly remembered the scissors incident from sixth grade. All those warnings about running with scissors turned out to be true. I was working on a paper-maché relief map of South America in Mr. Gehring's class when I slipped, fell, and the scissors cut my wrist. No stitches, but it bled pretty badly. The school guidance counselor referred me to the "talking doctor," Dr. Schwartz. Dr. Schwartz asked me to draw my family and thought it "intriguing" that I put Grannie in the middle instead of Mom or Pop. Then I had to say what a bunch of inkblots looked like. One reminded me of Mount Everest and another resembled the profile of former President Ford.

I never got the test results, but I must have passed because I didn't have to take medication or see the talking doctor again. It made me think, though, something new about myself. It was just a simple little accident, and if it had happened to Ingrid or Debbie

Schneider or even to Emily, no one would have worried. But apparently there was something about me, Wilma "Sunnie" Sundstrom, that made people think I might want to die. I had potential someday to kill myself.

I rose from the wet restroom floor, braced my hands on the sink and stared at my red, swollen, tear-stained face. *What do other people know about me that I don't know myself?* I wondered. *What do they already know that I still have to learn?* In the back of my mind I heard the echo of Pierce's challenge—*"How many fat girls ever get famous? Ask yourself—how many?"*

CHAPTER THIRTEEN

I left the Clark Oil station later that night, after the storm that Arthur had promised passed through and turned the streets slick and shiny, washing away the hazy afternoon patina of dust, hay, and manure. Still shaking, I walked the quiet residential streets of North Platte back to the depot and hid in a toilet stall until 8 o'clock the next morning, when I heard the announcement that "Santa Fe Trail," the bus replacing the cursed "Continental Divide," had arrived and was boarding passengers to Denver and all points west.

I was terrified to leave the bathroom, afraid that Arthur Burton was waiting just outside. *That's stupid,* I thought, washing my face and brushing my hair. *He won't come back. For all he knows I called the police. I'm pretty sure what he did was a crime, or if not a crime, then at least something he could get in trouble for. He's probably halfway to Denver with my duffel bag still in his trunk.* I felt sick thinking about his greasy hands pawing through my pajamas, my good luck scroll, and my carefully-constructed sit-upon.

I entered the lounge. There were only about thirty listless passengers present, draped over plastic chairs or standing around chatting, drinking vending machine coffee. *Someone must have refilled the machine,* I thought. *Lots of stuff has happened since yesterday afternoon.*

I walked outside into the bright morning sunshine and stared up at the long, sleek "Santa Fe Trail" with its high tinted windshield and articulated wipers. Chrome glistened from the front grille and the giant headlights appeared freshly polished. This was the nicest Big Blue Bus I had seen so far, its blue-and-silver sides decorated with images of the snow-capped Rocky Mountains and a sexy Statue of Liberty.

Our new driver was a portly, round-faced woman named Betty in a train conductor's cap and waistcoat complete with watch fob and chain. "All aboard who's goin' aboard," she called out, motioning us onto the bus.

"Los Angeles, huh?" She looked at my ticket. "Pick up the 'Louisiana Purchase' at Denver." She squinted, lifting an eyebrow. "How old are you, darlin'?"

"Not as old as I feel," I replied, hiking up the bus' narrow metal steps.

I recognized about twenty passengers on board from our original sixty stranded in North Platte. I was grateful to get my own row of nicely-upholstered seats up front, just behind Betty. I settled in, pulled down the window shade, and did some quick figuring. It was just after eight o'clock on Wednesday morning. I had left Horicon early Monday, a full two days before. According to the map, I was still one thousand miles from Los Angeles. After a vending machine breakfast I had $188 left for the trip, and Arthur Burton had taken something precious from me that I couldn't yet count; something of value, but without a clear price.

The only person who ever told me I was pretty turned out to be a sex maniac. Maybe this is what grown-up life is going to be like. I no longer had my jacket to use as a pillow so I laid my aching head on my backpack and sobbed. My good eye was level with Hello Kitty's face and I couldn't believe she still looked happy.

Once the journey was underway again, I got bored watching the broad Nebraska prairie stretching mile after endless mile, broken only occasionally by cattle farms and fields of corn, sugar beets, and barley. I slept deeply for several hours, the first real sleep I'd had in days. The bus rocked me like a cradle while the sunlight warmed my scalp and skin.

It was lunchtime when we reached the outskirts of Denver. The mountains surprised me, coming up suddenly, rising out of the eastern Colorado flatlands and soaring to snow-capped peaks lined with dense forests of evergreen, aspen, and fir.

The Denver depot was designed like an old log cabin with colorful Indian blankets hung from the windows and an elderly man with tiny glasses manning the old-fashioned cash register. Behind him were tall wooden shelves stocked with peas, sardines, and other canned goods. I looked around the station, clasping my backpack for dear life. *Arthur could be here,* I thought. *He could be waiting.*

As I sat on the narrow wooden bench inside the depot and waited for the Louisiana Purchase, I noticed a pay phone. Beneath the phone hung the Metro Denver Yellow Pages. I considered phoning Delia Burton and telling her what her father had done. Was that really a photo of his daughter and granddaughter he had shown me, or did he invent the whole story in order to win my trust? *If Delia and Trina are real, I sure feel sorry for them, having Arthur in their family.*

Someone tapped my shoulder and I jumped. I looked up at a young woman with lank, dark-rooted hair bleached a flat yellow-blonde, and round, hollow, hazel-colored eyes. Along with a battered suitcase and knapsack she carried a dented guitar case covered with stickers.

"Hey, sorry," she said, holding up her hands. "Didn't mean to scare ya there."

"That's OK." My voice sounded small and shaky.

"You got a cigarette?" She dropped her filthy knapsack on the floor and it landed with a thud.

"I don't smoke."

"Probably smart." She nodded. "Mind if I sit?"

"Go ahead." I shifted down the bench. As she sat I noticed an odor of incense, cinnamon, and onions.

"So how'd you get that shiner?" She indicated my eye.

After my experience with Arthur I had no interest in making friends. "Got hit in the face with a canoe," I said evenly.

"Ouch."

"Uh huh."

"My name is J.J. Reynolds and I'm heading to California." She held out her hand, adorned with cheap rings on every finger. As we shook, her long hair shifted and I saw that she had a red tattoo on her neck that said, "Lovely." She had more tattoos on her wrists and her feet, visible in her worn leather sandals.

"I'm Sunnie," I said. "Sunnie Sundstrom."

"Where you going?"

"Los Angeles. To see my aunt and uncle."

"Wow." She nodded. "All by your little old lonesome?"

I sat up straight. "I'm seventeen," I said. "I can take care of myself."

"Like sugar you're seventeen." A sly smile tugged at her lips. "What's the real story? You running away?"

"Not exactly." I looked around the busy little depot and decided I had nothing to lose. "I got thrown out of summer camp and boarded the bus to California to see Johnny Carson."

"Excellent! J.J. mightily approves. Heck, that's something I would do. If I were. . . ?" She raised one ragged eyebrow.

"Thirteen," I admitted.

"No way!" Her hazel eyes glowed. "I had you pegged at fifteen, at least."

"What can I say?" I shrugged. "I'm big for my age."

J.J. was nineteen, already married and divorced, from Arkansas originally, but now what she called a "citizen of the cosmos." She was a folk singer-songwriter on her way to meet a music producer in L.A.

"My demo tape blew his mind," she confided. "He wired me money for the bus and said, 'Get out here as soon as possible.'"

J.J. and I took turns guarding each other's belongings while we used the bathroom. Then we split a tuna salad sandwich and a Coke, alternating swigs from the same cold glass bottle. After she drank, I could taste the residue of her cigarettes around the rim. I was surprised to find myself trusting J.J., especially after Arthur. *Maybe that's good,* I reasoned. *He didn't screw up my life completely.*

When our bus arrived and the driver didn't believe that I was seventeen, J.J. stepped in and rescued me, claiming that I was her little sister and that we were on our way to visit family.

"I don't know how to thank you," I said as we staked out our own row of seats near the front of the bus. "If he didn't believe me I would have been stuck. The police are probably looking for me by now."

"Hey, no prob." She bounced on the seat, gauging its resistance. "I just wanna hear the truth about that black eye, instead of that phony canoe story."

The miles passed so much faster with J.J. at my side. We talked, we giggled, we made up funny stories about the other passengers. When she dozed, off her head fell against my shoulder and I felt safe with her beside me, her breath like a warm puppy's against my arm.

I watched out the window as we traversed the awe-inspiring Rocky Mountains and descended into the layered sandstone canyons of Utah. I couldn't believe how much of America I had seen in just a few days. I felt as if I had peered into the country's vast desolate center and had experienced the loneliness of the open highway, where opportunity and anonymity meet. I had heard the thin, high-pitched whistle of an invisible, but not-too-distant, train and the rumbling roar of heavy wheels on concrete. I had seen endlessly open fields and sharp old farm tools rusting by the sides of country roads.

How could I go home and start the ninth grade like any other kid? I had been different for so long—forever, really; as big as an adult from the age of eight-and-a-half. I had always been thoughtful and different, worrying in a way other kids didn't worry; aware in ways other kids weren't aware.

"Wilma, are you mindful?" Grannie would ask, and then pay attention to the answer. "Wilma, are you mindful?" That was her signal that I was thinking too much and that it was OK to retreat to my real age, the age of my body, and be a child again, if only for a little while.

"Sunnie? Wake up."

Something tugged my sleeve and I opened my eyes. My face was flush against the window and I stared out at the dark barren desert, broken by dramatic sandstone arches with moonlight flooding through, casting cool patterns on the rugged brush below.

"Hey Sunnie," J.J. whispered. She shifted, brushing my arm.

I rolled over and faced her. "Is it almost time to stop?"

"No. Not for another hour." She frowned. "Sunnie, you were crying. In your sleep."

"No, I wasn't." I touched my cheek and felt the dampness. "Oh. I guess I was."

"Was it a bad dream?" J.J.'s soft, smoky voice was barely audible above the rumble of the engine and the cycling of wind through the bus' massive wheels.

I thought for a moment. Arthur Burton's cold, dead-fish eyes hovered somewhere above my consciousness, but worse than the memory of my encounter with Arthur was the thought of what my absence must be doing to Mom, Pop, Ingrid, and Max. During the day I could keep thoughts of them at bay by reminding myself that I would be home soon, just as soon as I saw Johnny, but at night their fears invaded my dreams.

"I miss my family," I whispered to J.J. "They must be really worried wondering where I am. But a part of me doesn't want to go home, because that's where Grannie died."

"Wow. Heavy," J.J. said. "But you're lucky to have people who care about you. My Dad's in prison and my Mom threw me out when I turned eighteen. Ain't nobody home worrying about me."

"J.J., I'm sorry," I said. "I didn't realize." I couldn't imagine anyone not wanting to be J.J.'s Mom.

Her voice got tough again and her eyes looked brave in the darkness. "It's OK. You and me, we're cool. 'Til we get to L.A., we'll be family to each other." She wrapped her arms around my shoulders and drew me to her chest. I inhaled the warm cinnamon scent of her Army jacket and drifted back to sleep.

166

It was just after noon of the following day when the bus finally dropped us off in downtown Los Angeles. "This is perfect," I told J.J. as we stepped into the Southern California smog. "Johnny tapes at five-thirty. People will be lining up even now."

"I still think it's a little psycho that you like that old guy, but hey, whatever floats your boat," she said with a smile, lighting up her cigarette and squinting into the sun.

I watched her luggage while J.J. went to the pay phone and called Terry, her music producer. She came back scowling, kicking the dirt with her heels.

"What's wrong?" I asked.

"His old lady is giving him grief. I gotta wait here half an hour."

"Did you *know* he had an old lady?" I asked carefully.

She rubbed her chin. "He said they were separated."

"Should I wait with you in case he doesn't come?"

She put on her brave face again. "And risk you not seeing lover boy Carson? You gotta be kidding. Here, let me hail you a cab."

As we stood on the curb peering into traffic she opened her knapsack and tried to give me some cash. "It's gonna cost you to get to Burbank."

I curled the money back into her fist as a cab screeched to a halt in front of us. "That's OK," I said. "I've reached my destination. Nothing else matters now."

J.J. opened the back door and I hopped in. "Be careful," she said. "Be good. Don't talk to strangers."

"OK, Mom," I joked, tossing my backpack on the seat.

"Seriously. It's a dangerous world out there."

"I know." I paused. "Will I ever see you again?"

"Sure! Look for me on the Billboard Top 40!"

I had tears in my eyes as the driver pulled away. "Where to?" His lilting accent made me think of pomegranates and rubber trees.

"Burbank. NBC Studios, please," I said decisively. "3000 Alameda Avenue."

The driver nodded as a cute red convertible sporting a long-haired blonde and a golden retriever cut us off, the girl turning to wave and give us the finger. *I can't believe it was so simple,* I thought. *Just jump in a cab and recite that magical address. I should have done this years ago.*

I sat back in my seat, which stank of French fries and sweaty shoes, and watched the palm trees fly by. The busy L.A. streets were full of Taco stands, tattoo parlors, and pink neon. We passed leather-clad men on motorcycles and girls in knotted halter-tops wearing tight short-shorts. Everybody was super-tan; not a single person looked Milwaukee-pale.

I wasn't sure exactly where I was, but I enjoyed the ride. The only map I'd ever seen of Los Angeles was the map of the stars' homes that I'd ordered from *Rona Barrett's Hollywood.* Glancing out the window, I was sure I recognized Charleton Heston's palatial estate and Susan Anton's hip Spanish ranch.

The NBC Studio in Burbank—beautiful downtown Burbank, which was actually an affluent suburb full of exclusive car dealerships, law offices, and classy apartments—surprised me by being on an ordinary street, across from a gas station, a Whattaburger, and a row of modest ranch houses. The studio was a sprawling, fortress-like complex constructed of sand-colored concrete with dark slits for windows.

People were already lining up along Alameda Avenue to see the show, but I had the driver drop me off around back, near Studio 4, where tickets were sold for the studio tour.

After a 45-minute wait I reached the front of the line and saw a big sign on the ticket window that proclaimed, "TONIGHT SHOW TAPING: No One Admitted Under the Age of 18." I tried to convince the ticket agent that I was eighteen, but she didn't believe me. *Where's J.J. when I need her?* I thought.

I walked around the large parking lot behind the studio complex where a series of triple-wide house trailers were lined up side by side. I guessed they used these trailers as offices, with the filming done inside the studio itself. *So where's Johnny's office?* I wondered. *Inside or out here?* Several security guards patrolled the parking lot beneath a large sign that read, "All Vehicles Are Subject to Search Upon Exit."

Right, I noted. *That leaves out jumping in Johnny's trunk and waiting for him to find me when he gets home. What the heck should I do?*

I paced a wide circle around the parking lot, and when I reached the far side of the building, I noticed a shaded, narrow alleyway behind Studio 11. A delivery van with its double doors wide open was parked in the alley. I didn't see anyone else around. *Stormy would do it,* I told myself, sidling up to the van. *She wouldn't be scared at all.*

A small door opened from the alleyway into the building. I tiptoed through, allowing a second for my eyes to adjust to the dark. I heard muffled voices to my right so I turned left, nearly knocking into another door. I slowly pushed the door open and saw a narrow steel staircase. *Good,* I thought. *If this takes me into the basement, I might find an elevator back up to the studio.*

Heart pounding, I descended to the dark, drafty bottom of the stairwell, which was laced with cobwebs and smelled of mice droppings and mold. *I bet Johnny's never even been down here,* I thought. *If he had been, he'd have made them clean it up.*

I pushed on the heavy door in front of me and was amazed when it opened into a busy, brightly-lit, white-walled commons area. I looked to my right. The NBC commissary! I could see Sally Struthers carrying a plastic tray and talking to Melissa Gilbert. Behind the commissary was the NBC gift shop. *Oh yes! I bet I can get another picture of Johnny there, along with a mug like the one he keeps on his desk, not to mention some of those famous two-headed pencils!!*

I was reaching to get my wallet when a hand grabbed my shoulder. I nearly jumped out of my skin as I turned to face two security guards. "And just where are you going, young lady?" the younger man asked.

CHAPTER FOURTEEN

Dwayne and Mel, the guards who stopped me, looked like UPS guys in their manila-brown uniforms with matching buttons and tan epaulets. They carried no weapons, only walkie-talkies and big jangly keys.

"Where are you going, young lady?" Dwayne's big hand was clamped to my shoulder. He was about thirty, tall and skinny with thinning dust-blonde hair and a scraggly goatee.

"I'm sorry," I said, smiling through my fear. "I must have taken a wrong turn."

"A likely story." Mel hiked up his belt. About fifty, Mel had a round belly, bald head, and rosy cheeks. "This is a restricted area," he said. "Passes only."

"Sorry. I'll just be on my way . . ." I tried to break away.

"Not so fast," Dwayne warned. "You've breached a restricted area. We gotta write up a report."

"But this is all a big mistake," I insisted as they dragged me down a narrow corridor, Dwayne holding my left shoulder and Mel holding my right. "I got separated from my family. If you just let me go . . ."

Somewhere deep in the bowels of the studio complex we reached a small, stuffy room the size of a supply closet and filled with old *Tonight Show* props including several of the "We'll Be Right Back" placards, along with Art Fern's pointer, an old Carnac cape, and the swinging vine from Johnny's Tarzan sketch with Betty White. *How bizarre,* I thought. *I've seen all this stuff on TV, and now I'm seeing it for real.*

Instead of windows the room had several closed circuit black-and-white TVs. One screen showed the "Guest Services" entrance outside Studio 4, where I'd spoken to the ticket agent. A second camera revealed the growing line of people waiting along Alameda Avenue. A third camera was focused on the parking lot where Johnny's white Corvette was parked in the first space, beside a door that said "Artists' Entrance." *Johnny's car!* My heart leaped. *He's really here!*

"Sit down." Dwayne pointed to a folding chair. On a table sat a crushed bakery box and beneath the table a wire trash can was stuffed with candy wrappers, napkins, and tabloid magazines. As I sat, the chair squeaked. Mel closed the door.

"Something to drink? A pop?" Dwayne's voice was light and friendly.

I get it—good cop, bad cop. I remembered recent episodes of *Switch* and *Hawaii Five-O. Dwayne's being nice so Mel can go in for the kill.*

Mel dropped into the chair across from me, removed his cap, and pushed back his squiggly hair. "We're fresh outta doughnuts." He patted the bakery box. "We could get you something from the commissary."

Hmmm. Maybe I've got the routine wrong. "That's OK," I replied. "I'm not hungry."

Mel took a notebook and pen from his uniform pocket. "So you wandered away from the tour?" he asked.

I looked at Mel across from me and Dwayne standing, arms folded, behind him. *I'll never get away with this,* I realized. *They won't let me go until I'm reunited with my "family."*

In *Girl on the Lam* Stormy talks her way into Sing-Sing prison and finds the man who embezzled her inheritance. *Please Stormy, give me strength . . .* I put my elbows on the table. "Mel. Dwayne. May I use your first names?"

Mel and Dwayne looked surprised but they nodded. "Go ahead."

171

"You seem to be reasonable men." I glanced from one to the other. "Men I can trust with my true story."

Their eyes grew wide with interest.

"My name is Wilma Sundstrom, but you can call me Sunnie. I'm thirteen and from Milwaukee. I was at a summer weight loss camp where I fell in love, stole a canoe, almost killed my friend Cherise, and got put on a bus back home. But instead I came here to Los Angeles."

Just for a moment I caught it; a look of admiration in both men's eyes. "Your parents must be worried sick." Mel scratched his head. "I've got a teenage daughter, and I know I'd be."

"Why California?" Dwayne asked.

"Because of Mr. Carson," I answered proudly. "I've been a fan since second grade."

Mel frowned, but still managed to look fatherly. "Aren't you kind of young for Mr. Carson?"

I felt myself blush. "It's not like *that*," I explained. "Johnny lets me dream."

"About what?" Dwayne asked.

"About possibilities. Like getting on a bus and traveling across the country."

Mel nodded. "I gotta give you credit, kid. You've got spunk."

"And ball . . . I mean courage," Dwayne added quickly. "It takes courage to do that."

"So can I stay and watch the show?" I asked. "The ticket agent said I had to be eighteen."

Mel looked at Dwayne. "Call Shirley and see what you can do."

Dwayne left and Mel and I talked for a while. I learned all about his wife, Madge, his sixteen-year-old daughter, Violet, and his ten-year-old son, Clark, who was a crazy Evil Knievel fan. "The boy wants to jump motorcycles. Jeez-us! You kids today, I can't keep up."

"We're a new generation, Mel," I explained patiently, leaning back in my seat. "It's not the good old days anymore." While we talked, I kept my eye on the closed-circuit cameras, hoping for a brief, black-and-white glimpse of Johnny, who was somewhere, right now, inside this very building.

Dwayne returned and closed the door behind him, brushing dust from his hands. "It's all arranged," he said, smiling. "Mr. Carson will see you now."

"See me?" I felt like I was tumbling downhill.

"You betcha." Dwayne slipped his hands in his pockets and rocked back on his heels. "He's got a few minutes before the writer's meeting."

"But I don't want to *see* him." I struggled to speak. "I only want to watch the show and maybe get an autographed photo."

"Oh." Dwayne's long face fell. "You don't want to meet him?"

"No." I shook my head vehemently. "Absolutely not."

Of course I wanted to meet Johnny, more than anything else in the whole entire world. I had dreamed of this moment since I was eight. But in my dream, it was different. In the dream I was in my mid-twenties, tall and sophisticated and beautiful and thin, most importantly thin; not just average, but size-four thin with gorgeous clothes and stunning long blonde hair flipped back like Farah Fawcett's. In the dream I was a talented and successful writer-director who could sit beside Johnny and talk with authority and humor about my life and my career, and I would deserve Doc Severinsen's musical introduction; I would have earned the audience's respectful applause.

I'm still plain old Sunnie, and Sunnie can't meet Johnny Carson, I thought. *I'm thirteen and I'm fat and pale and dirty, with a black eye and a gashed arm. I'm not a screenwriter or a director, I'm not returning from Rio or Cannes or Dakar and whatever else I am, I am most definitely not a star.*

"Thanks," I told Dwayne. "But I don't want to bother Mr. Carson."

"Okey-dokey." Dwayne scratched his scraggly chin. "Let's see if we can get you that photo."

Mel shook my hand as I walked out. "Pleasure to meet you, Sunnie," he said. "Good luck on your trip back home."

173

"Pleasure to meet you too, Mel," I replied. "Take care of that son of yours."

Our steps were brisk and steady, tapping the concrete floor as Dwayne led me to a service elevator. *I just turned down the chance to meet Johnny,* I thought. *The* real *Johnny Carson.* I blinked hard. My stomach sank and for one horrible moment I saw the taillights of Horace Hellesen's racing motor car as he drove away, leaving Grannie's sister Wilma dying in the street.

"Don't let anything derail your dreams," Grannie had warned me, and when she said "anything," she meant anything; nothing could stand in my way. Even though she never admitted it, I knew that Grannie regretted never having had the chance to dance for Busby Berkeley. I pictured Grannie rubbing her ankle, touching the bone broken when she fell milking the cow. "It still aches sometimes," she acknowledged, "just a little bit at the end of the day."

I also thought about Mom, my chronically-disappointed Mom, back when she was still in high school, weighing only one hundred-eight pounds, dating the JV quarterback, and showing off her closet full of Pendleton skirts and all of her blouses with Peter Pan collars. She had been a girl with ambitions then; a girl who was going places, until her father died, she caught mono, and she gained a lot of weight. It was all downhill from there. It was clear that if I waited until everything in my life was perfect, I would never, ever meet Johnny Carson; and, like my Mom and my grandmother, I would spend the rest of my life regretting the opportunity I had missed.

I might always be fat, I realized. *I might never direct feature films. The Romulans might make fun of me forever. But I know what's here in front of me; what's available to me right now.*

I tugged on Dwayne's manila-brown sleeve just as the elevator slid open. "Dwayne?" My voice sounded small but steady. "I *do* want to meet Mr. Carson. I only said 'no' because you caught me off-guard."

Dwayne smiled. "Terrific." He ushered me into the elevator, then grabbed his walkie-talkie and clicked it near his mouth.

174

"Yeah, Erin," he said. "Let Shirley know I'm bringing the young-ster to meet Mr. Carson. Over."

We took the elevator up to the ground floor and past the wide double-doors to Studio One, where Doc and the band were warming up for the show. My heart was pounding and my stomach in knots. *Help me, Grannie,* I prayed. *I'm so nervous. What should I do?*

"Stand up straight, Wilma." Rocking in her wooden chair, Grannie folds her hands in her lap. "Shoulders back. Head high. There's nothing wrong with being tall."

I stare at my feet.

"And don't squint," she insists. "It makes your eyes look miserly."

"But what should I say?"

Grannie taps her bottom lip, considering. "Speak freely, but say nothing to embarrass the family. Your grandfather's brother Per had the honor of meeting Franklin Roosevelt himself and doesn't it figure, in his haste to shake the president's hand, he spilled pea soup all over the president's shoes."

"But Grannie, I'm scared."

She looks surprised. "You? Scared of meeting Johnny Carson?"

"Not scared of meeting him," I explain. "Scared of it ending. I'm only thirteen. What if after meeting Johnny there's nowhere to go but down? What if I realize in that moment that my life will never again be quite so sweet?"

"Interesting thought." She nods, rocking faster. "I can't answer that. But I know that if I'd been introduced to Mr. Busby Berkeley back in 1930, even if he hadn't liked my dancing, there would have been joy in that memory for the rest of my life. Joy, Wilma, joy. And joy is not a word I use often." Her slippered foot taps the floor.

"Never," I think, looking up. "In my whole life, Grannie, I never once heard you use the word 'joy.'"

Johnny's office was situated on a landing above and just behind Studio One, nestled within the heavy ropes and electrical wiring of the back-stage rigging. The office door was just plain wood with a little sign that said "Johnny Carson" at eye-level.

Please God, let me be as charming as Lola Falana, as smooth as Sammy Davis Jr., as adorable as Tatum O'Neal, I prayed under my breath.

Dwayne looked down, winked, then knocked.

"Come in," a voice responded.

Dwayne opened the door and there he was, Mr. John William Carson, all five-feet-ten-inches of him, standing at his desk with one hand on his hip, the other tapping a lit cigarette. He was squinting, skimming a sheaf of papers I could only guess made up the night's monologue.

"Mr. Carson, this young fan wants to say hello." Dwayne suddenly sounded nervous, as if he too were awed by Johnny's presence.

I scanned the office, noticing the coffee table with Johnny's drumsticks, several legal pads, and a stack of newspapers. On the wall behind his desk were framed magazine covers and photos of Johnny with favorite guests, mostly from the 1960s and early '70s.

"Yes Sir, Sunnie comes all the way from Minnesota," Dwayne continued. I was too nervous to explain that I actually came from Wisconsin; Johnny probably wouldn't care anyway.

"Is that right?" Johnny didn't look up as he took a deep drag from his cigarette. He was casually dressed in a white, short-sleeve polo shirt and tight blue jeans. He looked thinner than on TV, narrow through the hips and shoulders, with his distinctive puffed-up chest. He looked older too, with crinkly lines around his eyes and a patch of sunburn bleeding into his silvery hair. Still, rational went out the window as I realized that I was standing in front of the most handsome man in the world.

Dwayne nudged me and I stepped forward. "Mr. Carson," I said. "It's a pleasure to meet you."

Johnny glanced up and, seeing my age, stubbed out his cigarette. "Nice to meet you too." His blue eyes twinkled.

"This really is an honor," I continued. "I've admired your work for quite some time." *I admired his work! Yes! I remembered!*

"Quite some time?" He chuckled. "And how old are you now?"

I stepped closer to his desk. "Old enough to know that at twelve, you picked up *Hoffman's Book of Magic* and were hooked for life," I said. "I know that you first heard about Pearl Harbor while working as an usher at the Granada Theater in Norfolk, and that your first TV show was called *Carson's Cellar* on KNXT-TV in Los Angeles in 1951."

As the facts poured out I offered a quick prayer of thanksgiving to Mr. Matusak for assigning that seventh-grade social studies report. "In 1957, ABC hired you to host the game show, *Who Do You Trust?* The rest, as they say, is history."

Johnny looked surprised and delighted. Erin, the young NBC page Dwayne had called on his walkie-talkie, appeared at the office door holding an old-fashioned camera with a big flashbulb on top. "Mr. Carson, Sir," she asked timidly. "Can we get a photo?"

"Sure thing." Johnny strode to my side, placed his arm around my shoulder, and gave me a squeeze. "Well, Sunnie," he whispered, "if I ever need an official biographer, I'll know just who to call."

I nodded and my chin was only an inch below his. If we faced inward we'd be nose to nose. He drew me closer as the camera flashed and something fragile came alive inside me, dancing with humanity. For the first time ever I realized that Johnny Carson, in all his greatness, was still just a man of ribs and blood and muscle. Every night he spoke to millions and those same millions listened, but even so his heart, like everyone else's, was just an ordinary bird chirping in a cage of bone.

"Smile!" Erin insisted, snapping the camera again. "Come on, Sunnie, show us those thousand-watts!" I smiled my widest smile. I was standing beside Johnny Carson. I didn't care who thought my face looked chubby, as long as they realized that it was me.

A moment later it was over as Johnny dropped his arm. "So long, Sunnie," he said, stepping back behind his desk and gazing down on the monologue once more. "Hope you enjoy the show."

"Thank you, Mr. Carson. I know I will."

Erin and Dwayne escorted me into the hallway, each with a hand on my back. After a few paces I stopped, turned, and went back to Johnny's office.

"Sunnie, don't!" Erin whispered, hand to her mouth.

It was too late. There was something more I had to do. I peered around the open door and cleared my throat. "Mr. Carson?"

Sitting now, Johnny had a fresh cigarette and was trying, hands cupping the tip, to light it. He drew in a breath and the cigarette glowed. "Yes?" As he squinted I thought I caught a momentary flash of irritation.

"I want you to know that I'll be back," I said. "I mean I'll be on your show someday. As a guest."

He drew in a lungful of smoke and released it. "Is that right?" His face was neutral now, not believing me but not disbelieving me; just open; open to possibility.

"Yes. I'm going to write and direct feature films. The first is called *Girl on the Lam*, starring Kristy McNichol and Robby Benson."

His face broke into a bashful smile. "I look forward to it, Sunnie. Best of luck." He held up his hand, palm out, and gave me a brief half-wave. I understood that he was dismissing me, sending me back to the everyday world. My private audience with the king had ended, but I would go forth in confidence, knowing that his blessing was on my head, marking me out as something special: forever and ever the "real" Sunnie Sundstrom.

"What did he say?" Erin asked anxiously as I returned to her side.

"Never mind," I answered. "Just something between friends."

After my meeting with Johnny, Erin explained that the police had been called and so had my parents, who would be leaving the next morning to come and pick me up. A juvenile advocate from the Child Welfare Office was coming to supervise me until my parents arrived, but in the meantime I would be allowed to stay and watch the taping of the show.

"Excellent!" I said. "Who are Johnny's scheduled guests?" I had waited my whole life to ask that question.

Erin glanced at her clipboard and frowned. "Lorne Greene just canceled. Trouble on the set of *Battlestar Gallactica*. Tony Randall is filling in, along with Debby Boone and Joan Embery with marsupials from the San Diego Zoo."

"That's great!" I hoped some creature might pee on Johnny's head, and that that particular clip would be shown every year on *The Tonight Show Anniversary Special*. I could watch it with my children and my grandchildren and tell them that I was there that night.

I looked down at my dirty jeans and the torn sleeve of my T-shirt. I could only imagine how much worse my face must have appeared with my black eye and gashed forehead.

"I can't sit in *The Tonight Show* audience looking like this," I told Erin. "Is there any way I can wash up before the show?"

Erin smiled. "I think I know a couple of ladies who can help you." She took my hand and escorted me down the narrow back hallways to Hair and Make-up, where she introduced me to Carmen and Marlene, the NBC beauticians. Carmen washed, cut, and styled my hair, feathering it in Farah Fawcett layers around my face, while Marlene did my lips with liner and gloss and covered my black eye with concealer. After hair and make-up, Carmen went to wardrobe and returned with a long blue dress with a wide belt, a V-neck, and a pointy collar.

"It's so pretty." I stroked the smooth polyester sheath.

"It was left behind by . . . what's her name?" Carmen frowned. "That girl from *The Facts of Life*."

"Mindy Cohn?" I asked. "Natalie. The heavy-set girl."

"No, not her." Carmen tapped her foot impatiently. "The blonde."

"Blair?" My voice caught. "Lisa Welchel?"

Carmen's dark eyes glowed. "That's her name!" She snapped her fingers. "Nice girl. Used to be on *The Mickey Mouse Club*."

"Oh yeah," Marlene chimed in. "She left the dress behind last time she visited."

"It won't fit." I envisioned Lisa Welchel's curvaceous figure.

"I don't know." Carmen pulled out the tag. "Size fourteen?"

"Maybe." I stripped off my clothes. Marlene pulled the dress over my head and Carmen adjusted it. The belt didn't quite reach, so Carmen poked another hole with a hatpin and buckled it snugly around my waist.

"It fits!" I shrieked. "I'm wearing Lisa Welchel's dress!" I twirled, letting the fabric dance. I wondered if the dress had been washed since Lisa wore it, but decided it didn't matter. The dress was mine, at least until after the show.

When Carmen and Marlene had finished my transformation, Erin returned and escorted me back to the studio through hallways decorated with large framed stills from recent Bob Hope Specials.

Studio One as we entered was frantic with activity. Stage crew, sound technicians, and publicity personnel bustled around the high-ceilinged auditorium. The studio was smaller than it seemed on TV. The seats were divided into three sections and held only about five hundred people. The actual set itself was tiny, maybe thirty-five feet by thirty-five feet, with five big TV monitors hanging from the rafters so that everyone in back could see the show.

Erin led me to the front row, a few feet from where Johnny would be standing. I was close enough to see the stitching in the multi-colored curtain, and close enough to see Johnny's stage mark, a white star embedded in the shiny blue floor.

Erin knelt before me and the klieg lights caught sparks off her braces. "Sunnie, don't make any noise or you'll be escorted out by security," she warned.

"Can I say, 'How hot was it?' if Johnny asks?"

"No!" She frowned. "You don't see it on TV, but those people have to leave."

"Thanks. I'll behave." I smoothed the pleats of Lisa Welchel's dress. "I'm not even supposed to be here. I won't call attention to myself."

The double doors at the back of the studio opened and numerous NBC pages, dressed just like Erin in blue slacks, white shirts, and blue blazers, led the rest of the audience members to their seats. A big clock on the wall read 11:15, even though it was really only a quarter after five. *I get it—they set the clock to "show time" to put everybody in that late-night mood.*

While the audience settled in, murmuring "wow," and "it looks bigger on TV," Doc Severinsen took his place at the bandstand. *Oh my Gosh, that's really Doc!* I thought. *And he really does dress funny!* A stagehand lined up Johnny's cue cards while the brass section played a bluesy tune and the drummer practiced his rim shots.

"Come on," I whispered, looking up at the clock. It now said 11:22. "I want to see Johnny. We met only two hours ago, but it seems like forever."

Suddenly the striped curtain shimmered and split down the middle. Could it be Johnny? No, it was only the producer, Freddie DeCordova, whom I'd often glimpsed on TV. He looked exactly the same in person, handsome in a grandfatherly way, wearing dark, large-framed glasses and a beige cardigan golf sweater. After dropping a manila folder on Johnny's desk, he picked up a microphone and took center stage.

"Good evening, ladies and gentlemen, and welcome to *The Tonight Show*," he began in a warm, friendly voice, straightening the microphone's long cord behind him. "Before our show tonight gets underway, let's get better acquainted. First, say hello to the person directly behind you."

I turned in my seat and greeted Bob and Viola, an older couple from Forth Worth, wearing matching red sweaters and baseball caps with their tour group's name. After the introductions, Freddie joked about Doc and the band. Then Ed McMahon came out and told a few jokes while Freddie moved to a swivel chair at the end of the stage, about twelve feet from Johnny's desk and directly in his sightline.

As Ed finishes his jokes I look up at the clock. 11:29. A hush falls over the crowd. My heart starts to pound. I can't see him, but I know he's there, only a few feet away from me. Johnny is standing behind the multi-colored curtain, in the cold darkness, totally alone. This terrifying golden moment belongs only to him. I have stood beside this man. In my mind, I stand beside him again. "It's OK, Johnny," I say, grasping his hand. "Don't be nervous. You've done this a million times before."

Freddie cues Doc and Doc cues the band. They begin the familiar Tonight Show *theme. I cross my fingers and whisper, "Do Aunt Blabby. Do Carnac. At least do 'Stump the Band.' Yes, do 'Stump the Band' and call on me." I've got a song from fat camp all ready in my head, the regular words altered to poke fun at Randall-Anne. Or maybe it will be "Edge of Wetness." Yes. "Let the camera zoom in on my face and I promise I'll have a funny expression. Please God, let the Romulans and their parents be watching tonight, along with everyone else in the world who's ever made fun of me . . ."*

CHAPTER FIFTEEN

The show went by so quickly—one minute Tony Randall was trading quips with Johnny and then, after a brief word from the sponsors, Joan Embery came out with her baby marsupials, who were suitably cute but failed to pee on Johnny's head. The animals had barely vacated the stage when Debby Boone arrived in pink taffeta, singing with a chorus of deaf children whose dancing hands brought the music to life before our very eyes.

Johnny thanked his guests and the audience, then announced that next week's guest host would be Bert Convy. *See, I told myself. I stole the canoe at just the right moment. A week later would have been too late.*

Doc and the band struck up the theme song over what I knew would be the closing credits, scrolling down the TV screens at home. As the lights came up, Tony Randall rose from the couch and unclipped his microphone. Johnny shook Tony's hand and whispered something in his ear.

"Chasen's." I nodded to Bob and Viola behind me. "I bet Tony and Johnny are having dinner tonight with Bombastic Buskin."

Meanwhile, the stagehands got busy mopping the floor, struggling to remove the odor of excitable platypus and baby kangaroo that wafted through the studio.

I stood up and smoothed the powder-blue dress. Erin rushed over, clipboard in hand.

"What's wrong?" I asked.

"Nothing. I've just been told to keep an eye on you. Rumor has it you're rather feisty." She gave a pantomime wink and nudged me with her elbow. I realized that I liked having total strangers find me feisty.

"Where's my juvenile advocate?" I asked, peering around Erin's shoulder.

"Seems they're understaffed," she explained. "They can't send someone until tomorrow." Erin handed me a plastic bag.

"What's this?"

"Your clothes," she replied. "Marlene and Carmen said to keep the dress."

"Excellent! I'll never look at *The Facts of Life* the same again." I pulled out my T-shirt and jeans. They had been washed and mended, even the sleeve torn by Arthur's rental car door.

"Let's go." Erin turned me towards the studio doors. "Your car is waiting."

"My car? But I don't drive," I protested.

"No, silly." She giggled. "Your *car*. Your limousine? To take you to your hotel."

"My hotel?"

"Yes. Mr. Carson has arranged for you to stay at the Beverly Hills Hotel until this whole thing gets cleared up."

The Beverly Hills Hotel! I might see Kristy McNichol in the lobby, or find a producer for Girl on the Lam! The Beverly Hills Hotel was where, in 1972, Johnny celebrated *The Tonight Show*'s tenth anniversary and announced that he had married his third wife, Joanna, that same afternoon.

"That's just like Johnny," I told Erin confidently, "choosing a place that will be special in *both* of our lives."

As Erin led me down the hall we passed Ed McMahon. He was still dressed for the show, but he had a towel around his neck and a drink in his hand. He waved jauntily, offering a hearty "Hi-Oh."

"Oh my God!" I squeezed Erin's arm. "Did you see that? Ed just waved!"

"Sunnie," she said patiently, "he waves at *everybody*."

"Yes, but this time, he waved at me!" I had barely recovered from that encounter when Freddie DeCordova motored past in his little golf cart, tooted the horn twice, and then raised a hand in greeting.

I'm part of The Tonight Show *family now,* I thought. *Johnny initiated me into the club.*

As Erin and I stepped out onto Alameda Avenue, the sunlight temporarily blinded me.

"You forget what time it is in there," Erin said, nodding back at the building.

"That's for sure." According to the studio clock, *The Tonight Show* taping had ended at 1 A.M., but in fact it was still only 7:20 P.M. and the sun was hanging heavily, low in the sky, skirting the Hollywood Hills.

I shielded my eyes as a limousine pulled forward, looking like a big black submarine on wheels. The driver parked and got out, coming around to the door. "Guillaume, this is Sunnie Sundstrom," Erin said. "Sunnie, Guillaume will be your driver."

"A pleasure to meet you, Madame," Guillaume said with a tight little bow. He was a tall, elderly, white-haired man in a tuxedo and tails. He whisked open the back door and I ducked into the vehicle.

"Oh my gosh!" I smoothed the leather seats and settled in with Hello Kitty. The limo had a fully stocked wet bar complete with champagne, plastic glasses, and a bucket of ice. There was even a mini-fridge and a small-screen TV in the padded console in front of me. "If only Emily and Jerry could see me now," I whispered. "They totally wouldn't believe you could have a refrigerator inside of a car."

I flipped up the armrest at my side and found a handset with several multi-colored buttons. I pressed all the buttons at once. As we sped off into traffic, I realized that I could raise and lower the tinted glass screen that separated me from Guillaume. I raised and lowered the screen several times, enjoying its futuristic sound effect, until Guillaume glanced back and asked, "Madame, could you please refrain from doing that? It is rather a distraction."

"Sorry," I mumbled, leaning back in my seat.

Traffic was still heavy as we slowly worked our way out of beautiful downtown Burbank and towards Beverly Hills, past palm trees and nightclubs and brightly-colored Mexican murals, straight onto Sunset Boulevard. Neon and billboards gave way to broad grassy boulevards, elegantly manicured lawns, and million-dollar mansions. We passed one mansion with a huge wrought iron gate that I could've sworn, based on my old map of the stars' homes, belonged either to Paul Anka or Engelbert Humperdinck.

At last we turned into a tree-lined drive with a green sign at the entrance, announcing "The Beverly Hills Hotel." Palm trees rose high above us in a single-file line, swaying in steady unison, leading towards the acres of lush tropical gardens surrounding the massive pink and green palace.

Guillaume parked in the circular drive, expertly nestling the limo between a Rolls Royce and a Bentley. He helped me out of the limo and together we followed the red carpet—a real red carpet!—up the broad steps to the front entrance.

We entered the lush, floral-themed lobby with Guillaume carrying my backpack, holding it slightly out to his side to avoid dusty contact with his immaculate self.

A dizzy whirl of sophisticated men and beautiful women were flirting shamelessly or making deals in the Sunset Lounge just off the lobby, drinking cocktails while dazzling in diamonds, sundresses, and solid gold watches. I'd never seen so much visible skin, with everyone a color somewhere between French Toast and cocoa.

We reached the front desk and Guillaume introduced me. "Miss Wilma Sundstrom," he said. "A guest of Mr. Carson's."

The receptionist looked skeptical, but searched the register for my name, finally nodding. "Here it is." She looked down at me. "Are you staying alone, Miss Sundstrom?"

"Yep." I winked. "Unless I get lucky." I wasn't sure what that meant, but I now had my feisty reputation to maintain.

"Miss Sundstrom is a minor child. A juvenile advocate will arrive to supervise her later this evening," Guillaume said patiently. "I suggest you keep an eye on her until that time."

As Guillaume bade me good-bye I slipped him a fifty-dollar tip. "So much, Madame?" he asked, surprised.

"Of course," I answered. "My journey is over. What do I need money for now?"

I took the elevator up to the fourteenth floor and opened the door to my suite. "Oh my God!" I shrieked, dropping my backpack. "This is bigger than the whole downstairs of Emily's house!"

The rooms—a bedroom, a sitting room, and an enormous bath with Jacuzzi and shower—were all done up in the hotel's signature color scheme of forest green, pale pink, and cream. The bedroom featured a king-sized canopy bed with real silk sheets, pale yellow bolster pillows, and a cream-yellow silk sash draped from the top of the canopy down to the floor, spreading out in waves as sleek as rippled milk. The sitting room had an oriental tapestry, a long green leather sofa, a writing desk with a high-backed wooden chair, a folder of stationery, and my own private telephone. Fresh-cut flowers decorated the glass coffee table, lilies with long white petals and curved green leaves.

The bathroom was a wonder, full of deep emerald-green marble surfaces, gold fixtures, and piles of fluffy white towels so thick and dense they barely stayed folded, springing open at a finger's touch. I hadn't been clean, really clean, for over a month, since before fat camp started, so I opened everything I could find: the complimentary soaps, the little bottles of shampoo, conditioner, and hand lotion, along with, for good measure, the shoe shine strap, the shower cap, and the miniature sewing kit.

I poured the entire bottle of shampoo into the Jacuzzi and watched the tower of bubbles rise higher and higher, overflowing onto the marble floor. I turned the water off, but left the jets running as I undressed and carefully hung Lisa Welchel's dress on the hook behind the door.

Before getting in I looked at myself, really looked at myself, in the full-length mirror beside the tub. Marlene's make-up job had held up well, giving my skin a smooth, even, pinkish glow. But there were dark circles from a week with little sleep, and my black eye was reemerging from beneath the heavy concealer.

"I'm not beautiful," I whispered to the mirror, stroking my face. "I'm not pretty. Only someone with weak eyes and a generous heart would dare to call me 'cute.'" Even after this amazing journey I was still Sunnie Sundstrom from Mrs. Tooley's fourth-hour social studies class, with the same stubby nose, determined little chin, moon-shaped face, and size-nine, C-width feet.

I stepped back three paces and watched my body in the mirror, considering myself from head to toe beneath the harsh bathroom lights. I was covered with bruises that could be read almost as a map to events of the previous weeks. I had bruises on my thighs, back, and butt; hand-shaped, thumb-shaped, button-shaped, crowded-bus-seat-shaped. Some were fresh blue-red, some had turned eggplant purple, while still others, nearly healed, were close to the surface and as yellow as straw.

I was bruised, I was lumpy, and without a doubt, I was fat. I pinched the excess flesh of my upper arm, then shook my leg and watched my thigh quiver until it stilled. I sat down on the closed toilet seat and watched my stomach fold into several pudgy rolls. The Summer Slim-Down Retreat had been a failure, just like Pierce had predicted. Even with seven pounds gone, I still weighed about the same as before Grannie died.

I was about to cry when a new thought popped into my head. "OK, so I'm fat," I said. "But look at what I've accomplished: I won a truckload of jam; fell in love with Asher Gideon, and stole a canoe to prove it; traveled across the country by bus; escaped the disgusting clutches of Arthur Burton, and met Johnny Carson himself. If I did all that while fat, why bother being skinny? How could being skinny be better than this?"

I watched in the mirror as a slow smile spread across my face. "This is Sunnie," I said decisively. "Every inch of her. This is who she is."

I stepped into the Jacuzzi, plunged my head under the steady water jets, and rubbed my face clean, gingerly avoiding my tender black eye. When I surfaced again I made a huge hat of shampoo bubbles, twirling it higher and higher like a pointed turban atop my head. "This is Sunnie," I insisted, watching myself laugh in the mirror. "This is who she is. The *real* Sunnie Sundstrom."

After my bath I wrapped my hair in a towel and put on one of the robes that said "Beverly Hills Hotel" on the pocket, then curled up in the king-sized bed. After reading through the room service menu I called and ordered everything that appealed to me: three appetizers, two bowls of soup, several entrées, four desserts, and two extra-large Cokes. I had just sat back to watch TV when an awful thought occurred to me: *When Johnny gets the room service bill, he'll think I'm fat* and *greedy. That could ruin our whole relationship.*

I called room service again and asked for a more reasonable, and respectable, order of pâté de fois gras on toast points, a Caesar salad, a filet mignon (medium rare), and a creme brulée for dessert. I had no idea what any of these items were, and I especially wondered how toast could be pointed, but I was ready for an adventure. *Just think, one week ago, I was eating gruel. Now I'm eating stuff I can't even pronounce.*

It wasn't yet nine o'clock and I could barely keep my eyes open. But I had to stay up for *The Tonight Show*, just to check if the camera, panning, had caught a glimpse of me with my new haircut and my Lisa Welchel dress.

I went to the TV and flicked through the channels. There was a Heckel and Jekyll cartoon, *The Rockford Files*, *Hawaii Five-O*, and *The Harvey Korman Show*. I moved higher on the dial to the UHF channels where an old black-and-white movie caught my eye. The screen was dark at first with only a woman's face in the spotlight, singing "The Lullaby of Broadway" as the camera moved in closer.

Suddenly there was a knock at the door. "Supper!" I said with delight. I tightened the belt on my robe and hurried to the door.

It wasn't room service at all but a teenage bellboy with a rash of pimples and an organ grinder's cap. "Miss Sundstrom?" he asked.

"That's me."

"This just arrived for you at the front desk." He handed me a brown 9" x 12" envelope. My name was scribbled on it in ball-point pen and beneath that someone had printed, more neatly, "DO NOT BEND."

"Thank you," I said, taking the envelope and closing the door. I returned to the bed and sat down, cross-legged.

"What the heck?" I tore open the gummy seal, reached inside, and pulled out something flat and shiny. As it caught the light, I squealed.

"OH MY GOD!!" It was an 8" X 10" color photo of me and Johnny Carson! The picture Erin had taken in Johnny's office earlier that afternoon! Every detail in the photo was as clear as day: Johnny's drumsticks, the newspapers and legal pads, the monologue spread across his desk, the cigarette in the ashtray. Johnny's arm was around my shoulder and both of us were smiling. At the bottom of the photo Johnny had written with a red marker, "To my friend, Sunnie. Best of luck. Love, Johnny Carson."

I pressed the photo to my heart, not daring to cry for fear of smearing the ink. I was Johnny Carson's friend. He even said so himself. Pride swelled inside me, yet I felt humbled, touched. For the few seconds that Johnny spent signing this photo, our lives overlapped and our souls were as one. I was real to Johnny, for at least part of an afternoon. Even if he forgot all about me by next week, I had reached out and touched something bigger than myself. My life would always count for something from now on. I possessed something that no one in the world, not the Romulans, not Randall-Anne, not even Arthur Burton, could ever take away from me. I had worried about that moment in Johnny's office being over, fearing that life would never again be as sweet. But now I realized that the moment's ending only meant that I needed to find some new and bigger dreams.

I looked up at the TV as the "Lullaby of Broadway" continued. The woman's face in the spotlight had been replaced by a group of handsome men in tuxedos and beautiful women in crop tops and shorts tap dancing on a series of soaring metal risers. One by one the girls fell backward into the mens' arms, revealing their long, shapely legs. Dick Powell, handsome and suave, emerged singing from the crowd and took the arm of little Ruby Keeler. I suddenly knew why the movie seemed familiar. It was *Gold Diggers of 1931*. I had seen it once on TV in Grannie's room, she in her rocking chair, me lying back on her bed. This was the movie that Grannie had hoped to audition for, the film that had sent Busby Berkeley to Iowa searching for big-boned girls from good Scandinavian families.

"That could be you, Grannie," I had said, watching the vibrant ladies dance and smile, kicking up their heels and tossing back their blonde bobbed hair with wild abandon. "That could be you on screen right now."

"Foolishness," Grannie insisted, shaking her head. "That's no kind of life. I met your grandfather. Had my family. That was the Lord's plan all along." Without thinking, she stroked her petulant anklebone.

On the TV screen in my hotel room, Ruby Keeler stepped onto the balcony and Dick Powell kissed her through the glass. A mass of dancers pressed forward and the window inched open, pushing Ruby from the ledge. She fell backward, twisting and turning, many stories to her death. A commercial came on, lightening the screen. When I looked up and saw my face in the mirror across the room, I realized that I was crying.

CHAPTER SIXTEEN

T he next day a juvenile advocate from Child Protective Services, Mrs. Mariah Pye, finally arrived at my hotel room at 7 A.M. and caught me in the middle of a room service breakfast, courtesy of Johnny. "You're a hungry one," she said, surveying my tray of sliced melon, Oysters Rockefeller, Maryland crabcakes, and a Brie-and-lobster omelet.

"Hungry? You have no idea," I replied, helping myself to a third cup of coffee heaping with cream. "Care to join me?"

"No, thanks, I've eaten." A tall, rumpled woman, she settled down on the sofa, folding her hands and shifting her oversized purse beneath her feet. She watched me carefully, eyes squinted with suspicion. Again, my feisty reputation had preceded me. I could tell that she was determined to keep me in her charge until my parents' arrival, but I had one last mission to complete and I understood that Sunnie, when she put her mind to it, could do anything she wanted.

Mrs. Pye didn't know that I had already spoken to Mom and Pop. After watching *The Tonight Show* the night before with the photo of Johnny and me propped up beside me, I had picked up the old-fashioned telephone and called home. My hands were shaking as I dialed the number.

Mom was so furious that she could barely speak, while Pop said very little, and what he did say came out weak and husky. I listened with the uneasy notion that I was the only person in the world who had ever made my father cry.

I volunteered to take the bus back to Milwaukee or, if they wired me money, fly home alone, but Mom and Pop said no. They had already arranged tickets on the first flight from Milwaukee and would arrive late in the afternoon.

"Stay in the hotel until we get there," Mom ordered. "Don't open the door for strangers, and don't swim in the pool until an hour after you've eaten."

"Yes, Mom," I said dutifully. "I love you, you know," I whispered before I hung up. I'd never said that to anyone before. Mom and Pop didn't respond, but I could tell in their stunned silence that they were trying to find a way to forgive me.

Escaping Mrs. Pye was disappointingly simple. I said I was going to get some ice and even took the engraved plastic bucket for good measure, dropping it discreetly at the door to Room 464. Hailing a taxi from the hotel's front entrance would be too risky, so I sneaked out the back exit behind a cleaning lady's cart. I tiptoed around the azure-blue Olympic-sized swimming pool, ducked between the dense garden rows of hibiscus, bougainvillea, and azaleas, and darted to the bus stop across Sunset Boulevard.

The bus headed east into Hollywood with me, an expert bus passenger by now, in a front seat behind the driver. I followed the route with my thumbnail on a Map of the Stars' Homes, excitement building as we passed the supposed homes of Lindsay Wagner, Buddy Epsen, and multi-award-winner Rita Moreno.

I got off on North Orange Drive and walked the last three blocks to Hollywood Boulevard until I reached the old Roosevelt Hotel, a cream-colored Spanish-style building that dominated the busy street corner. Although still only 10:30 A.M., it was hot, humid, and hazy, with smog wreathing the hills. In the distance I could just make out the HOLLYWOOD sign as the intense August sun beat down on my brand-new feathered haircut, my Camp Muknawanago T-shirt, and my now-mended jeans.

The Hollywood Walk of Fame was jam-packed with hawkers selling maps, tourists speaking German, Japanese, and Spanish, and flailing arms, flashing cameras, and baby strollers every-where, the thickening crowd of tourists nearly rodeoing me into a bank of pay phones.

I walked quickly, head down, my feet covering the forgotten stars of Ward Bond, Claire Trevor, and Lupe Velez. Meanwhile, I counted the steps to my destination, barely noticing the postcard shops, the wooden carts selling sunglasses and chewing gum, or the record stores and tattoo parlors along the way.

Mann's Chinese Theater was set slightly back from Holly-wood Boulevard, creating the large open forecourt famous for the cement imprints of stars' hands and feet. The theater was smaller and tackier than I expected, with fewer cement squares. The squares themselves were different shapes and sizes and in four distinct colors: green, red, dark gray, and beige. The oldest squares were split down the middle and faded by the sun, with their once-deep impressions worn nearly smooth. All that remained of Betty Grable was her signature, along with two dots from the spikes of her stiletto heels.

A Judy Garland look-alike nearly bowled me over as I strode across the squares of Red Skelton, Dorothy Lamour, Irene Dunne, Cary Grant, Henry Fonda, and Don Ameche. I was growing dizzy from the heat and feared I'd be caught.

I pushed through the crowd of tourists towards the western edge of the courtyard, near the small fountain wishing well where at least I could get some air. Near the theater's back gate and the stairs up the side entrance I found what I was looking for. It was small, dark, and neglected, sandwiched between Carole Lombard and W.C. Fields.

I knelt and touched the ground. The concrete felt hot, even in the shade; a heat that came from years of baking in the sun. I gazed at the square and let my eyes soak up the words:

William "Busby" Berkeley
October 28, 1935
"We're In The Money $$$"

Someone nearly tripped over me in his or her haste to see more famous names, but I took my time tracing his handprints: his palms, his thumbs, the perimeter of his wrist, sunk slightly deeper in the concrete. I pictured him as a small-boned man with long elegant fingers. "He touched this," I thought. "And I am touching it now."

"Busby Berkeley? That old-time director?" A man's shadow spread over my shoulder and darkened the square like a cloud obscuring the sun.

"Yes." I glanced back at the man. "But he was much more than that."

I stood, brushed the dirt from my hands, and centered myself in his footprints, pressing my heels to where his had been so many years before. My size nine sneakers were a perfect fit.

I raised my arms and smiled, squinting into the sun. "Grannie," I whispered. "Can you imagine? It took nearly fifty years but you met him in the end. Say hello to Busby Berkeley, the famous director himself."